P9-ARK-875

EVERYTHING SAD IS UNTRUE

(a true story)

EVERYTHING SAD IS UNTRUE

(a true story)

DANIEL NAYERI

LEVINE QUERIDO

MONTCLAIR · AMSTERDAM · NEW YORK

This is an Arthur A. Levine book
Published by Levine Querido

www.levinequerido.com • info@levinequerido.com

Levine Querido is distributed by Chronicle Books LLC

Excerpt from "Terence, This Is Stupid Stuff" by A. E. Housman • Excerpt from "Childe Roland to the Dark Tower Came" by Robert Browning • Excerpt from untitled poem by Iraj Mirza • Excerpt from "The baseness of the foul interpretation given by the fly" by Rumi • Excerpt from "Run Red" by Rachel Pollock reprinted with her permission. Excerpt from *Shahnameh: The Persian Book of Kings* by Abolqasem Ferdowsi

Library of Congress Control Number: 2019909484

ISBN 978-1-64614-000-8

Printed and bound in China.

Published August 2020
Third Printing

When I was a kid in Isfahan, I would tell my mother that someday, I would build her a castle at the top of Mount Sofeh. I could see it from my window. A castle in the sky. I didn't know that life would make a liar out of me. I'm sorry, Mom. I didn't forget. I just never managed it. I wrote you a book instead. I know it isn't even close.

It seems like only yesterday that I believed
there was nothing under my skin but light.
If you cut me I would shine.
—Billy Collins (approximately), "On Turning Ten"

The people of the world say that Khosrou is an
idol worshipper
Maybe so, maybe so
But he does not need the world
And he does not need the people
—Amir Khosrou

I believe like a child that suffering will be healed and made up for, that all the humiliating absurdity of human contradictions will vanish like a pitiful mirage, like the despicable fabrication of the impotent and infinitely small Euclidean mind of man, that in the world's finale, at the moment of eternal harmony, something so precious will come to pass that it will suffice for all hearts, for the comforting of all resentments, for the atonement of all the crimes of humanity, of all the blood they've shed; that it will make it not only possible to forgive but to justify all that has happened.

—Fyodor Dostoevsky, *The Brothers Karamazov*

ALL PERSIANS ARE LIARS and lying is a sin.

That's what the kids in Mrs. Miller's class think, but I'm the only Persian they've ever met, so I don't know where they got that idea.

My mom says it's true, but only because everyone has sinned and needs God to save them. My dad says it isn't. Persians aren't liars. They're poets, which is worse.

Poets don't even know when they're lying. They're just trying to remember their dreams. They're trying to remember six thousand years of history and all the versions of all the stories ever told.

In one version, maybe I'm not the refugee kid in the back of Mrs. Miller's class. I'm a prince in disguise.

If you catch me, I will say what they say in the *1,001 Nights*. "Let me go, and I will tell you a tale passing strange."

That's how they all begin.

With a promise. If you listen, I'll tell you a story. We can know and be known to each other, and then we're not enemies anymore.

I'm not making this up. This is a rule that even genies follow.

In the *1,001 Nights*, Scheherazade—the rememberer of all the world's dreams—told stories every night to the king, so he would spare her life.

But in here, it's just me, counting my own memories.

And you, reader, whoever you are. You're the king.

I'm not sucking up, by the way. The king was evil and made a bloody massacre of a thousand lives before he got to Scheherazade.

It's a responsibility to be the king.

You've got my whole life in your hands.

And I'm just warning you that if I'm going to be honest, I have to begin the story with my Baba Haji, even if the blood might shock you.

But don't worry, dear reader and Mrs. Miller.

Of all the tales of marvel that I could tell you, none surpass in wonder and coolness the one I am about to tell.

COUNTING THE MEMORIES.

Baba Haji kills the bull.

My very first memory is blood, slopping from the throat of a terrified bull, and my grandfather—red-handed—reaching for my face. I would have been three at this time.

Maybe I have memories before that. I don't know.

If I did, they'd be flashes of tile patterns, or something.

I can make it up, if you want.

But really, it was the blood. And the bull braying. And the gurgling sound.

People ask, "Really? Really was it blood?"

They ask because they don't believe me.

They don't believe because I'm some poor refugee kid who smells like pickles and garlic, and has lice, and I'm probably making up stories to feel important.

I don't know what the American grown-ups have for memories, but they can't be as beautiful as mine.

So they laugh. They don't touch me. But they roll their eyes. "Okay," they say.

"It is," I say. "It's one of two memories I have of my Baba Haji." I promise. I haven't been careless with it. My heart clenches it like a fist.

Like gripping a ball bearing as hard as you can. The fingers dig into the palm and you don't even know if it's still in there. The knuckles are white and you're afraid it fell out and you didn't even notice. You're just clenching nothing until your nails cut into your palm and you bleed.

The memory is small. Barely a few pictures. His face is one still image.

IT BEGINS IN A big gold car. It isn't real gold, just painted the color. It was so big the seats were two couches on wheels.

The car drives on a dirt road through a desert in the middle of Iran. Specifically, on the road to Ardestan.

That doesn't mean anything to you, probably, if you even bothered to pronounce it. I could have said, "on the road to *skip-this-word-you're-a-dumdum-stan,*" and it'd be the same. It was a desert in a faraway land.

You want a map?

Here's a map.

When I say the words, people think it may as well be Mars. Or Middle Earth. I could say we drove a chariot pulled by camels and they'd believe me.

But it was a Chevrolet. And we were normal back then.

I wore sneakers with Velcro and had a dad.

He had a bushy red mustache and could make weird faces to be funny. He would blow out his cheeks and furrow his eyebrows like a super serious chipmunk.

He drove. My mom sat beside him and handed us pieces of pistachio cardamom cake. The road went up and down like an ocean.

On either side was sand that could suck down half the car before we could even get out. Some places, the sand blew over so you couldn't see any road at all.

My dad drove so fast it was like a boat going up a wave and crashing down the other side. My sister and I would shriek as our butts lifted off the seat. My mom would say, "Akh. Masoud, slow down. You'll kill your children."

But this was the road my dad knew by heart, because he was born in Ardestan, and he was going home. He drove hungry for his mom's stew and yogurt. His dad was my Baba Haji.

This trip happened every weekend for a while. So this part isn't my first memory. I'm just telling you how it happened *every* time.

The drive would have happened before I saw Baba Haji slaughter the bull, but I'm not certain. The cake could have been rose and honey. My mom could have said, "Akh, Masoud, not this again." His mom could have made kebab and yogurt.

But those aren't differences that make a difference.

The next image is parking outside of the stone walls of my grandfather's courtyard. I see myself, because this part is not my own memory. It was described to me by my mom. So imagine from up by her head, looking down at me. I'm three years old.

I wore corduroys. I carried my stuffed sheep, Mr. Sheep Sheep, in one hand and a stick in the other. I wanted to be a shepherd. My cheeks were chubby, and people pinched them constantly, so I scowled a lot. I was the serious chipmunk.

"Akh. So cute. The cutest boy you have ever seen," my mom would say.

I am now in school in Oklahoma and no one agrees with this.

I am told it would be dusk in the village of Ardestan by the time we arrived. The sun shined red behind a dusty mountain. The house was surrounded by a wall, ten feet high. It was six hundred years old and made of stone.

The garden was inside the wall. It was lined with mosaic tiles. The trees were almond, peach, and fig. At the center was an inlay fountain that cooled you with its whisper. In the corner was the well.

But we hadn't seen any of this that first time. I just know it because it's a place in my mind. I could go there now if I wanted. When teachers brought us to the sod house in Oklahoma and told us it was ninety-eight years old, I asked why they'd made a museum out of it.

The teacher looked at me like I was simple.

"Because we preserve and cherish historical things," she said.

"But no one lives in it?"

"No."

"So every ninety-eight years, people move out of their houses and turn them into museums?"

She looked away at this point, probably because her answer would have been, "What're you, simple?"

"Okay, class, hold a buddy's hand and keep moving."

The first time we went to Ardestan, the time I'm telling you about, we got out of the car outside of the walls, and heard the sound of men shouting and hooves clonking on the stone.

My dad said, "Stay here," and ran around to the entrance, to see if it was one of those demons who hide behind the hedgerows.

We didn't stay there, of course. He wasn't the kind of father you listened to.

I remember approaching the gate. Louder and louder the men shouted. Curses. "Yalla! Yalla!"

I turned the corner.

In the courtyard, by the well, was a bull.

Four grown men from the village struggled to hold it down.

A giant beast. Its eye was black and bigger than any marble in my collection. In it was a swirl of panic.

Sweating.

Shaking.

Insane with fear.

A knife lay on the stone where one of the men had dropped it.

The bull saw me.

Its eye looked at me.

I remember this, because it was the only time I have ever been begged for anything. The bull let out a sound I can only say was like opening your mouth and trying to push all the food out of your stomach.

One of the men slipped off the wet hindquarters and fell.

My dad ran over to help.

But before he reached them, my grandfather emerged from the house. He wore sandals and his muslin pants were rolled up to his knees. I knew it was my Baba Haji even though I think this was the first time I had seen him.

He stepped off the porch and walked toward the confusion. He shook his head at the mess they had made and sucked his teeth in disgust.

In a single motion he leaned over, picked up the knife, and pushed aside the man grappling with the bull's horns. I heard him say, "Here," like, "Here, let me do it."

Then, with one hand, he grabbed the bull's horn and pulled it sideways. I could no longer see the bull's eye, only its exposed neck. With the other hand, my grandfather stabbed the knife into the bull, below its ear, then pulled down and around to the other ear.

The whole neck opened.

Blood poured onto my grandfather's bare feet.

The bull's legs buckled.

I heard a gargle.

The men stepped back, relieved and embarrassed.

It collapsed.

My mother must have been the one who screamed.

My vision went black. She had covered my eyes. I heard her say, "Akh, Masoud!" as if my dad should have known.

Underneath her hand was the color red.

My next memory is back at the car, outside the walls. Mom very angry. Dad kinda laughing cause whatever, farm life, you know? He thinks she's overreacting.

She won't go back until they clean up the blood.

He explains the men were running late. The bull should have been slaughtered hours ago. My grandfather's only grandson (me) had come. What else did she expect?

It occurs to me at this point that the feast was for me.

The bull must have known I was the right person to beg.

I could have saved it.

My three-year-old brain doesn't know what that even means.

When I tell this whole story, I don't tell anyone about that part. I was just a little kid back then. Still. They'll think I want their pity. In America they distrust unhappy people. But I don't want pity. I just wonder if they've had that feeling too. The one where you realize it's your fault that something beautiful is dead. And you know you weren't worth the trouble.

When I opened my eyes, my Baba Haji was looking at me. This is the only memory I have of his face. It was craggy, his beard white and red. He had a knit skullcap and a permanent squint from working in the sun.

He reached for my cheeks.

He smiled at me.

His hands were still red with blood.

Behind him the animal was bleeding on the stone. The blood pooled and flowed toward the drain. A red river.

Oklahoma also has a Red River.

It is not red.

In some places, it's not even a river.

THAT WAS MY FIRST MEMORY of my grandfather. My second memory is not a true one. It is the kind you invent in your head because you need to.

On the phone once, with my dad—I was in Oklahoma, he was in Iran where he stayed—he said, "Your Baba Haji has a picture of you on his mantel. Every day, he weeps and kisses it."

I imagine him doing this.

I don't know what the mantel of his home looks like, so I make one in my mind out of rough stone. I don't know the picture he had of me, so I make it the one from Will Rogers Elementary School in Edmond, Oklahoma.

He holds the frame in his shaking hand.

He cries for me. "Akh!"

My dad tells me Baba Haji's only wish is to see me before he dies.

I say, "Okay."

It is my job to give this to him. If he dies before he sees me, he will be the bull. It will be my fault. I make up this whole memory of Baba Haji, the vision of him by his mantel, so that I can hold it every day.

That is all I know about him for sure.

I don't want to speak about it anymore.

OF MY GRANDMOTHER MAMAN MASSEY—Baba Haji's wife—I have three memories.

The first is of her feeding me sweet dates dipped in thick yogurt she made.

The second is her sitting on a wooden stool weaving a Persian rug in the dark on a giant loom hidden deep in the cellar of their house.

The third is her voice on the phone from across the world, when I realized I would never see her again.

HERE IN OKLAHOMA, THE KIDS like to fight me because they know I won't tell anyone.

Our bus is 209. The teachers call it "the troublesome bus," because the kids are so bad a substitute driver once stopped in the middle of the route, shouted that we were all hooligans, and walked out. Everybody sat there, then everybody screamed and shot even more paper clips at each other and Brandon Goff pinned me down and shoved spitballs in my ear.

Bus 209 is also known as the poor kid bus, because it goes to Brentwood Apartments and Forest Oaks, which are the bad neighborhoods with houses that don't have basements for when tornadoes come.

We sat there for thirty minutes until the vice principal came and drove us. He gave a speech, but I couldn't hear it because Brandon Goff wouldn't let me take the spitballs out.

I **SHOULD INTRODUCE MYSELF.**

Name: Khosrou Nayeri

Age: 12

Hair color: I dunno, black.

Favorite movie:

You know what? I'm not going to introduce myself. You will know me by my voice. In your mind, we are sitting together. You've given me your eyes. I could show you a hill, with patches of grass. Or a peanut butter sandwich. I could help you hear the bells on the neck of a sheep. *Ting ting ting.*

In here, you host me. I am your guest and you probably think of me like you think of yourself—human. We're so close. You can maybe hear my heart beating, scared. I have one, just like yours. I'm scared all the time.

If you saw Khosrou Nayeri on a class sheet, it wouldn't even look like a name to you.

Male or female.

Elvish or Klingon.

You couldn't even say it. It has that *kh*, which is a thrashing sound, like you're trying to hawk up a loogie. It's just spit in your mouth. The sound a warthog makes. And the *r* after the *s*, that's one you have to roll on your tongue, like a cat's purr.

But I'm no beast.

I'll be a good guest and pay for your hospitality with tales of adventure. You can call me Daniel if you want. The other name? Don't bother with it.

Khosrou. You wouldn't like it.

It was a king's name, actually.

Khosrou the First was born in Ardestan—my Baba Haji's village—fifteen hundred years ago. He defeated the Romans at Antioch and when they begged for peace, he gave it to them. The legend goes that one winter he was tired of the cold rain, and so he commanded his artists to create a new season.

The shah of shahs wanted spring.

And so the great craftsmen of the day made a giant rug 150 feet long, woven with gold and silk and gems. The soil was made of gold, the rivers made of crystals. The petals of flowers were rubies, sapphires, and amethyst. The leaves were emeralds. The spring carpet of Khosrou defied the weather of the world.

It lay at his feet.

About a thousand years before Europe discovered toothpaste, Khosrou stepped onto a magic carpet that shined brighter than a meadow in May.

That's the legend.

Khosrou. That name ain't for your mouth.

But the hero's always less than his legend.

Khosrou's just a twelve-year-old kid with a big butt.

You can call him Daniel.

When you think about it, the king could stand on the jewel-encrusted carpet—the kaleidoscopic radiance of human greatness—and yet, if he stuck his head out a window, it'd still be raining.

YOU MIGHT BE THINKING, "What kind of twelve-year-old talks like that?"

And I would say, "The kind of twelve-year-old that speaks three languages."

All my life, people have told me I speak weird. In Iran, my Farsi was baby Farsi (because I was basically a baby) so I made up my own language.

My mom said it was brilliant so my sister and cousins tried to prove I was faking. They asked me the word for a bunch of things like "ladder" and "chicken" and they wrote them down. Then two days later, they asked me again, and guess what? I said the same words because my new language wasn't some punk baby babble.

Also, maybe because it's not that hard to remember fifty words somebody asked you two days ago.

The only words I still remember from that language are "finigonzon" (beautiful girl) and "finigonz" (beautiful boy).

That is not one of my languages anymore.

In Italy I spoke gibberish Italian because we lived in a refugee camp with Roma and Kurds. The people didn't want us there, so if you said, "Buena sera," they'd say, "Good evening," back because they didn't want us to stay. They didn't even want us to learn Italian.

In Oklahoma I spoke like a kid who learned English from a book. When I pronounced the word toilet "twa-lette," everybody thought I was slow or something. When I used old words like parlor instead of living room, they thought I was trying to act superior.

It's been three years and my English is A+ now.

It's easy to tawk lahk one them Okies. Just gotta loosen yer jaw a bit 'n' never let yer teeth touch. Mostly, it's slow and comfortable, imaginin' you own a house and it has a porch and yer sittin' on it.

Or you can watch the black people on TV and talkin' like them ain't hard. If you're around 'em, just nod and go, "wut up." No question mark. (Nobody in America likes grammar Nazis. Not even the neo-Nazis who live in Owasso, Oklahoma.)

Then be cool.

And don't talk too much, and they'll be "chill."

If it comes up, you can tell them a joke about the weather or yo' mama. I wrote a bunch of these down in my notebook when I heard them at recess. So I could always refer back to that if we're about to be friends.

One rule in Oklahoma is that if a grownie talks to you, speak like an Okie. If a finigonzon talks to you, be "chill."

So I speak well now. And I've memorized tons of words.

But if you want the kid version of the story, here goes:

Golly gee, hiya! I'm just a dumb kid who likes ice cream. I was born in Iran—happy face! To a family so wealthy that my grandpa's grandpa was called a king in the history books. There was murder and intrigue and Ferris wheels in the desert, and a house full of swans, a sapphire blue river, and a chest full of gold doubloons—we'll get to all that.

Then my mom got caught helping the underground church and got a fatwa on her head, which means the government wanted her dead—"oh-no" face!

We had to sneak out of the country, but my daddy stayed behind—disappointed face, maybe not-even-all-that-surprised face.

We were guests of the prince of Abu Dhabi for three hours, then homeless. There I cut my head open and they sewed it back together. And then we went to a refugee camp in Italy where I became a great thief, until we got asylum in Oklahoma, where we try to act normal—raised-eyebrow face like you don't believe it.

I think I skipped the part where my grandmother (mom's mom this time) tried to assassinate her husband, failed, and was exiled instead. And most of the blood. And the secret police. And the torture.

Sigh face.

Listen.

The quick version of this story is useless. Let's agree to have a complicated conversation. If you give me your attention—I know it's valuable—I promise I won't waste it with some "poor me" tale of immigrant woe.

I don't want your pity.

If we can just rise to the challenge of communication—here in the parlor of your mind—we can maybe reach across time and space and every ordinary thing to see so deep into the heart of each other that you might agree that I am like you.

I am ugly and I speak funny. I am poor. My clothes are used and my food smells bad. I pick my nose. I don't know the jokes and stories you like, or the rules to the games. I don't know what anybody wants from me.

But like you, I was made carefully, by a God who loved what He saw.

Like you, I want a friend.

MY DAD CALLS ONCE a month, on a Sunday afternoon.

"Allo?"

"Yeah, hello?"

"Allo, Khosrou?"

"Yeah, Baba, it's me."

"Allo?"

"Yes. What."

"You son of a dog, why didn't you answer me?"

"I did."

"Don't speak to your father that way."

He speaks in poetry by the great Persian writers. Hafez, Rumi, Ferdowsi. It is two in the morning in Isfahan. I imagine him sitting in the dark house where we all used to live together. The doves in the aviary are asleep.

My sister tells me he is probably drunk or on a drug. I think he is in the trance of a thousand-year-old verse. I stand in the kitchen of our house in Edmond, Oklahoma, watching our cocker spaniel sleep in a sunny spot by the back door.

In my ear, my Baba's deep voice murmurs the refrains. "'*Uncheh shiranrah konad rubbeh mesaj, ezdevaj ast ezdevaj ast ezdevaj.*' Do you understand?" he says.

It's an ancient Farsi that I can only sort of catch.

"No," I say.

"You are forgetting already. You're forgetting your own family. And your history. These are the poets you should be reading in school."

"Tell me what it means."

"It's a clever joke. Your Baba Haji made it from a common phrase. It says, 'The thing that turns a lion into a little fox is need.' Do you understand that?"

"No."

"Akh. Okay, so lions are strong champion creatures, yes?"

"Yes."

"And a fox is a coward, yes?"

"Really?"

"Yes. In Persian literature, a fox is a coward."

"In America it's a tricky animal."

"Persian literature is ten times older than America!"

"Okay, okay. Fox is a coward, got it."

"So the riddle asks, what makes the champion a coward?"

"Need?"

"Yes. The weakness of needing something. Now the lion must beg for it. He is no king if he needs anything."

"Okay, how is that a joke?"

"Because your Baba Haji changed the word 'need' to 'marriage.' Now it says, 'What turns a great lion into a needy fox? Marriage.'"

I pause.

"Because '*ehtiaj*' rhymes with '*ezdevaj*,' so the change is clever."

"Okay."

If ever there was cleverness in the joke, it has been wrung out like a dish towel.

"I was a lion," says my father.

He wants me to understand so badly. He wants me to know the Persian poets like I know American rappers. I feel desperate to give him the connection, but can't.

"I was a lion," he says, "and I married and now I sit by the phone and beg to speak to my children. Do you see?"

His voice crumbles.

I imagine the telephone wire going from my hand into our wall into the ground under our yard up the telephone pole across the flat prairie to the Gulf of Mexico under the water under the Atlantic past Gibraltar across the Mediterranean under Turkey into Iran over the Zagros Mountains to Isfahan to our street to our house to my Baba's chair to his ear where he sits crying. I listen to him weep into the phone.

When he's finished, he says, "Are you doing well in school?"

"Straight As."

"Good. Good. You're my champion of champions."

"Thank you," I say.

"Okay, be good."

"Okay."

"Send pictures."

"Okay."

And we say good-bye.

THEY SAY MY FATHER'S family got their land from the king of India, in gratitude for saving his daughter's life.

This was generations upon generations ago, before Oklahoma was even a state. No one ever told me exactly when. There was never enough time for details. There were no lazy Sunday afternoons sitting beside the fountain in the courtyard with aunts or uncles, no moment to ask, "Was this ancestor around when they had horse-drawn carriages? Or was he around when the phoenix flew its fiery wings over hillside villages? Did he know the prophet Daniel, when he came to Persia, or did he know the doctor Ibn Sina twelve hundred years later? This greatest of grandfathers, was he from the age of myth, the age of heroes, or the age of history?"

Dastan. Persia. Iran.

The boundaries of these three countries are nothing but ten feet of fog.

In Dastan land, the mythical age, my great-great-great-..great-grandfather was a doctor.

Nobody in Mrs. Miller's class had trouble believing this, because doctors aren't all that special anyway. It wasn't like I said he was a beast master.

Anyway, he was a doctor. Not a rich guy with a stethoscope. Don't imagine that. More like a young man who spent all his time in the library of the university, or the private archives of the local magistrate. He spent his money on herbs and plant roots and oils to make things like ointments for burns and cuts.

And he spent the rest of his money on paper and ink so he could take notes on what worked and what didn't.

He was poor, they said, but generous.

He lived in an ancient city.

"How ancient," Jared S. said, when I told this part to my class.

"It's just a city," I said.

"Like from *Aladdin*."

"Yeah, like that."

In myths they don't spend time describing things like cities.

The herbs aren't fenugreek, wormwood, and yarrow.

They're just herbs.

He's not a specific man, with shoulders built strong on his father's plow. He's just a guy who left home and became a student.

A myth is only an explanation, not an exploration.

This one explains how my father's family became kings.

But if this was a story in the heroic age, they would give my great-grandfather a name, Jamshid, and a personality—ever-laughing Jamshid with a limp in the foot his father crushed with a plow. Jamshid who took even a broken finch as his most honored patient.

He lived in Isfahan, the city of covered bridges. The city that smelled of jasmine.

The young doctor was soon famous for his willingness to help the poor and the untouchables. He even sat with those who weren't sick, only sad, broken-hearted, or lost.

They would sit in his small garden under an apricot tree. He would give them tea and sesame cookies, and he would listen.

"Doktor, I am going to die."

"Come now, sir, don't say such things."

"It is true! I am half-dead already! Three quarters almost."

"What can I do, then?"

"Hemlock."

"I can't."

"It must be hemlock."

"Hemlock is poisonous."

"Then belladonna."

"Also poisonous."

"I know, Doktor, I know."

"This is about that lovely Maryam, isn't it?"

"Akh! Doktor, send me now to a world without her. I am the unhappiest of men."

"She refused your offer of marriage."

"Yes. Well, no. I don't know."

"So you might also be the happiest of men?"

"I don't know!"

"Sir, please. Let go of my hand."

". . ."

"If you don't know, don't you think we could wait a little and find out?"

"But you see, this is my problem. This is my problem."

"Waiting."

"No. If she says yes—Maryam, who loves me, and I who love Maryam—we will be richer in joy that the great Xerxes."

"It sounds nice."

"Except her brothers have sworn to poison me. I will die. She will be widowed and left to those villains."

"I see. And if she says no, in order to prevent all this?"

"That one is obvious, Doktor."

"I see."

"So, the hemlock if you please, Doktor. A large gunny sack of it."

"Right away."

"No one will blame you. I'll tell everyone I got it from a dervish."

"You're too kind. But first, have you heard of Mithridates' antidote? Could I offer you the story?"

"Doktor, I don't want to be rude."

"You're pressed for time, I understand. It will be short."

"I don't go to the baker for soap. And I don't go to the storyteller for cures."

"But you've come to a doctor for a killing drink."

"Of course! A builder can make and unmake a house. Both are his job."

". . ."

". . ."

"The price of my poison is to hear my story."

"Akh. Very well, Doktor. Only because you have been kind to my mother."

"Once upon a time . . ."

"Don't get greedy, Doktor. A quick anecdote, if you please."

"The father of the great king Mithridates was assassinated at a banquet. He'd been poisoned, you see."

"As I would be if I married my love."

"Yes. Now you see the connection. And so Mithridates went into hiding. He wandered the forest, and vowed to become stronger than his enemies. Every day he drank a sublethal dose of poison until his body became accustomed to it. And so when he returned to his kingdom, he imprisoned his mother and brothers, who he suspected had killed his father, and he threw a banquet. 'They put arsenic in his meat and stared aghast to watch him eat; they poured strychnine in his cup and shook to see him drink it up.' But Mithridates was immune to such a death. He smiled and drank. Then he offered each of them a sip from his own goblet. They were his friends, after all. They couldn't refuse. If they did he would know that *they knew* that it was poisoned. And so each drank, and each died, and the poets say, 'I tell the tale that I heard told. Mithridates, he died old.'"

". . ."

". . ."

"So."

"So."

"So you think I should ambush her brothers with such a ploy?"

"No. I think whatever grievance you have with your future brothers, you should offer forgiveness, and ask them for theirs."

"That is not what the story said, Doktor."

"Sure it is."

"It said Mithridates foiled the plans of his killers."

"It said his friends hated him. It said he killed his mother and brothers."

"Yes, but he died old."

"Kill everyone at a party, and you are the life of the party, but that doesn't make you good company."

". . ."

". . ."

"I think your story needs work, Doktor."

"You're probably right."

"To explain that Mithridates was unhappy with his decision. And perhaps add the idea that he did not become strong by drinking poison daily. He only became full of poison himself."

"That's good."

"His poisoned heart beat poisoned blood."

"I will work on it."

"No, no. I think you should stick to physician's work."

"Very well, then."

"I'll ask Maryam's brothers to sit with me."

"That sounds like a good plan."

"One of them suffers in his back, when he sleeps."

"I will give you an ointment. He'll sleep like a mountain bear."

"Thank you, Doktor. The thing is that I don't have money."

"It's my wedding gift, then."

"I must tell Maryam."

"Go."

"She'll make you her honey cake."

"I would be honored."

"Best in Isfahan. Her hand sweetens the honey itself."

"I'm in your debt."

When I tell this story to Mrs. Miller's class, I don't do the talking parts. There is just too much to explain. I only say, Jamshid was famous for taking his payment in whatever patients could offer. Honey cake. A chicken that laid hard-boiled eggs. Three bottles of jam made from his garden's apricots.

"That's super weird," says Jennifer S.

Jennifer S. thinks everything that isn't in a mall is weird.

And so the legend goes, that he was a good man, peculiar, and not very good at explaining stories clearly. But see, this is the thing with legends. They are more detailed than myths, but not always more accurate.

So the telling goes, the young doctor of Isfahan was summoned to the palace of a great pasha. No one knows the details, so let's imagine them. Maryam's cousin—a merchant of rare furs—knocks on the doctor's back gate. He has returned from the court of a Parsi king who worshipped the Hindu gods. In the bazaar, as he haggled, he saw a magistrate climb onto a mountain of rugs (despite the rug merchant's protests) and shout over the crowd.

"The pasha—generous and merciful—"

At this point Jared S. interrupts. "Wait. Who's the cousin?"

"I'm confused," says Jennifer L.

"Can you make him do his reports on horses or normal stuff?" says Doug P.

"No," says Mrs. Miller. "I would hope that everyone does the research assignment and writes a report on their actual family, Douglas."

Doug P. made up a bunch of stuff about horses in case you didn't figure it out.

Anyway, Jared says, "Is the cousin the same guy as before who wanted the poison?"

"No, that's Maryam's husband," says Jessica, who is the best listener.

"It doesn't matter," I say. "None of these people are important. The only person to remember is Jamshid. The rest are just people for the story. The only part I know for sure is Jamshid."

"Then get to the point," says Jared.

The point was that the pasha's daughter suffered a supernatural illness. Magistrates (like the pompous one in the bazaar who did not purchase a rug after all that) were sent to every city to find doctors to help her. And the cousin—doesn't matter whose cousin—had the letter of invitation for the doctor of Isfahan, which he had promised to deliver in exchange for a meager fee.

When my father tells it, he skips all of this guessing, because he's the greatest storyteller of the family, and he has a nose for when the strange turns of history begin to sound too much like myths.

He only speaks what we know for certain.

He says, "Your great-great-great-grandfather earned all this land. He was a doctor, the best in Isfahan. At that time a pasha in India had a daughter who was sick—probably with a mild schizophreniform disorder, but back then, they had no diagnosis for these things. So he prescribed a sedative. She calmed down and eventually grew out of it."

That's it.

To me, this was tightfisted.

What about the court of the pasha?

Was the daughter beautiful?

I will tell you, reader, that I imagine her like Kelly J., who looks nothing like a pasha's daughter, but very much like a Disney princess.

How long would it take the doctor to caravan to India, and what did he do in the heat of the day, as the camels lay on the ground resting?

I would imagine he walked into the palace and looked up to see the daughter watching from a terrace above him in the grand hall. At that exact moment he fell forever in love with her.

But she was wracked with convulsion and delusion and horrific visions.

In her bedroom, he would submit the full weight of his knowledge to healing her condition, knowing all the while that his success would only separate them forever.

And she too might have loved the Persian doctor. Cursed though she was with illness—she might have come to prefer it for his company.

The tragedy of love would unfold as the doctor could never sit by and watch the princess in such pain. He would heal her and together they would suffer the duller ache of longing. I would imagine him trudging behind a long caravan back to Isfahan, broken.

But my father would make no concessions to mythmaking, when the truth was available.

"The pasha gave him his weight in gold," my father would say, "and once again in jewels. And your great-great-great-grandfather returned home. He bought all the land around Ardestan."

That was all we knew. He returned with enough treasure to buy thousands of acres. Enfolded in them were mountains, and a river, and enough villages to make him a local government unto himself.

"If only he had been fat," joked my father, "we'd be twice rich. But your father's fathers were all cursed with heroic fitness."

"Sure, Dad."

"It's true," he says. "You don't think it's true?"

When we have this conversation I am in the kitchen in Oklahoma, where they make fun of kids with hairy arms and bubble butts. I imagine my father, a portly bear who I have never seen move faster than a brisk walk.

"Well, it's true. You descend from kings. Good-looking ones."

Suddenly, I realize he's saying that because my mom told him about school. About Brandon Goff pointing at how my shirt doesn't go straight down my back, and shouting to everyone that I have a bubble butt.

This happened in the halls, and Kelly J. wasn't around, but still.

I didn't say anything to my dad because I'm not even sure how he knew. I guess my sister saw me stretching out my shirts on the back of a chair and told my mom, and they figured it out. I didn't say anything to my dad. It's not like he could do anything but talk on the phone anyway.

We don't live in the heroic age. Our separation isn't any great poetic struggle. It's just pain. It's just ripping bodies apart.

Anyway, that's how come we had all that land.

In Oklahoma we are the opposite of kings.

Everything we own is inside a hard gray suitcase. It is mostly coats and papers. There is one squished shoebox full of photos that my mom guards, and cries over when she thinks we're asleep.

We left all the toys, and the books, and my candy bars. It has been years since we left Iran—but I wonder about the candy bars.

One of my last memories of Iran is my dad coming home with a case of Orich candy bars a few weeks before we had to escape. When people here ask me what kind of candy I like, I say, "Orich!"

And we go through the exact same script every time.

They frown. So I explain. "They're chocolate-covered coconut."

"Oh, like Mounds bars. We have those here."

Everyone is always insisting they have things here, but they do not have Orich, or my father. That is two things.

They have everything else here.

The grocery stores scared us at first. They have chips that are all the same shape and stack on top of each other in a tube. But they don't have Orich bars. I say, "Like a Mounds bar, but they taste different."

"Oh?" say the grownies, as if they don't believe me. "How?"

I don't know how to explain. I barely remember the taste of Orich. I only know I ate a Mounds bar and it wasn't my favorite most amazing thing in my mouth . . . so it must be different.

I usually say, “I also like Kit Kat.”

They smile, because I finally answered something normal.

I don’t say that in Iran, Kit Kats aren’t broken into bars; they’re one flat square.

Whenever my dad brought home a case of candy bars, we ran to the door. I was just a five-year-old kid. My sister was eight. Our dad had such a habit of bringing home cases of chocolate that my mom had made me a place to store them. She took a clown doll and sewed giant baggy pants around it that ruffled out with dozens of little pockets. Back then she sewed us all kinds of toys. She even made a step stool the shape of a big red bus—stuffed with cushions so I could reach my bed.

Anyway, we’d run up to my dad. “Baba!”

He was a dentist who worked above a candy shop. They used to joke that it was the perfect arrangement.

We opened our mouths so that Baba could look.

I remember the taste of his thumb better than Orich.

He would look in my mouth, push on my molars to make them perfectly straight. I used to think my Baba could change the shape of teeth as easily as the great hero Rostam could move mountains.

After he checked our teeth, I would hug his right side, because he kept cigarettes in his left breast pocket.

This is a memory that has no sound, but probably it should have my Baba's laugh, which was such a rich and resonant chortle that it fills rooms of my memory that he was not even in.

He was still thin at that time, with a bushy red mustache. I only remember him eating kebab and ice cream.

He presented the last case of Orich—probably thirty or forty bars.

From here, the memory splits into three dessert-oriented stories.

The first is the myth of the Baker and Tamar.

The second is the legend of my sister's cleverness.

The third is the history of a clown's underpants.

YOU SHOULD KNOW SOMETHING.

In school they have dances that other kids go to. There are about six reasons I don't go. One, they're at night and you need a ride. Two, I don't know what they are like. Three, I don't dance. Four, Brandon Goff goes. Five, his friends still call me bubble butt and it's become a "thing." Six, no one ever asked me.

But last week, I was standing in the courtyard after lunch and Jennifer S. walked up to me. She had to walk all the way over from where people are, so it took forever. She was trying not to laugh. I checked my armpits for sweat and stuff like that. I tried to straighten my hair down. I dropped the acorns I was holding, cause it's weird to count acorns.

When she arrived she said, "Hey, are you going to the dance?"

I said, "Hi Jennifer."

She said, "Are you going to the dance?"

I said, "No."

She turned around and walked back.

You should know, reader, that Jennifer S. is a finigonzon, for sure. But I have a crushed heart for someone else. I won't tell you about her yet, because sometimes love has to be kept secret. If other people find out, they attack it.

I thought maybe Jennifer S. was asking me to the dance. But then I saw her walk back to her group and they all laughed, and her friend gave her back her purse. So maybe it was a dare. I don't know.

THE MYTH OF THE BAKER and Tamar, and its relation to my dad and candy bars and the love of his life.

In my hometown of Isfahan, there is another town—a hidden town completely surrounded but separate—called New Jolfa.

In 1606 the shah Abbas created the city of Jolfa and gave it to the Armenians, who were running from the Ottoman emperor because they were Christians. In Jolfa, they were allowed to be Christian and to build churches. But if they ever spoke to the people of Isfahan about their faith, the shah would cut off their heads.

And so you can imagine, Jolfa kept to itself.

As the centuries passed, the little city prospered. By the time I was born in 1982, they were kings of pastry. And the undisputed king of kings—the shah-in-shah—of these bakeries was Akh Tamar. The people of Isfahan ventured to the center of the strange neighborhood to stand in line, before the famed bakery of Akh Tamar, just for six of his cream puffs.

They said he was the padeshah of pâte à choux, the ruler supreme of rosewater and cream. He was an old man by the time I ate one of his pastries. I was just a little kid. He might have even been dead like McDonald's. I don't know.

I remember eating a cream puff in our kitchen in Isfahan and counting the guests to see if I could have another. A man, I don't remember if it was my uncle, I don't even remember his face, said, "That Abbas is king."

I think the baker's name was also Abbas.

The man started to tell the story that Baker Abbas was once a poor son of New Jolfa with a heart overfilled with kindness.

"Very handsome, very handsome," agreed the women listening. The man in my memory goes on. "And though the Armenians had no king at this time, they had Tamar, who was so beautiful she shined

as she walked through the bazaar.

There is no notion as important as love.

Abbas saw Tamar one day and fell into an ocean of it. And she, when she saw him—a delivery boy for a greengrocer at the time—she fell into a kind of heartsickness that can only be described as an equal mixture of love and grief.

She was a governor's daughter, of course.

And the rich never forget the social order. Tamar at this moment knew she was hopelessly in love with Abbas, and also that her love was hopeless.

It is no magic to guess what happens next.

They meet and speak electric words to each other.

'Hi.' 'Hello.'

They flit around each other when she orders from the greengrocer daily. They steal kisses in the shadows of her father's vaulted staircase.

She weeps in his arms and tells him they can never marry.

Her mother sees them from her window. She promises her daughter to some fancy boy who once visited Paris.

Abbas pours himself into his pastry craft.

He races time. He races the courtship of Tamar to what's-his-name.

He sculpts chickpea cookies with a steady hand. They are each individually perfect. None crumble. He takes a stall in the rear alcove of the bazaar and sells them. He makes saffron rice pudding, stirring patiently, pulling the pot from the fire with a troubadour's timing. It is a perfect sunrise yellow.

He layers his baklava generously with walnuts and cardamom. His almond cakes are subtle and the cherry puree on top is joyous, bold, even a little wanton.

Soon no one remembers Abbas the greengrocer's errand boy, only Abbas the master baker of all Isfahan.

His first large order is from a governor who wants a thousand cream puffs for the wedding of his daughter—Tamar.

Abbas dies here.

His heart crumbles into chickpea flour.

Late in the evening the merchants of the bazaar hear him weeping in the rear alcove, as they shutter their stalls.

Here is something I would like to tell you—stories get better as they get more true.

The sad truth of this story is that Abbas was truly and completely ruined.

His tears—they said—were the warm water baths that steamed up his oven. His trembling hands whipped pastry cream as light as a shroud.

When the guests at Tamar's wedding ate the cream puffs, they could taste the truest thing in all the world at that moment—the baker's pain.

They didn't understand this, of course. To them, they were simply the most delicious pastries they had ever eaten. They toasted the merry couple.

When Tamar tasted one, it was a love letter. She ran to her room and sobbed into a pillow.

This is how the greatest bakery in New Jolfa came to be called Akh Tamar. The sound of a punch to the rib—Akh!—Oh!—Oh! Tamar! The sound of the old master baker weeping in the back kitchen."

In my memory of this story's telling—in our kitchen in Isfahan—the man finished his tale and popped another cream puff into his mouth. I can almost squint and see him.

Yes, I think he's my uncle Ahmad, who fancied himself a storyteller.

Memories are always partly untrue.

It could have been his brother Reza.

A **PATCHWORK STORY** is the shame of a refugee.

IN OKLAHOMA I GO to the library sometimes. My mom drops me off on Saturday mornings before she goes to work. It is a small one-story building with gray carpets.

It does not have a Persian section. The first thing I read are comics about Calvin and Hobbes. He is a boy who seems to hate the world as it is and love the world that ought to be. The tiger is his sane mind, which goes to sleep too much, so that he never knows what to believe. And never knows which world he is in. I like him because he speaks better than a kid.

When you are spending the whole day at the library, it is important to do stuff in chunks. First, read all the new comics. Then, look at the new magazines with sports on them and write down the phrases that are cool, like "the whole kit and kaboodle," which means "everything," and "put on a clinic," which means "taught." When the Chicago Bulls put on a clinic and took home the whole kit and kaboodle, it means they won.

In the afternoon, the old people are gone so the next thing to do is find the section that has poems that tell stories. It's easy to learn languages when the sounds rhyme. There's one poem about a kid named Roland who is walking from one country to another, and he's scared. When he looks down at the wet field, he thinks the grass looks like ugly hair sticking up from a bloody head. He says, "Thin dry blades pricked the mud which underneath looked kneaded up with blood."

And then he sees a stiff blind horse and thinks it's the saddest thing he's ever seen. But he doesn't know what to do to help him. He can't just leave it there in the bloody field. But he doesn't have a way to help either and he wants to keep going. Suddenly he starts to talk himself into caring less about it. Little by little, to make sure his heart doesn't break, he makes himself immune to the pain of the horse with its "shut eyes underneath the rusty mane." Then he says, "He must be wicked to deserve such pain."

Just like that. It's the horse's fault. I don't believe that, reader. I think Roland is a dumb kid who just wants to forget he ever saw the horse.

My mom usually gives me an egg sandwich to eat, but people hate the smell of egg sandwiches so I eat it in the bathroom.

The librarian at the Edmond Library is a woman named Helen Brown, and she is the kindest person I have ever met, and would never leave a horse in a field or blame it for anything.

Mrs. Brown gave me my library card. I am allowed to check out thirty-five books and can visit the library every two weeks. That is seventy books a month. In one year, I will read 840 books. I don't care what they are about, only that they contain English.

Mrs. Miller says this is the only way to learn.

One time, I found a book on Persians in the myth section. It said:

> Akhtamar—The largest of four islands in Lake Van (Turkey). According to folk legend, an Armenian princess lived on the island. Every night she held a lamp so that the boy she loved could swim from the mainland to meet her. One night her father caught her and smashed the lamp. The boy was lost in the lake and drowned. Locals claim to hear his dying words, "Akh, Tamar!" to this day.

THE LEGEND OF MY sister's cleverness is a family story that people mention anytime they want to call me mazloom.

Mazloom is a word I can never tell you what it is in English.

It is someone who is cute and pitiful.

Mazloom is a puppy. But not a happy puppy, a kicked puppy.

Mazloom is something you just want to hold and say sorry to. A victim.

When I was four and wanted to cry, I knew they would laugh at me—what grief could a chubby toddler feel?—and I knew I could not run, so I would clench my fists and roll my eyes up to look at the ceiling as if maybe the tears would go back down into my eyes. I would stand in one place and tremble and wish the welling tears would just dry up. But tears are like genies. They will never go back into the bottle.

My sister would say, "Akh, he's so mazloom! His cheeks, and those little fists."

In the story they would say, Khosrou was always so mazloom that he had no idea when his sister would trick him. When Masoud would bring home a box of Orich candy bars, he would run and put his portion into the pockets of his clown. She would say, "Khosrou, let's have a race to see who can eat their candy bar first."

At this time, Khosrou loved his sister and would agree to anything she proposed.

He would shove the entire candy bar into his mouth. She would say, "You're so fast. I can't keep up."

As soon as he had swallowed the Orich bar, she would reveal hers and nibble it slowly while his mouth watered. "Mmm. This is so good. I'm just going to enjoy it forever."

Khosrou's fists would clench and his eyes would roll up to the ceiling.

That's it.

She was very clever.

HERE IN OKLAHOMA WE DON'T talk very much. She hates Ray and wants our dad back.

I don't know. We just don't talk. What else is there to say? She is the best student the teachers have ever seen. They can see it in her eyes. They are not begging eyes. They are watchful and hungry. They want something that—for now—school can give. If she gets A+ in everything, and starts a club, and builds an after-school program, and scores perfect on all the state tests, they will have to love her. But she doesn't understand that people are immune to the happiness of others too, not just their pain. They're numb to everything. They don't even see her.

I think she thinks I forgot our dad and accepted Ray or something.

THE HISTORY OF THE CLOWN'S underpants is a secret history and I will never tell it. But if you think people are stupid and mazloom and all you ever do is take from them, then they eventually learn how to survive you.

They learn to hide away everything they love, where you can't touch it. And they won't just hide it someplace easy to find, like a clown's pockets, or anyplace in this world.

They'll create a new world, with its own language, and they'll hide everything there—all the favorite jokes they won't say around you, all the best books, the spot on the wall that looks like a keyhole, being safe and free and comfortable—all those things, and you won't even know they exist.

And when you've gotten your hands on the one Orich, and you've laughed at the badly hidden tears, you won't even know there was a secret zipper in a bus pillow where the rest of the bars were really hidden. Not some obvious clown. You won't know because you believed the weak can't do anything.

But hiding is something to do while you wait to get stronger.

Deep hiding.

Hiding so sneaky that it's hidden below tears that you *think* are trying to hide themselves—but they're actually decoy tears. Not real ones.

Why did I even start talking about desserts?

I don't remember.

I guess the point of all this is to say I don't like the cream puffs here in Oklahoma, which they call Twinkies.

HERE IS A LIST of foods we discovered in America:

Peanut butter.

Marshmallows.

Barbecue sauce. (You can say, "Can I have BBQ?" to a kid's mom at potlucks and they'll know what you mean.)

Puppy chow. (Chex cereal covered in melted chocolate and peanut butter and tossed in powdered sugar. They only give it if you win a Valentine friend.)

Corn-chip pie (not a pie). (Chili on top of corn chips with cheese and sour cream (not sour).)

Some mores. (They say it super fast like s'mores.)

Banana puddin. (They don't say the *g*. Sometimes they don't even say the *b*.)

Here is a list of the foods from Iran that they have never heard of here:

All of it.

All the food.

Jared Rhodes didn't even know what a date was.

I **HAVE A NEW FATHER** here in America. Did I mention this already? It's called a "stepdad." His name is Rahim, but he tells Americans to call him Ray. My sister says the only reason Mom married him was to give me a male role model so I'd know how to grow up into a man, and so we wouldn't be on welfare.

Ray is thin and doesn't have a beard—the opposite of my dad. My dad drinks alcohol, but Ray quit when he quit smoking (my dad is a chimney). My dad quotes the great Persian poets—Rumi, Hafez, Ferdowsi. Ray only reads the Bible.

Ray cuts his hair kind of like Bruce Lee, because he says Lee is the only martial artist who deserves to be feared. Ray is a third-degree black belt in tae kwon do. I would rather face a villain with a gun than a man with Ray's 360 back kick. There is no one in Oklahoma as good at fighting as Ray.

We don't talk much after what happened the first Christmas we spent in apartment 404. Except for nights when he comes home with an action movie. He wakes me up and we watch all the greats—Bruce Lee, Jackie Chan, Bolo Yeung, Phillip Rhee, Jean-Claude van Damme.

Ray covers my eyes when there are naked women. He pauses the fight scenes and quizzes me on the best techniques. "There, did you see that?"

"He kicked the guy into the spears."

"Before that."

"It was a side kick."

"Look at him chamber his knee."

He'll fiddle with the VCR till it pauses on the exact moment of van Damme holding his knee up to his chest before exploding it out sideways into a guy's stomach. "The power is here."

Ray stands up and moves the table so he can show me properly. He'll stand in front of the TV on one foot with his knee chambered just like van Damme. He's the Persian version of the Muscles from Brussels.

"From here," he'll say, "you punch out into a side kick, or you can rotate your hips and swing around into a lead-leg roundhouse."

He extends his leg into a perfect side kick, then brings it back and does the roundhouse. He's standing on one leg the whole time. One fist is at his chin, the other by his ear, the whole time.

"Or, if he comes in, you chamber, he flinches, you put down the knee, switch feet into a swing kick."

He does the maneuver and swings his back foot right up to my temple. He stops a hair away. I don't flinch.

It would ruin the movie if I flinch.

I know all the best kicks from thirty-seven rated-R movies.

The axe kick in *Best of the Best.*

The side kick in *Enter the Dragon.*

The 360 back kick in *Best of the Best 2.*

The roundhouse in *King of the Kickboxers.*

I've done each of them a hundred times. Actually, I've done the other guy. The one who telegraphs his punch and misses with his other arm down and leaves himself open. Ray whizzes the famous kicks right past my nose, so close it tickles.

By the time the movie's over, I have to go back to bed because I have school in the morning. I have no idea where Ray goes. He's usually not there in the morning.

Someday, I will be strong enough to break his jaw.

I don't hate him, but it will be my job to fight him.

I will not miss.

THE MYTH ABOUT RAY—the one I heard in a whispered voice from my mom—is that he was one of sixteen kids in a part of Iran so far north that it bordered the Soviet Union. His mom died when he was five, and his father remarried a woman who had more kids.

The dad was a giant brown bear, they said. In the mornings he would scrabble out into the woods and return in the evening. No one questioned him. One day when Rahim was ten, he dropped something—a bowl or a cup, doesn't matter—and broke it.

They say his dad stood up, grabbed Rahim by the hair, and dragged him across a lawn to the first tree on the forest's edge.

He took off his belt.

He pushed Rahim up against the trunk.

He wrapped the belt around the trunk and Rahim, and tightened it.

He tore a long green branch from the boughs of the tree and whipped Rahim until he bled from his neck and arms and cheeks and ears.

Then he left.

Rahim was tied to the tree for two days. He stood there, unable to sleep or sit down. He cried out for a while but was afraid only the bear would answer. Only his new mother dared to help him. At night, she snuck out of the house with rags to wash his cuts, and gave him food and water.

That was how he knew she had accepted him, even though she wasn't his mother. And that was how he knew his siblings weren't ever going to help him.

After the two days, Ray knew he was alone. When he turned seventeen, his dad sent him to America to earn money.

When he arrived, he had no English, no place to stay, and less than twenty bucks.

But more than language, and more than money, and more than a house—he knew he needed an axe kick strong enough to cut down a bear.

He walked into a dojo in Oklahoma City run by an old Korean man named Master Moon. Years later, when I signed up at a school, Ray called it a toy gym, cause it was run by a guy named Kerry, and it was full of rich kids with brand-new head protectors on sale in the back.

Moon's Gym was just a room off the highway with exposed cement beams and heavy bags held together with duct tape.

Ray said they would do so many roundhouse drills that all the skin on the ball of his pivot foot would rip off and the blood would start pooling on the carpet—at first the size of a quarter, then a plate.

They would stand in line, holding one knee up and Master Moon would attack their shins with bamboo rods until they passed out. Everybody in Moon's Gym was a super stud. They weren't afraid of anyone.

Master Moon was a sixth-degree black belt.

I know now that this part isn't true, but I used to think Master Moon had the Death Touch—where he'd hit your chest with an open palm and the impact would burst your heart like a Gusher.

He was a knotted-up old Korean guy, and since Ray couldn't pay any money, he made Ray a deal. Ray went to live at Master Moon's house. In exchange for a room and tae kwon do training, Ray would clean the Moon family house and make their meals.

Mrs. Moon had a condition where she couldn't work anymore, but she would rather die than eat some Iranian kid's teenage cooking. So she would sit in the corner of their tiny kitchen and yell at him in Korean. Neither spoke English, so she'd say, "Cut the radishes," in Korean and he'd say, "Pick up the knife?" in Farsi.

"Now cut the radishes," in Korean.

"What should I do with the knife?" in Farsi.

"The radishes. Radishes."

"Cut these?"

"No, long ways."

"Like this?"

"No!"

Then she'd scream, and screaming is the same in Korean, Farsi, and English.

Until years passed and Ray finally knew how to make bulgogi, kimchi, bibimbop, mumallaengi—all the super serious Korean foods.

That's how Ray became a third-degree black belt.

And how he got that bear-slaying uppercut that he only ever used on single moms.

IF YOU REALLY WANT to know the truth, it's the forgetting that hurts most. Not the secret police trying to murder us. Not Brandon Goff shooting paper clips at my neck. Not Ray. Not everyone thinking I'm gross.

Those pains are pains that make me strong.

I imagine the more they bleed me, the more I become like jerked meat—a dried bull, a hard leather.

But no matter how hard I clench my fist, the memories pour out of it and disappear. When you kill a monster in *Final*

Fantasy, it makes a sound like a groan and disintegrates into sand. None of them are strong enough to keep two grains together once they die.

You could imagine the Elemental Fiends clenching their toothy jaws—but even they just crumble.

That's what forgetting your grandpa's face feels like. There's no good in it. Nothing to gain but nothing. A piece of your heart makes a sound like a groan and disappears. Then you poke at it sometimes, trying to remember what was there by the shape of the hole. That's it. You are less.

The truth is that's why I'm writing all this. Behind me is the elemental fiend of my memories crumbling into powder. I watch an arm disintegrate and instantly forget what was there.

Did I ever hug Baba Haji? What was that like?

Did he smell like a farmer or a shepherd? He was both.

Did his arms feel strong?

You don't get to choose what you remember.

A patchwork memory is the shame of a refugee.

Did I tell you that already?

I could still tell you how I left the toys in my room. How many Orich bars I left in that bus cushion. But I couldn't tell you what it feels like to have a grandpa.

I also forgot Italian when I learned English.

I also forgot all the bad things about my dad when I met Ray.

I also forgot my granddad on my mom's side, but he's less important because I think he's a killer who married a child bride.

THE FARTHEST BACK I can remember on my mother's side is a meadow outside the house of my great-grandmother—who we called Aziz.

Cutting straight across the meadow was a secret tiny river no wider than the length of my arm. I could hop back and forth, or straddle it like a giant. The green grass on either side was tall enough to flop over the banks and hide the river—that's why it was secret.

If you looked from the house window, you'd see a crazy kid jumping ziggy-zaggy across the field. But the almost underground river wasn't a brook or creek. The water flowed through it at river speed. If you slipped when you did a straddle jump and a foot went in the water, it would grab your ankle and yank.

I remember squatting by it and staring at the clear water rushing over the stones. My little hand wasn't enough to block it. A few yards up the river, my sister put her hand in the river, but her hands were bigger, so every once in a while the water would stop and the stones would glimmer and tiny fish would flop between them. I would shout and she would lift her hand, and the water would come rushing back.

I believed—as deeply as you can believe anything—that one of those fish would pop its head above the water and speak to me like in the *1,001 Nights* stories, because I was the one who told my sister to make the river flow again.

It would say, "O, happy boy, may the wise and eternal God bless you for saving me."

I would reply, "He is wise indeed," showing I'm a good guy in the story who believes in God, and not one of those djinns who speak against him.

Then the fish would go on, "But still, I am drowning in sorrow if not in air. I was once the prince of a great green city on the banks of a river one thousand times bigger than this, with skiffs and feluccas, and galleons sailing on it to bring my people silk, spices, and animals as you have never seen from the corners of the world."

"What happened, honorable prince?" I would ask, "What brought you low?"

The fish would say, "I will tell you a tale passing strange and wondrous as a *warning*, so that what happened to the ox and the baker and my great green city might not happen to you."

"Tell me," I would say, "Tell me, please, Mr. Fish. Tell me the warning."

Even though I would ask three times, the prince fish would dart suddenly back into the water and swim downstream.

To lose something you never had can be just as painful—because it is the hope of having it that you lose. The hope that in this world, there are magical fish who will give you advice and warning, when really, the future is unknowable and infinitely dangerous.

The story of the magical fish is just a nice thing I imagined. I never had anything like that. I remember hearing my sister walk across the meadow from upstream. "Hey Khosrou," she said. "What're you doing?"

I shrugged. The magic fish was long gone.

"Let's play a game," she said.

We played a game where she would stand upstream and drop a combination of wildflowers into the river. I would wait downstream and shout what I saw. "Yellow, red, red, blue."

"No, it was red, yellow, red, blue."

That was it.

Not really a game.

I would scoop the flowers out of the water and arrange them into piles. I could give them to Aziz, I thought. She would forgive that we had emptied her meadow.

The last set of colors was, "Yellow, blue, brown—"

When I scooped it out, I screamed, because it was a wet mushy poop. I threw it down. I smelled my hand. There was some left. I shook my hand and wiped it on the grass. I stuck it in the river, but my sister said, "There's more in there."

A new bulb of sewage flowed past. I pulled my hand out and shuddered. "There's a woman up there washing diapers," said my sister, nodding upstream.

My pile of flowers was ruined.

My magic river was just a drainage gully.

The game all along was to get my hand in a sewer.

I HEARD THIS ONCE:

When the immigrants came to America, they thought the streets would be paved with gold. But when they got here, they realized three things:

1. The streets were not paved with gold.
2. The streets were not paved at all.
3. They were the ones expected to do the paving.

THE TRUE STORY OF AZIZ is more interesting than a magic fish anyway, and took place beside a real river called the Aras. When she was a little girl, she lived in a big house surrounded by saffron fields. Do you know about saffron? Should I explain it? Okay, I'll explain. It's a spice that comes from pulling tiny threads from the middle of a flower. It's delicate and impossible to harvest with machines—you have to pinch them out of the flower by hand. In fact, I bet it's even more valuable than gold.

Aziz's dad was a khan for owning all the fields. They say he rode his horse in top hat and tails—he was a gentleman farmer.

And they say he was kind to his workers. When the girls returned from the fields to the big house, everyone at the house could hear their laughter, because saffron has an aroma that makes people happy. Sometimes a warm rain would soak the fields and the flowers would give off their deep red color—rivers of red, like the yolk of sunset burst over everything. The workers' hands would be stained yellow; so would the ankles of the khan's white horse.

Aziz was the little princess of the khan's grand floral sea. She read her books in the open courtyard sitting on the inlay tiles of the fountain, one foot dangling on each side, with an eye always on the horizon.

When her father's hat peeked over the hill, and the laughter of the harvesters was a far-off chime, Aziz would run into the house to tell everyone, "They're coming! They're coming!"

Aziz ran back across the orchard to the bonfire. The old cook got his kiss on the cheek from the princess, waited for her to leave, and began barking orders. The whole house prepared for the feast. Even Aziz. Her job was to fill two bowls with fresh yogurt from the sacks hanging in the basement larder, where the floor was packed dirt, and where the old cook kept his pickling jars.

Soon the dinner carpet was full with trays of kebab, grilled onions and tomatoes, platters of fresh chives, green and purple basil, cilantro, radishes, and dill. The mountains of steaming basmati rice were capped with drizzles of saffron butter. A stew of chickpea, lamb, crispy shallots, and fried mint was the khan's favorite.

Aziz always sat beside him and made sure his plate never wanted for anything. He did not talk much, but held his wife's hand as much as possible. You can already feel it, can't you, in all this happiness, that some horrible darkness perched outside the houses watching Aziz.

And those nights in the saffron fields would be the best she ever got.

LISTEN TO ME FOR a second.

The life of Aziz is a tragic one.

It was a real life. She was a happy mazloom girl in this part, but I only knew her as an old woman—bent in two, with a face like dry soap, shut off from the world, shuffling around her little sod house by the ravine in her coverings like a black ghost.

She would look at me—I remember because she would smile and the lines in her face twisted into unfamiliar shapes—almost like a grimace, almost like she was looking at me from the bottom of a well.

She offered sesame candy from a dish beside the lamp that also had buttons in it. I remember because it was the first time in my life I refused candy.

Those are the only two memories I have of Aziz: the little river of flowers and sewage, and a sad old grin giving me stale candy. I'm telling you this because it's important to count the memories. The rest is other people's memories. Stories they told me some thousands of nights ago.

Now that we are here in Oklahoma, I will never see Aziz again, because she is too old to travel and I can never go back.

Sometimes on the bus to school, I think of her and hope she has a gentle death. I hope she has more memories that I do, and I hope she forgives me for the ones I have of her. In my head, I tell her I will always think of her as the princess of a kingdom of laughing flowers.

But the truth is that we are both exiles and will never go home again.

THE DAY AZIZ BECAME an exile is also the day she lost her father, the great khan, forever.

The legend goes that the khan had to take a long trip. His fields stretched from northern Iran into Azerbaijan, which, at the time, was a part of the Russian Empire. For centuries,

Russian and Persian dynasties fought over it—but at this time, it was peaceful and the khan rode back and forth without trouble.

In the stories the calamity is sudden. Somewhere else in the world, a mad king sent out his army.

Not an important king.

Aziz wouldn't even know his name. But the stars and the moon and every heavenly thing aligned to make the worst of all outcomes. And so the far-off kingdoms of Europe and Russia tumbled into the second Great War.

The drums of war had not yet silenced the laughter of the harvesters, but Aziz felt the first pinch of heartache when her father didn't return on the appointed day.

They say he was in Azerbaijan when the war began, and the borders were closed. I imagine it like an iron fence shutting behind him and scaring his horse. No one knows what happened after that. His fields on that side of the Aras River were taken by faceless enemies. And the khan was never heard from again.

It's easy to imagine it from our side of history. To see the khan's horse rear up at an encroaching darkness that pounces on him like a pack of wolves.

To imagine him immediately drowned.

To see his top hat floating away in a red river.

But Aziz and her mother didn't have the comfort of certainty. To her, the darkness across the river was a cloud of endless unknowing.

At any moment, she might see her baba emerge with tales of adventure and a pocket full of sesame candy.

Until the very last day, Aziz stared in the direction of the northern fields and wished for the khan's return.

But that was months after he disappeared, and by then her uncles had already done their evil.

FOR MY CLASS PROJECT, I would like to present the *1,001 Nights*, which will unconfuse you about some very important things.

First, you have to know about Shahryar, who was a Persian king—not in true history, but in myth history.

He had a wife we will not name, because it would be embarrassing to her family. In the story everyone except Scheherazade is a shame for their family, but the queen is especially shameful because she's an oath breaker.

The king finds his wife in the garden copulating—that means sexing, but I use the official word because Mrs. Miller would freak out if I said "sex" in class and Tanner would make kissy noises and Kelly J. would say, "Gross!" either because of Tanner being slurpy or because she thinks I'm gross and "sex" reminded her to remind me.

So anyway, the king finds her cheating on him and goes crazy.

He has everyone killed, which is why we'll just call him "the king" from now on. In the story he mends his broken heart by turning it to stone.

Every night after that, the king marries a young woman and kills her in the morning. The night he marries Scheherazade, we are not told what number wife she is.

This is how the thousand nights begin, with Scheherazade entertaining the king with a story. Before she can finish each one, we are told "the morning overtook Scheherazade, who lapsed into silence," leaving the king burning to hear the rest.

And so each morning he spares her life in order to hear the end of the story. And each night Scheherazade weaves the tales together so that they always end on a cliffhanger. The brilliant part is that the king always thinks it's his idea for them to keep going. And at important parts, she stops and lets the king fill in the story so he feels good.

For a thousand and one nights she does this, but really, it's forever, because we don't have all thousand and one stories recorded. Nobody wants them to end. They're all the stories people tell after dinner, over glasses of tea. Like with the phrase "Once upon a time," a storyteller will say, "And so the following night, Scheherazade began her tale once again."

There are endless variations from teller to teller. *The Tale of the Three Brothers and the Djinn* might be a comedy if you hear it in the market in Isfahan, or it might be a hero's journey around a bonfire in Ardestan. Every possible version exists somewhere. In the mind of Scheherazade there are a thousand times a thousand times a thousand tales.

She tells them forever without stopping.

Even this is one of them.

But lunchtime has overtaken me and I cannot finish my report on what I did this summer.

WHAT DOES THIS HAVE to do with Aziz as she awaited her father, you might ask.

How does this unconfuse anything?

The answer is that now you know two true things.

One, every story is the sound of a storyteller begging to stay alive.

And two, the story of Aziz could have gone a million different ways.

IN A DIFFERENT TALE, the khan has an odyssey in the Azerbaijani hill country.

He dances with every member of a village of lepers, and heals them with nothing more than a kind touch.

He steals a key ring from the horn of a sleeping djinn and throws it to a mermaid imprisoned on a salt stone at the center of a pink lake.

He sits for tea in the den of a demon who believes in God and together they write the saddest of poems, a poem so immeasurably sad that it quenches the flames of the demon's seat in hell.

And he returns in time to tell it.

The khan returns in the final moment to save his daughter from her uncles.

But this is not what happened.

After just a few weeks, the khan was considered dead, and the mansion in the saffron fields fell into decay.

The world's war found Aziz and her mother and the old cook and the harvesters—and put its calloused hand over their mouths.

The fields went fallow.

Hunger came on them like a bandit.

Her mother sat all day with an untouched glass of tea and watched it cool. Aziz began to feel that her mother had also left her, and would only return with the khan.

Aziz spent those famine days at the front window of the house, in a state of half-reading. Carriages drove past the open courtyard, taking people to the cities to find work. One woman stuck her hand out of a carriage and let a man cut the bracelet from her wrist in exchange for a loaf of bread.

The day her uncles came, Aziz witnessed the old cook carrying a pot of barley stew from the bonfire on the other side of the orchard to the main house, when a gang of people attacked him, spilling the pot onto the dirt. They pushed the cook aside. And then they fell to all fours and plunged their faces into the stew and the mud.

IMAGINE YOU'RE EVIL.

Not misunderstood.

Not sad.

But evil.

Imagine you've got a heart that spends all day wanting more.

Imagine your mind is a selfish room full of pride or pity.

Imagine you're like Brandon Goff and you find poor kids in the halls and make fun of their clothes, and you flick their ears until they scream in pain and swing their arms, and so you pin them down and break their fingers.

Or you spit in his food in the cafeteria.

Or you just call him things like cockroach and sand monkey.

Imagine you're evil and you don't do any of those things, but you're like Julie Jenkins and you laugh and you laugh at everything Brandon does, and you even help when a teacher comes and asks what's going on and you say nothing's going on, and he believes you because you get A-pluses in English.

Or imagine you just watch all of this. And you act like you're disgusted, because you don't like meanness. But you don't do anything or tell anyone.

Imagine how much you've got compared to all the kids in the world getting blown up or starved, and the good you could do if you spent half a second thinking about it.

Suddenly evil isn't punching people or even hating them.

Suddenly it's all that stuff you've left undone.

All the kindness you could have given.

All the excuses you gave instead.

Imagine that for a minute.

Imagine what it means.

WELL, ANYWAY, DON'T GET too upset.

You can always find somebody worse-acting than you and say, at least I'm not as bad as *that* guy.

And you can feel good and go to the mall and go back to being evil.

HER EVIL UNCLES APPEARED on a cold early morning, right after Aziz walked into the courtyard and found her mother dead.

Aziz was only ten. She stood over her mother and thought, How will I tell this news to Father when he comes back? That was how out-of-touch she was, probably. She knew he was dead, but also, in a different story, he was temporarily dead. She wanted to live in that other story.

In a different tale her mother would have died of heartache for her missing husband (in this one, disease).

That was the story that actually happened. Aziz lost her dad, then lost her mom, then the uncles arrived as if they had heard the news of their sister already. As if they knew Aziz had become the orphan heir of all the khan's estate.

She had no one but the old cook, and the steward family who kept the orchards, and the harvesters who lived in the village. But they couldn't defend her against her own kin.

The uncles—I don't know what they looked like or how many. Let's make two. Both younger brothers to Aziz's mother, both squat and shaggy.

No wait, one is pinched and thin.

Together they look like a bird and an onion.

One is the kind of villain who wants more for himself.

The other is the kind who wants less for others.

The one who looked and moved like a bird was the first to walk into the house and inspect everything, as if he'd just walked into a bazaar. The uncle who looked and smelled like an onion stood by the door, sweating.

So the story goes that the uncles had whispered with a clerk in the village and given him gold. In exchange, they took the deed to all the khan's fields.

And what about their orphan niece?

They would keep her, of course.

She would care for the house.

There is no more description of this time in Aziz's life, because no one ever talked about it.

The harvesters refused to call the uncles "khans." Under the watch of Mr. Bird and Mr. Onion, they marched into springtime fields so full of purple flowers they looked like carpets in the house of God. But Aziz never heard the harvesters laugh again.

As she washed and mended, she only ever heard them say, "Don't worry, Aziz joon. Soon you will come of age and claim the khan's inheritance."

No one knows if Aziz felt better when she heard that sort of thing. Because Aziz would never say. But it would have been better if she put her head down and helped the cook prepare the private meals for her uncles. It would have been better if Aziz never dared hope anything in those long five years.

Because the version where she grows and takes her father's house back—that's not how the story goes.

PEOPLE GET MARRIED FOR all kinds of reasons.

I said that once in Mrs. Miller's class and Julie Jenkins said, "Like love."

And I said, "Or money. Or protection. Or just to talk to somebody," which is what I thought at the time, because my mom married Ray. It seemed to me she just wanted someone who spoke Farsi like we did, and he was the only one we met when we got here. Mrs. Miller didn't know that, so she said, "Thank you, David. Let's stay on task."

She called me David for the first few weeks, even though we told people to call me Daniel. They're both the same to me, so I didn't correct her. "Ma and Pa love each other," adds Julie. And we go on reading *Charlotte's Web*.

We lived in an apartment before Ray. Brentwood Apartments. It was a nice place. I once saw a kid explode his tongue with a car battery, so I guess it was the kind of place where they value education.

His name was Tanner and he was trying to kill the cockroaches in a drain ditch behind the apartments. He had the two prongs of jumper cables with the other end attached to the car battery. And he'd put them on the cockroaches.

I was only there because Ray was shouting at my mom and they'd sent us outside. I played in the cement drainage area because Tanner told me someone had killed a kid in the woods last year. So I stayed away from there.

"Come check this out," said Tanner.

I didn't move.

He jabbed the prongs into the ditch, under an open grate, and laughed. "I think you could kill a turtle with this."

"Don't," I said.

That made Tanner look up, because I was telling him what to do. He could have probably killed me if he wanted. "What'd you say?"

I would have run home, but Ray hit my mom a lot back then, and it was worse if we were around. I said, "Nothing. I thought . . . is there a turtle in there?"

"No, idiot."

He stuck the prongs in again. They made a zap sound.

"It could fry up a bird, easy," he said.

When I had a dad, in Iran, we had a house and it was so beautiful. I dream about it sometimes. There's a smell I smell in those dreams. It could be a fake memory, because one of the pictures we still have—a baby picture—was me in the backyard standing in front of a wall of white jasmine flowers and red roses. I'm smelling one in the picture—my sister says, like a sissy. Like a sensitive boy, my mom would say.

I dream about that sunny jasmine smell.

And we had a pool.

And between my room and my sister's, the wall was one giant sheet of glass. Between us was a room with trees in it—inside the house—for doves to perch on. The ceiling of that room was glass too. Light shined down all day on the potted trees and the birds sang to each other. You could see it all from both rooms. I would watch my sister through the glass room playing. She wouldn't let me go around to play with her. But the memory is that flower smell, the glare of the glass, squinting to see my sister on her side with her dolls, and the birds in between sitting safe in their orchard. When I was a kid I thought everybody had a glass bird room in their houses. I only ever remember birds being nice to me. I thought, Why would Tanner want to kill them?

With Tanner I ask, "How strong is it?" The battery. He's got a pile of dead roaches already.

He shrugs.

I wonder if we'll go to the hospital today and tell them my mom hurt herself. And Ray will buy us dinner at a restaurant.

An idea worms its way into Tanner's brain. He looks at the two prongs attached to the car battery. Like a bird, he cocks his head sideways.

I say, "Don't."

He slowly raises the prongs to his face.

I don't have anyone to shout for, because all the other kids in my class live in houses across town and the apartment families won't talk to us because they say they may be poor, but they ain't dune coons that make foul-smelling food and yell at each other in gobbledygook.

Tanner opens his mouth and looks at me, big-eyed. He stands up to brace himself. But I don't dare him to do it.

"That's gonna hurt—"

I don't finish, because he jabs the two prongs onto his tongue and the zap sound is a juicy water balloon sound.

Tanner's mouth is suddenly full—like he's blowing out his cheeks.

He drops the cables and falls to his knees.

I hear a scream from an apartment window.

Tanner opens his mouth and a water balloon worth of blood pours out.

More screams.

Tanner's still coughing, like moms do when they get punched in the stomach. A chunk of his tongue is in the pool of blood.

I run to get help and hear an ambulance coming.

It could be for Tanner or my mom.

Anyway.

Sometimes people get married just so he'll buy them a house—not one with a bird room—a little one with cockroaches. Maybe it's love most of the time. But that's a reason too. And it doesn't have to be because they want a father figure for their sons. That would be a terrible reason.

You shouldn't put that kind of blood on a kid's head. Cause he would have said he didn't even want a house or a stepdad, if it was all for him like my sister said.

Sisters can be evil like that.

They tell you all the nightmares you ever had were your fault, and you were the reason somebody broke your mother's jaw.

Anyway, Tanner came back three months later with a forked tongue. He'd stick it out like a snake—two nubs wiggling around.

And anyway maybe Ma and Pa in *Charlotte's Web* do love each other.

Maybe I could have just read that and had a father figure to teach me how to treat mothers. Anyway, the only reason I said anything was that sometimes marriages give people houses and sometimes they take them away.

Like for Aziz. She lost hers.

HERE'S A VERSION OF the rest of the story that is mostly true.

By the time Aziz turned fourteen, she had stopped glancing across the orchard every time she passed by, hoping to see the khan riding up the road.

She had buried him in her heart.

The saffron fields—under her uncles' control—were just a great big red river of blood. Every day, she would wake the rooster who slept by the fountain in the courtyard. She would lean into the open grate of the reservoir and pull out five stones the size of cantaloupes that stopped it up. The water would flow into the paved channels in the courtyard to feed the apple trees and the grape vines.

The truth is that she was lost after that. She wandered.

One evening her uncles appeared as she sat on a blanket pitting cherries and spreading them out to dry in the sun. Uncle Bird liked to stand when others sat. Uncle Onion sat and began eating the pitted cherries.

Aziz was polite, but she was also a thousand worlds away.

"We have news," said Bird.

"Mmm," said Onion, and then, *shlorp shlorp shlorp*, which was the sound of cherries mushing in his mouth.

"News that will make you happy," said Bird. "Do you want to hear it?"

"Yes, Uncle. You must both be hungry. We have dinner."

But Onion was content devouring her day's work.

"We should tell you now," said Bird. "It's a family matter."

In that moment Aziz dared hope.

Was he alive?

Had he returned?

"You are a married woman now," said Bird.

"Congratu—*shlorp shlorp*!" said Onion.

"He lives in Karaj. His name is Hassan."

Aziz had never been as far as Karaj in her life. It was as far away as Edmond from the Gulf of Mexico. She said, "Dear Uncles, am I not helpful?"

"Of course," said Onion.

"And as owners of this house, couldn't you let me stay?"

She referred softly to the fact that her uncles had long ago stolen the deed to the estate. There was no need to send her away. She would never inherit.

"Yes," said Bird, "but we have reputations to think about. You're a woman now, Aziz."

Aziz opened her mouth.

Then closed her mouth.

Then closed her eyes.

WHEN SHE OPENED THEM AGAIN, she was on a horse cart to Karaj with a small trunk of clothes, and nothing to help her remember her mother or father.

She never returned.

OF COURSE, SCHEHERAZADE WOULD never let the morning come at the end of a story—or else the king would have no reason to keep her alive.

Reader, you are the king, so let me tell you, when Aziz married Hassan, the two were already in love and one of them was already destined to die.

IN MRS. MILLER'S CLASS WE make goody bags for American soldiers in the war and it is very important that I help as much as I can to prove whose side I'm on.

"Class," she says, looking at me, "be sure to sign your name at the top of the card."

Jared S. draws a bunch of fighter jets shooting arrows at monkeys on camels. Mrs. Miller comes by and makes her lips a straight line but doesn't say anything.

Brianna is the best at bubble letters, so she writes, "We support the troops," and Kelly J. helps her color the American flag with hearts where the stars should go.

The soldiers are in Iraq to kill Saddam Hussein, who's evil.

I raise my hand and Mrs. Miller calls on me from her desk.

"Saddam Hussein is evil," I say.

"Don't write that, please," she says.

"Okay, but I hope we win," I say.

Some of the kids have uncles in Iraq and lots have family who work at Tinker Air Force Base in Midwest City, Oklahoma. A lot of them think my family is Mexican, which is what "wetback" means, but if they see Ray's beard or hear my mom talking to us in a grocery store, they come up and tell us, "My brother-in-law works every day at Tinker to protect us."

At this moment we will be trying to pick out juicy oranges, so my mom will say something like, "Yes. Good."

Then they'll say, "We support the troops around here," and walk off. Some say, "Eff Saddam!"

I want to tell them that when I was three, Saddam was at war with Iran. He bombed Isfahan every night trying to kill people and my uncles fought him. One of them has a twitchy face from the chemical attacks. One night, when I was a baby, the building next to ours was hit and the whole thing collapsed.

My mom says she ran into my room and I was still asleep.

I was a super fat and sleepy baby—which is the best kind of baby. And I even slept through bombs.

So the point is that Iran is not the same country as Iraq. This should be obvious because they have different names. But then Doug C. leans over and says, "Hey, you from Iraq?"

"No."

"If I ever see a dune coon, you know what I'd do?"

"What's a dune coon?"

"Arabs."

"I'm not Arab."

"Okay, but you know what I'd do?"

"What?"

"Iraq, Iran," he says. "I-rack," he says again, "I-ran . . . I'd kick 'em in the balls."

He laughs. I kinda laugh, because it's joking and joking is a shared thing. Mocking is a joke that is not shared. I laugh a little to acknowledge that he has shared his joke with me.

Then I tell him, "I signed my name 'Daniel.'"

"Good for you," he says.

That way the soldiers won't think I'm trying to poison them with my tin of cookies.

Also, I don't have a problem with Arabs. I'm just not one.

Also, kicking someone in the nuts and then running is a coward thing to do, but I guess there isn't a country for I-rack, I-gloat.

I AM IN LOVE WITH KELLY J., who thinks I am disgusting even though I finish worksheets faster than all the other boys. She seems to value Tyler L. for his shirts with surfing lizards on them.

There is no helping this.

I do not have the T-shirts that she likes, because they are from a store called Gadzooks, which is in the mall of new clothes. I only have my love, and used clothing.

I used to believe that you could not choose who you love any more than you could choose the picture on a used shirt.

But the truth is that no one is innocent in love, and nobody forced me to love Kelly J. I don't want to stop just because she laughs at me. I want to stay in love with her until she realizes I am a person. It is a complicated thing that a little kid, or even a fifth grader, can't understand, that we are always choosing situations that hurt us.

We choose them so deeply that we don't know we chose them. We think we had to. We think the world did it to us.

And then we think, what a horrible world that makes a weapon out of love. That stabs you with it, even when you can't defend yourself and the other person hates you and wants to see you cry.

It's a miracle that anyone would ever fall in love with someone else and—of all the people in the world—that person loves them back. Like if you fell off a building and landed in a pillow truck, somehow.

It doesn't happen, basically.

Which means we end up with someone and there's lots of choosing to do. Choosing to forgive strange smells or choosing that Gadzooks is not the only place that boyfriends can shop.

This is the work of love.

I never had a grandpa to tell me this stuff, so I could be completely wrong.

I mean, I only have the memories of people quitting love. So I've seen it. I've seen love take hard work that they don't want to do anymore. They just decide their own kids aren't worth it (my dad). They tell themselves it's okay to give up, because love should be like the shows on TV, where you float uncontrollably on the smell of the other's perfume. They lie to themselves with stories of Aziz and Hassan, whose love—they say—was like Khosrou and Shirin, a legendary love, a love so big that if it was a mountain it would sink the earth to the bottom of the well of the universe.

HERE IS AN INTERESTING question that I heard once in church. Can God create a mountain so big that He himself couldn't lift it?

It's trying to put God in a corner, because if He can or if He can't, He's not all-powerful.

But the question is silly, because it assumes God is as stupid as we are. If you're as big as God, there's no such thing as "lifting." It's all just floating in a million universes you made. If you made an object of some insane, unusual size, then it'd still be *a thing*.

And God is as big as everything at once. And as small.

Physical stuff is too simple.

The better question is, Can God create a law so big that He himself has to obey it?

Is there an idea so big that God doesn't remember anything before it?

That answer is love.

Love is the object of unusual size.

AT FOURTEEN, AZIZ WAS a beauty.

But this would be difficult for anyone to know because girls at that time stayed home.

So a boy didn't know who to call on (which meant going to their house and asking the parents if he could court their daughter (which meant sitting in a parlor with her and talking to see if he wanted to get married)).

So moms came up with strategies. At the public baths, they would look for the beautiful girls and tell their sons to go calling at their houses.

Or people would look at the brothers. If the brothers had soft flowy hair and nice cheeks and pretty eyes, people would assume his sister would too, so she'd get a bunch of callers.

But if the brother was a hairy boar, like if he spit a lot and had a giant nose, people would imagine it on a girl's face and that sister would have lots of time to read.

The word for those guys was "sister ruiner."

Aziz didn't have any of that when the horse cart rode into Karaj: the brother to help or hurt her reputation, the mother to watch out for her at the baths, or the father to stand at the door and look strong.

She was beautiful and alone.

I do not know how the story goes exactly.
Only that Persian love stories are all tragedies.
To explain love, I have to tell you three stories:

The first is the myth of Khosrou and Shirin.
The second is the legend of Aziz and her husbands.
The third is the history of how I broke my thumb at my mom's church.

THE MYTH OF KHOSROU and Shirin and its relation to my mom, and the Miami Dolphins and church.

When I was a kid (before Oklahoma), my name was Khosrou and everybody could say it, because everybody knows Khosrou was a shah in the year 500. I told you that already, didn't I? Scheherazade repeats herself all the time, just so you know.

Khosrou—I'll stop writing it so you can stop skipping it—was the famous king who made the carpet called "The Spring of Khosrou," where the rubies and emeralds were flowers in a golden field. It was one of the legendary treasures of the Old World. You remember this, yes?

I always imagined the king laid the rug in his audience hall so that anyone who came to petition him would step on the greatest treasure in the kingdom. This would be such a Persian thing to do.

A farmer walks in and doesn't even realize it until his muddy boot treads on a bouquet of jasmine made of pearls and he says, "Oh."

And then realizes he's soiled the magic carpet of the greatest empire in the world and says, "Oh!"

And the Persian king, being super Persian, goes, "Come in. Come in. No matter the carpet."

"A thousand apologies," says the farmer, falling to his knees to wipe the pearls with his shirt.

"Don't trouble yourself," says the king.

This is how Persians host. There are very important rules to treating guests with honor. The farmer would just keep apologizing. They would go back and forth. Until the farmer wiped the rug clean.

"Forever my deepest apologies, O King."

"You are more valuable to me," the king says, "than any rug." (Even though the rug is more valuable than three countries.)

"I will leave," says the farmer.

"No, no," says the king. "But perhaps—"

"I will remove my shoes," says the farmer, finally catching on.

"That might be good, but only if you'd like to."

"Of course, of course," says the farmer, retreating to the entry and pulling off his boots.

"I will have someone bring you my own boots."

"No, I could never," says the farmer.

This is called "tarof," by the way, this politeness that goes on forever.

"Of course. Or perhaps my socks."

"I am unworthy of the king's socks. But if the king pleases, so I don't muddy your sacred hall, may I—"

"Have a basin to wash your feet?"

"Yes. If you please."

"Of course!" says the king.

And they go on like this for hours, honoring each other. So you should know when a Persian tarofs you, there are rules. I can't tell you them now cause I'm in the middle of a story, but you should know those rules because they're just trying to give you respect. Otherwise you end up making everyone feel like garbage. Like, you already know the American rule that when you walk into someone's house, you don't go, "Nice couch," and then climb all over the couch with your shoes on. It's that kind of thing.

In Oklahoma, when people from church come to our apartment, they don't ask if they should take their shoes off. They just walk on the rug. But then our rug isn't very nice, so maybe they aren't embarrassed when they get mud all over it. It's the most expensive thing we have, because our TV is a hand-me-down. But it's still not that nice. My mom doesn't say anything because they never start the tarof and they never realize when she's doing it.

Khosrou had a son named Hormizd IV, who had a son named Khosrou II. It was the grandson who grew up and fell in love with a woman named Shirin.

Like Aziz, Khosrou II had two evil uncles who killed his father, Hormizd, so that they could control him and take everything.

This was when the Persian Empire was so big that uncles and princes each got their own countries to play with. The saddest moment, I think, is that when his brothers grabbed the king in his palace, they blinded him first. I imagine one version of the story where the king falls to his knees before his ungrateful guests and looks at his father's great gold springtime carpet, maybe focuses on a single poppy flower made of rubies stitched around yellow diamonds with one black pearl at the center—and he watches as the boots of traitor soldiers tread it with the blood of his loyal servants. And that's the last thing he sees before the hand of eternal darkness covers his eyes—a poppy, red like blood.

No one ever told me if Khosrou II was part of the plan to kill his own father. I never imagined the king looking up to see his son standing in the poppy field. They probably didn't tell me because I'm named after him and it would be a curse to be named after a treacherous son.

All my mother ever said was that Khosrou II had his uncles killed and he was the best-looking boy in the fifth grade.

As for his love story, here are the lessons:

When Khosrou was a young man, his friend told him about an Armenian princess named Shirin—which means "sweetness" in Farsi.

Anyway, Khosrou fell in love with her, just from the descriptions from his friend, that she was a super finigonzon, with peridot eyes and one of those noses that look like a pinky finger and not a thumb.

The lesson here is that you can fall in love with a story you have in your head.

And the same happened to Shirin, who fell in love with Khosrou just by looking at a picture of him. You can imagine people a certain way and it's like you created them. Like a whole new Kelly who doesn't roll her eyes so much.

So the boy is all googly-eyed over the story within the story of the girl, but this isn't a Disney movie, so he doesn't just float over to Armenia. What happens is a warlord named Chobin shows up with an army at Khosrou's palace.

Chobin had been a general in Khosrou's dad's army and had been dismissed for losing a battle. He was humiliated and there's nobody more dangerous than a kid who feels like that.

Chobin's rebel army probably all felt like that. Fighting with tears in their eyes and embarrassed for being babies who cry.

And that army—the mazloom army—that one always wins.

So Khosrou had to run away and Chobin became the king of the Persian Empire. When Khosrou reached Armenia, he wasn't any better than a refugee, and Shirin was as blond as Kelly J.

The lesson here is that people have scales in their heads and they measure other people for their value and ugly refugee boys are near the bottom and pretty blond girls are at the top. This is not a happy lesson. But you either get the truth, or you get good news—you don't often get both.

Anyway, Khosrou was actually handsome, so that helped. When they met they fell into magical love. In the story,

Khosrou sees her naked while she's bathing and Shirin says she'll never marry him unless he gets his kingdom back, so maybe that tells you way too much about magical love.

Then Khosrou goes to Constantinople to ask the caesar for an army to go back and defeat Chobin. The caesar says, "Okay."

"Okay okay?" says Khosrou. He was probably expecting some tarof, some backing-and-forthing, but the caesar gets right to the point.

"Okay, you can have my army, but you have to marry my daughter Maryam."

"Which one's Maryam?" says Khosrou.

And the caesar points to a girl picking her nose in the corner.

The lesson here is don't ask anybody for anything you can't pay for. Or maybe it's that nobody cares if two lovers get together—that's like a cake only they get to eat. But nobody likes to watch someone else eat cake.

I don't know the lesson exactly at this point. Honestly, Mrs. Miller, not everything has a lesson. It's a complication that Khosrou agrees to. He marches back to Persia with an army and a wife, and smacks Chobin so hard for wrecking everything that Chobin flees to Fergana, which is like saying he runs away to Mars. And even then, Khosrou's so furious about having to beg the caesar and being homeless when he met Shirin, and being forced to marry Maryam, that he hires an assassin to sneak into Chobin's fortress and stab him to death.

A tip-top love story so far.

But by the time Khosrou finished with Chobin, he heard a rumor that broke his heart—like maybe he was in the library during lunch and his friend came in and told him—that a finigonz named Farhad, who was some kind of sculptor with dimples and everything, had started hanging out with Shirin after school.

"Sculptors can't be rivals to kings," said Khosrou, so he sent Farhad into exile to a mountain called Behistun and told him he couldn't return until he carved a staircase into the stone cliffside—all the way up the mountain.

"Rival for what?" said Maryam probably.

"Uh," said Khosrou.

The lesson here is that if you watch the side characters in a love story, you might notice the lovers treating them like garbage, with the excuse that they're doing it for love.

But another lesson might be that maybe you're not the hero of every story, and maybe Farhad was Shirin's true love, or maybe there isn't just one person designated for everybody. Maybe there's a lot more to it—maybe you choose and you practice, and that's what makes the love true.

Farhad had chosen to love Shirin and threw himself into the task of sculpting the face of the world. He carved the stone of Behistun into a staircase—one step at a time—all the while dreaming that he'd reach the peak of the mountain and by then he'd have changed the world. He could fly directly into the arms of Shirin. And all that pain would become gladness.

When Khosrou heard that Farhad was making progress—that day and night he worked at carving the rock and loving Shirin—Khosrou was filled with jealousy.

He sent a message to Farhad.

It reached Farhad on the mountain, by a bird.

Farhad held the creature in his calloused and dusty hands and pulled a roll of parchment from the tube tied around its leg. It said, "Shirin is, unhappily, dead. Do not return. Here is a list of more mountains."

On the back was the list, but Farhad didn't read it. He had reached the top of Behistun. The last step.

He could see—if he squinted, and if his eyes weren't full of tears—all the way to Armenia. And he thought of all the pain he had eaten to see Shirin again. Her face.

He screamed words in the unknowable language.

And he jumped.

And he did not fly.

THE LESSON HERE IS that your happiest memories can become your saddest all of a sudden.

KHOSROU WAS SO STUPID in this story that he thought he could have Shirin, now that Farhad was dead.

He never thought about poison.

How it might infect his own life to hate his wife, and kill some innocent man to get what he wanted.

That's a metaphor kind of idea.

His heart had festered with murder and jealousy—so little by little he boiled away all the loving parts.

But in this story, there is also real poison.

When Shirin heard that Farhad had jumped off the mountain, she must have known the reason. She must have known the truth about Khosrou.

But people get married for all kinds of reasons, so she still wanted him.

One thing that is interesting is that lots of poisons taste sweet. They're not like acid. They're like syrup.

This is interesting because you can imagine Maryam taking a drink of mulberry cordial one night and saying, "Mmm, shirin," which is the word for "sweet," and also the word for her killer.

Maryam died clawing at her own throat, trying to scrape or squeeze the shirin poison back out as it ripped her apart.

But remember, this is a love story.

And the lesson here is that people are unlikeable. They have the irritating habit of believing they are as important as you are to the story. I might be especially unlikeable to you because I'm not beautiful like Scheherazade, or funny, but I still have her job to entertain you.

And I want to be good.

I want to give you something you treasure.

I want you to like me, as if I was a person in your life.

That doesn't make me beautiful.

But wanting to please you is important too.

That's what you want, after all: to be pleased.

You'd be shocked how few people want what you want.

FARHAD AND MARYAM WERE conveniently dead, leaving Khosrou and Shirin to their love.

Except it was poison love now.

They had both murdered someone for it.

And if you thought this ended happily, then you haven't been paying attention. These stories are epic, so by this time, Khosrou had a son with Maryam (before Shirin killed her obviously). The son was a teenager and into girls. Uh-oh, you might be thinking.

And "uh-oh" is right, because the kid kills Khosrou so he could be with Shirin (the lady who killed his mom (but he probably doesn't know that)).

But before he could force her to marry him, Shirin went to the grave of Khosrou and drank poison.

The end.

There is a love story for you.

Really makes your tummy tingle.

The lesson here is that love is a many-parted thing.

There is the part when you see someone beautiful (naked in a bath or not naked), and you want to be near them.

There is the part when you decide not to marry anyone else (which Khosrou didn't do).

There is the part that makes you improve yourself—makes you practice controlling your fear and jealousy. There is the part where you choose every action so that it doesn't hurt the one you love, even indirectly. There's a lot more to love than smooching.

People are also many-parted things.

Two Persian poets—Ferdowsi and Nizami—tell it differently. As if both of them lived with Shirin and remember her with their own flawed memories.

In one telling she's a mazloom finigonzon who suffers. When she dies, it's because she was too pure for this world, and too sad. That one doesn't mention her poison stash.

In the other telling, she's the jealous maniac who murders Maryam and decides to kill herself when the son insults her pride with a proposal.

In the version I tell, she's a mix, like Mithridates who drank all that poison so it wouldn't hurt him while he was exiled, and then returned and killed everyone. She's half defending herself, half burning the world down. Sometimes I add to Shirin's story by having her do the same thing. She was paranoid that someone would poison her like she did to Maryam, so little by little she made herself immune. And then my twist in the last scene is that she drinks a whole cup to kill herself and nothing happens.

NOW YOU KNOW HOW Persian love stories go.

It's okay to be scared.

WHEN YOU ASK PEOPLE in Oklahoma how their great-grandparents died, they say—almost all of them say:

"Cancer."

Or:

"Heart disease."

Or if you get lucky:

"Kicked in the head by a horse."

Other than the horse one, you have to nod and agree with them that cancer and heart disease are totally normal and respectable ways to eat it.

But if you say, "Poisoned by the town doctor in a blood feud," then you get looks. Courteous looks. Like, "Isn't he precious" looks.

And only then would you regret being agreeable when they said theirs.

Why should you believe them?

How would they know that their great-grandpa died of cancer?

It's just a story someone told them. They weren't there.

They just expect everyone to take their word for it.

And people do, because the story is boring. Nobody cares the second after they hear it.

It goes:

"Cancer."

"Oh."

"Yeah. He was young too, only forty-seven."

"Wow. Wanna get tacos for lunch?"

Don't be fooled by the "wow." That was an "I don't care" wow.

People are like that.

They're immune to the sadness of others.

KARAJ IS A MOUNTAINOUS city so far away from Behistun—where Farhad carved his love letter to Shirin—that you could fit fifteen Edmond, Oklahomas in between.

But in the shadow of every mountain, there is at least one lover who looks up and sighs and wonders if the world could be so easy as to give him love, if he just climbed to the top.

There are no mountains in Oklahoma.

This is why people like the myths of Hercules and Rostam. The clarity that if they just completed their challenges, they could get what they wanted.

But love stories are never so easy. You might climb the whole mountain and return only to find out that mountain climbers aren't your crush's type.

My great-grandmother, Aziz, who was fifteen, loved Hassan, who was in his twenties, and the best thing I can say about it was that their love was clear.

It was clear that Hassan did not need to cleave a mountain to win Aziz.

Hassan owned the only auto parts shop in town. It was clear that Aziz liked this about him, because she always called him a businessman, even after he met with the Karaji physician one day in the winter, and he called Hassan a cart donkey—and which eventually led to Hassan's death.

They were in love—that much is clear.

It was sometime in the 1940s. That part isn't very clear, because I never asked about dates.

They lived in a house. From the kitchen window, Aziz could watch each day as the snowcap marched down the mountains till winter.

She made warm lunches of beef cutlets in tomato and saffron sauce on fresh bread, and walked the muddy path to Hassan's shop with extra crisp radishes and a thermos of hot tea in her gunny sack.

Karaj in the wintertime is a snowbound city, and cars driving on the mountain road would often crunch into potholes and drop transmission parts or hubcaps. They were probably old-timey cars too. This was the time when horses became cars, and great khans became mechanics.

If the people didn't care about cars, they would drive straight into puddles and flood their engines, as the physician did one day, when Aziz made a dish of chicken stewed with plums. She brought the lunch to Hassan wrapped in a scarf that she imagined her father had given her. Hassan kissed Aziz quickly, so the greengrocer across the street and his wife—who spoke to their individual cats more than to each other—would not spread rumors that the young couple were indecent.

Aziz only ever weeps when she remembers this story, and never tells it, so I will make up a scene to show what my mother told me, which is that Hassan and the physician had a misunderstanding that led to a bitter feud.

A truck pulled up in front of the auto parts shop just as Hassan raised his glass of tea. The sugar cube he held between his teeth was still dry when a man slammed the passenger door of the truck and marched toward the shop. He was shaped like a cashew, pushing his belly out and his forehead back.

"How can I help you, Doktor?" said Hassan.

Or, wait. Maybe it starts even worse, like, "Hello, sir, how can I help you?"

"Doktor," says the doctor.

"Oh. Very sorry. How can I help you, Doktor?"

Wait. No. This isn't working.

He's the only doctor in the neighborhood, so it would be unlikely that Hassan wouldn't know him.

In fact, straight-to-your-face rudeness isn't a very Persian thing. It would be more subtle. Like the doctor wouldn't barge in. He'd look at the little carpet that Aziz had put down in the shop and he'd sneer, but he'd never say the rug was too dirty for him to step on. He'd just smile and say, "Oh, I don't want to bother you while you dine," and he'd use a word for "dine" that means being a little lazy in the middle of the day.

Hassan would tarof and say, "Please, share some of my wife's tea," but the doctor would refuse, not even with a long, drawn-out compliment. He'd just say, "Thank you, but I'm in a great hurry."

Can you imagine something that rude?

That his hurry was somehow more important than a person offering tea. And even worse, his wife's tea, while his wife is standing right there.

The doctor may as well have spit in Hassan's face.

He just pushed past the part of the conversation where they would honor each other as humans, and started making requests, as if Hassan was a servant.

"My car is stuck in the mountain pass," said the doctor.

"Were you driving it?"

"When it got stuck?"

"Yes."

"Yes. It sputtered and just stopped."

"You flooded the engine."

"How do you know?"

"Was there smoke?"

"No."

"You flooded the engine."

"It happened after a big puddle."

"Yup."

Aziz would have found something to do in the back of the shop, since it was getting heated and her presence would have made it worse.

The doctor would have let the silence hang, as if everything was obvious.

"Well?"

"Well, how can I help you?" Hassan would say, which in this context would mean, "Get the hell out of my shop."

"I need someone to tow my car and fix it."

This would be the moment that Aziz—peeking from between a row of spark plugs—would see her new husband stop up a volcanic rage, as if it was a bottled djinn.

"I'm *not* a mechanic."

"You sell auto parts?"

"Yup."

"So you're like a hospital without an ambulance?"

"I'm like a grocer who doesn't make you dinner."

"You just sell the ingredients."

"Yup."

"Well, I have some advice if you'd like to improve your business."

"Oh? Does it need an X-ray for a hangnail?"

The doctor would suck his teeth and narrow his eyes at Hassan. To say the doctor pushed for expensive tests was like calling him a thief. Worse than a thief, a liar. He turned and walked away.

And from that moment, Hassan and the doctor were sworn enemies.

The way the doctor would tell it, when he described the fight to anyone who'd listen, was that Hassan was a lazy mechanic who didn't want to work on his lunchtime. The way Hassan would remember it, the doctor made impossible demands, treated him like a cart donkey, and insulted his wife.

Memories are tricky things.

They can fade or fester.

You have to seal them up tight like pickles and keep out impurities like how hurt you feel when you open them. Or they'll ferment and poison your brain.

SOMETIMES IN A VILLAGE in Iran, or Edmond, Oklahoma, a dog and a cat will have such a vicious fight that both of them are changed forever. The cat limps where the dog's teeth got it right in the hind leg. And part of the dog's nose, cut by the cat's claw, dries up and stops working.

The cat and dog make some kind of boundary and stick to their territory, so they can pretend they won a kingdom the size of half a town, when really they lost a limb the size of the other half.

This was Hassan and the physician, who would not even share a butcher between them. Hassan would go in the evenings after closing his store, and purchase from the butcher's wife, while the physician went in the morning to shop from the butcher's son. Neither asked about the other, even though everyone knew their veiled comments about the villains in town were attacks. If you asked the butcher himself, he'd say, "Don't worry about that," because he was the kind of person who hated gossip and just wanted to work. And then he might say, "A man can hold two hearts in the same hand and not let them touch."

And if you asked him what that meant, he would just tell you he needed to get back to work.

The many-hearted butcher was right, of course. Hassan and the physician's feud wasn't good for anyone. And so most of the town ignored it.

Like Mithridates the town became—little by little—immune to the bickering. And so it never solved itself. No one ever said, "Akh, Doktor, please!" or "Akh, Hassan, enough with this madness." And so the bitterness fermented in its jar in the dark cellars of their minds.

Love and lives are complicated, so I will tell you only two things that happened over the next few years, though you can imagine a thousand little slights between the physician and Hassan.

First, Hassan and Aziz had a baby girl—my grandmother, my mother's mother—and the only person who didn't visit was the physician. He left it to the nurses to care for Aziz in her bed.

"If anything had gone wrong," said Hassan, seething.

"Nothing has gone wrong, Husband. Look at these pudgy arms."

And second, Hassan began to come home in the evenings complaining of angels.

"A shaft of white light from the ceiling," he would say, "but deep in the back of the shop, where there are no windows."

"It appears suddenly?" asked Aziz as she held Ellie (who was called Ehteram then, which is really احترام, but who later became Ellie and so let's go with the one you can read).

"So bright I close my eyes and still see it burned into my vision. And a headache for hours after."

When the complaints began to include a dry snapping sound, Aziz's worry became desperate.

She was not yet twenty and her daughter was not yet two when the love of her life collapsed. She found him behind a row of timing belts when she brought a lunch of scallion pancakes. There are moments in your life where you are alone with two cups and you have to pick one to drink.

There are moments when the decision will change everything.

Farhad on the mountain.

My dad at the breakfast in Dubai.

My mom in the safe house.

You'll hear about those later.

For now, there is this one, Aziz with a fallen husband. To let him die was unthinkable. But to beg the physician to save him was equally so, since Hassan would only wake up to hate her forever.

In the short minutes, Aziz decided it was better for him to be alive, to love Ellie, if not to love her. She ran across town, knowing the physician would relish every moment of Hassan's wife begging for his life.

The story of Aziz and Hassan is a love story with poison in it. When the physician came to their tiny house, he saw his opportunity. He gave Hassan a bottle of medicine and left as quickly as he could.

For three days, Aziz fed Hassan the medicine, and for three days, he got worse and worse, until he died in her arms.

In the morgue they discovered that Hassan did not die of disease or from the collapse in his shop.

Aziz realized it was the medicine that killed Hassan. Can you imagine what that felt like? Like your heart is an engine flooded with black acid, drowned and clenched and clotted.

She ran back home from the morgue to find the medicine bottle, to give it to a judge, to convict the physician who had murdered her husband. But when she returned, the window of her kitchen was broken, and all the evidence was gone.

Maybe the lesson is that you never know the damage you might do, when you're trying to help. Or that a feud is a profoundly stupid thing.

There is no lesson maybe.

HERE IN **OKLAHOMA** PEOPLE don't poison each other except with canned green beans that have a vague medicine flavor. I don't think they taste it, because they've gotten used to it, little by little.

At church potlucks they play a secret game of dumping random cans of food in casserole dishes and pretending their grandmothers gave them the recipe. Jell-O is their favorite. Campbell's mushroom Jell-O goes on everything. So does Velveeta, which is a cheese Jell-O that only sort of hardens.

My mom is scared of their unnatural foods. She whispers to us that it's why the cancer rate is so high in America. It's a bored disease for rich people. I told that to my science teacher once—that preservatives cause cancer—and he laughed. He said the science was a little more complicated than that. My mom's a doctor and he is just killing time before coaching volleyball, so eat all the Fritos and corn syrup you want.

My mom makes cream puffs like they had at Akh Tamar and someone always asks what kind of store-bought whipped cream she used. One lady wouldn't even believe you could make your own by whipping heavy cream. Like people in history didn't have whipped cream until a company started selling canisters that squirt out runny foam.

Anyway, this story is embarrassing so I'll tell you a few things first.

One, I have a cap now, which is what they call hats.

A baseball cap, even though mine is for a football team called the Miami Dolphins. I have never been to Miami and never seen a dolphin. My newest friend likes them. My mom bought it for me so that we can declare our friendship. Other kids like the Cowboys, and can never be best friends with a dolphin.

The second thing to know is that I did not cry, even though when you're imagining this story, you'll probably imagine tears on my face when they took me to the hospital.

Well, don't.

AT THE POTLUCKS OF poor people churches in Oklahoma, the BBQ is always good. My friend who supports Miami wasn't there, because his family goes to the big church across town where they serve banana puddin and put out, like, seven different kinds of Pringles, which are the best chip.

This story happens during the time Ray didn't live with us, because he'd broken my mother's jaw and we spent Christmas in First Baptist Hospital. He bought us Pringles and Peanut M&Ms for dinner from the hospital vending machines, and my sister and I told the police it was an accident. And by the summer, they were divorced.

That was just the first time, though.

Anyway.

Summertime potluck.

Good BBQ.

Terrible everything else.

No Ray.

One Dolphins cap.

A youth pastor named Jonboy used to roam around the buffet with a group of high school kids, smiling for the old ladies and asking if any of them needed work done on their lawns.

He had a truck—which all good men in Oklahoma have—with blue neon lights shining underneath it—which they don't.

He argued with his dad, the head pastor, about the difference between old country music, which had grit, and new country music, which had music videos.

Jonboy didn't like me.

His blue truck lights meant he represented the Cowboys.

Some weeks he would refer to matches I hadn't watched. That particular dinner, he saw me by the BBQ and told me the Cowboys would beat the Dolphins again next week.

I said, "Pfft. The Cowboys are the worst team in the league."

Jonboy blinked at me. One of the high school boys named Wes laughed. It turned out the Cowboys had won the Super Bowl last year, so they were the *best* team in the league.

Wes had a brother my age named Bobby, who was standing behind me. He snatched my cap and ran back to Jonboy with it.

"Hey!" is a stupid thing to say that I said.

I looked around. All the grownies had their plates and were sitting at the tables talking about horses or whatever.

"Give me my cap," I said.

Jonboy was a refrigerator-size man wearing a silk Hawaiian shirt that would fit me like a tent. Wes was a wiry hillbilly.

Bobby was a scrub. He gave the cap to Jonboy.

"Give it," I said.

"Or what? What'll you do?" said Wes.

I stared at Jonboy. He grinned at me.

"Careful," said Jonboy. He had a peanut butter cream cookie in his hand. He held it like he was going to smash it inside the hat. "I might ruin it."

I couldn't tell if he was "joshing me," which is when grown-ups pull a kid's leg.

"It would be an improvement," said Bobby.

I didn't know what was supposed to happen.

I didn't even know the Cowboys played the Dolphins.

Jonboy brought the cap and the cookie close together.

"Crush it," said Wes.

But Jonboy said, "Just say the Dolphins suck and you can have it back."

I was alone. My new friend would never know I said it. It's the sort of lie that wouldn't cause any harm—and some people say it is not a sin to do that. But then, some people say Edmond, Oklahoma, looks like Italy in the springtime. Some people are idiots.

I reached into the tub of BBQ and grabbed a handful of sloppy pulled pork.

Jonboy's eyes got serious.

"Give me my cap," I said. A drop of BBQ sauce fell from my hand.

No one ever explains their sense of humor. You have to guess if they're serious. In Oklahoma they call these Mexican standoffs, where everybody has a gun on everybody else.

"Don't," said Jonboy.

"Crush it!" said Bobby.

"I'll throw it," I said.

"Say the Dolphins suck," said Wes.

"The Cowboys suck," I said.

Jonboy smiled and put the cookie into the cap, and started crunching it in his fist.

I threw the pork as hard as I could.

It splattered all over his silk Hawaiian shirt.

Bobby cackled so loud that everyone turned and looked. I ran up and grabbed my hat with my clean hand.

"You ruined my shirt," said Jonboy. His voice was suddenly adult—calm and disappointed. His smirk was gone. It was like he was his dad all of a sudden.

"You ruined my cap," I said.

"Look," he said. And he showed me the peanut butter cookie. He'd crushed it in his hand under the hat.

"That's not fair," I said. He'd tricked me. Now I was the bad one.

"This shirt was expensive," he said.

But I had told him I would throw it. I didn't lie. I said I would.

I thought, My mom doesn't have the money to pay for the shirt.

I didn't even *like* football back then.

"I'm sorry," I said.

But Oklahoma sports stories are all tragedies.

So Bobby snuck up behind me again and snatched my cap again and ran out of the fellowship hall.

I chased him.

I heard Jonboy shout after us, "Bobby, give it back!"

Here is everything I remember after that:

I hit the double doors of the church and left a smudge on the glass.

Outside was a summer night chill.

I caught Bobby in the parking lot before he even reached the park on the other side.

I tackled him to the gravel.

I grabbed for my hat.

It was under him.

I was on top.

I turned him over. He was laughing.

I grabbed for my hat.

My hand still had sauce all over it.

He had bent the bill in half.

He thought it was hilarious.

I was going to punch him, but I felt a shoulder smash into my back.

It was Wes.

He had his arms around my waist, trying to pull me off his brother.

Bobby started shouting.

His lip was bleeding.

I was screaming, "Pedar sag. Meekoshamet!" They didn't understand me.

Wes pulled at my waist.

I had my hat scrunched in one fist, and Bobby's ear in the other.

Jonboy shouted something, who cares what.

I hated all of them.

Wes pulled until he slipped and had me just by the arm.

I tried to wrench my arm away from him.

I wanted to punch Bobby square in his nose.

I didn't think I had punched him yet.

Wes yanked on my hand that was holding the hat. I wouldn't let go of it. Wes tried to pry my fingers off of it. He finally pulled so hard I felt my thumb snap and separate to go with him.

A white light, like a shooting star, blinding pain.

He pulled again.

I felt all the muscles in my hand stretch and tear around my thumb, like he was pulling a drumstick off of a roast chicken. I screamed and let go of Bobby.

Wes and I fell to the ground.

Jonboy ran out of the church along with the pastor and my mom. He said, "What do you boys think you're doing out here?"

And that is all I remember before going to the hospital.

If I was Scheherazade, I would stop here and say, "O great and clever king," except I'd say, "Reader . . . I have never lied to you, even when a lie would save me the humiliation of the truth."

And then I'd skip over the part in the hospital when the doctor said, "Hold on, son," and snapped my thumb back into place.

It's not lying if you leave it out.

The next Sunday the team of Cowboys beat the Dolphins.

Wes never spoke to me again. Bobby said it was because I was probably one of those people who sue Americans for money and he had to protect himself. Pastor Jonboy saw me in the church hall and said, "Whoa! Guess we should call you Lefty now."

I didn't say anything. Nothing I remember anyway.

He grabbed my cast and said, "Here, lemme sign it."

I don't have any other memories involving these people, so you can forget them.

The only reason I'm telling you this was that as Jonboy tried to use a ballpoint pen to sign my cast, as he scraped back and forth over my wrist so he could write, "Go Dolphins!" I thought of Aziz and wondered what horrible thing she'd left out of her story. I thought, Maybe she'd had to go to the hospital to see her husband—and his murderer was chatting with nurses in the hall. I dunno. There was so much left unsaid in her story, that we saw playing in her eyes, as she spoke only part of it.

We don't owe anyone our sadness.

Bones break over and over and you can get used to it.

Like Mithridates with his poison, you could even break your bones on purpose, put your arm in a drawer and slam it. Little by little, they still fuse back stronger.

Eventually, you might even become unbreakable.

Just knowing they could never hurt you—that would scare people.

Somewhere in their animal brains they know you've become a different kind of creature.

If anyone ever grabbed you, their fingers would shatter.

I know what you're thinking.

You're thinking, What about hugs? What about Mithridates' lonely curse?

You might even say, "We don't owe anyone our sadness, but the sharing of it is what friends do. It makes the sadness less. Friends don't care if you like the same football squad."

And you're probably right, brilliant reader.

You're right.

I cried in the hospital when they pushed my hand on the X-ray table.

And I cried again when they set the bone.

And I cried the whole time Wes was pulling me off of Bobby.

I didn't understand any of it.

I even cried when I threw away the hat.

THERE IS AN AMERICAN filmmaker named Orson Welles who said, "If you want a happy ending, that depends, of course, on where you stop your story." And Doctor Hamond (pastor, not a doctor) says, "It'll be alright in the end, folks. If it's not alright, then it's not the end," which means Doctor Hamond thinks the world is going to end at his birthday party.

But my point is don't worry.

Scheherazade lives at the end of the thousand and first night.

This is not a Persian love story anyway.

It ends in America. And it will have a happy ending.

But this isn't the end, so Khosrou and Shirin died bloody, Aziz became a widow, and I spent a summer with a bag around my arm every time I showered.

That's it.

Those are the facts.

LIKE I SAID, RAY WASN'T around for a while because my mom divorced him after Pastor Hamond told her it was okay—that Jesus would forgive her because Ray had broken her jaw—and we went to live in an apartment complex behind a gas station where the kids would run up behind me and punch me in the ear on my right side—where my cast was—so I couldn't do anything about it.

I got hit in the jaw about twice a week, but nobody ever broke it, because none of them had a third-degree black belt.

A few months later, Ray went to Pastor Hamond and told him he was repented—which meant he was sorry—and Pastor Hamond told my mom she should marry him again, because we didn't have any money and it was worse to Jesus if we were on government welfare.

So that was the second time they got married—in the pastor's office—and they didn't tell us about it until Ray started hanging around again. He just showed up one Sunday with the stuff to make his special Korean ribs, which had to be marinated for three days—so I knew he was planning to stick around.

When he saw my cast, he said, "What happened?" while he grated an onion into a bowl.

"I got jumped," I said. I was holding the fridge open, but there wasn't anything to eat except food that I would have to warm up in the microwave behind Ray.

"You got jumped," he said. He laughed maybe cause it sounded like I was in an action movie or something. He didn't know there were three of them.

I told him I was just trying to get my cap back and the bigger kid got on top of me and yanked till he broke my thumb. I tried to make it sound like I hadn't used any martial arts so he'd keep teaching me.

He just said, "Wow."

Over dinner three days later, they told us they were back together and that we were all moving into a house.

That was when I learned if you can't fight, you don't get a vote in anything.

COUNTING THE MEMORIES.

Grandma Ellie the exile.

Aziz and Hassan had a daughter before he died. That girl grew up to be my grandma Ellie, who plotted to kill her husband and was exiled to England. I met her there once and discovered that KittyBix and peanut butter is a good breakfast.

My only memory of her is early in the morning in her apartment in London—she's smiling and reaching out to take my box of KittyBix. "Khossie," she says, "that's cat food." And she laughs.

But first let me finish Aziz.

In any story the two hardest things to be are a widow or an orphan. Those are the bad cards to draw from the deck marked "life."

Because those are the two moments the people you love the most die. It's heart break. Heart shatter. Heart starve.

It's so much loss that it's easier if you just died and started the game over. But you can't. You have to wander. Part of it is losing your tribe and being homeless. Part of it is being alone in the dark.

I won't lie to you. The deck marked "life" is stacked full of bum cards.

Aziz was both an orphan and a widow, and the dark nights must have seemed unbearably long. Long enough to lose every memory and become a blank-faced animal.

But every good story has a turn and a twist.

The deck has a joker in it.

The turn for Aziz came two years after Hassan died.

She met and married a man named Agha.

He adopted her daughter.

And he loved Aziz.

And they all lived happily until their daughter grew up and got married and had kids of her own.

But here's the twist:

That daughter was thirteen when she got married (that's a seventh grader).

And Agha wanted his own kids eventually, but they couldn't have any when they tried. They went to the physician—who had a good relationship with Agha and who didn't even remember Hassan. He told them they would need a fertility test. Aziz wanted to spare Agha the humiliation, and so she said, "It's me. I'm barren. It's my fault."

She assumed Agha would say, "No no. That's impossible. You already had a daughter. Of course it's me."

But he didn't. He sat in the physician's office blank-faced, red in the cheeks. He said, "I want a divorce."

And suddenly, Aziz was in a room with the man who took her first husband from her, and the one who took her second.

The word Agha had used, setalagheh, was the kind of divorce reserved in Islam for men who have threefold anger. Men so angry they would never regret the decision, never return or remarry their old spouse.

That was the twist, I guess.

The twist is sometimes a knife.

Aziz was alone again, this time for the rest of her life. When she was very old, she married again for companionship. He was the one who liked sesame candy, but never ate it because he was bedridden.

And so by the time I met Aziz, she was the old woman who offered stale candy and whose house smelled like sadness.

She would play love songs she used to listen to with Agha (or Hassan, I don't know) and cry. I would run out to the little river. She would shut herself off from the world. And if you listened real hard for the sound of far-off girls laughing as they returned from the saffron harvest, you wouldn't hear it. It was too far away.

ALL MY LIFE, MY GRANDMA Ellie (Aziz's daughter, my mom's mom) has lived in England. The legend was that her husband, my grandpa, forced her to go or else he would kill her. His name was Arman and I have zero memories of him. Not one.

I can bring up his face in my mind, but only because my mom had a picture of him in her shoebox while we were escaping Iran. When we would look through it, there was always the one of him. Not with his kids. Not even with the new wife he had at that time—a woman whose name I don't know.

The photo is just Arman from the waist up.

It's black and white.

His skin is a light gray. He is very thin; his lips are thin too. His nose is thin and pointy. He is bald and unsmiling. His eyebrows are thick and corded. His eyes look directly at the camera, impatient, as if he has someplace to be.

Once, a long time ago, he killed a bunch of kittens in a burlap sack (probably threw them into a river because the family couldn't keep them). My mom told me this story to make him seem like a responsible person who had suffered under the weight of his obligations or something. That's the best she could do.

I said, "He looks really mean."

"No," she said, not like she disagreed, but that you shouldn't say such things about elders. "No," she said again, but it was obvious she didn't have any evidence. "He worked very hard," she said. That was all she could come up with. "And he wanted all his kids educated. That was very important," which if you know my mom, you know is a case for him being a villain. All her life she wanted to be a farmer. His pressure made her go to med school.

But whatever. She tried to defend him. The problem was you'd look at the picture of his pursed lips and cruel eyes and you knew the whole story.

"He was a very important man, a governor."

He was only seventeen when he married Ellie (thirteen), so he had to work hard to grab power.

Good for him, I guess.

At one point the four kids—my mom was the second—had a cat named Sherry that my uncle Salim loved more than anything or anyone in the world. He was young then, and Sherry (who was a boy cat) would wander at night.

One morning Sherry was at the door with another cat, this one trailed by a bunch of bleary kittens. Salim saw them and immediately adopted all of them.

And at this point, Ellie was probably around twenty-three and Arman twenty-seven, and they already had four kids (and the one cat), so it was already a crowded situation. But then one day Sherry got sick and their dad took him to the vet. The vet told him the cat wouldn't get better and would probably cause infections in his human kids.

So he put all the cats in an empty sack of rice.

"He drove them outside of town," said my mom, "but they came back the next day."

She paused here. To her, the picture of Arman came with a thousand memories. She seemed to admire him. She never said a word against him—even though, trust me, he looked like he would kill the camera man if the picture took one more second to take.

So he drove them to the creek and put them in the sack.

"Geez," I said, so she wouldn't finish.

He came back. That was the first time she ever saw her dad cry.

"He said he shouldn't have done that. We would be cursed forever for hurting the mazloom creatures."

And they were. Salim didn't even know he had been injured, but he was never again whole. They just told him that all the cats ran away.

I guess if you think regretting it makes Arman a nice man, then this story works for you. I don't have an opinion.

Because I don't have a memory of my own.

He's just a picture my mom likes to stop and stare into.

The difference between him and my Baba Haji is exactly one memory.

Those are my two grandfathers.

But the space between zero and one is all the world, and everything in it, so they aren't exactly neighbors in my head.

FOR MY NEXT REPORT on Robert Frost, I will count the memories of my uncles.

Please note, Mrs. Miller, that the "connection to the assignment" is that it involves two roads diverging—not in a yellow wood, like in Frost's poem—but someplace else. But that's a really good A+ connection.

THERE ARE SO MANY people in your life that you've only kept for one memory.

Think about them.

That person with scars you've never seen before.

Or the teacher you never had who yelled at you once in the halls.

And there are single memories you have of people you never met.

Like the bad guy in *Terminator 2*.

Or people who visit churches in the summer and give testimonies about China.

I have three uncles on my dad's side and two memories between them. Which means I have more memories of Jonboy the pastor's son than all my uncles combined.

One memory is my dad's youngest brother, Reza, who had such red hair and so many freckles that he was probably a descendent of Genghis Khan.

(Genghis Khan had red hair. Look it up.)

I remember riding on the front of his motorcycle barreling down the dirt road to Ardestan. So fast we would hit bumps and fly in the air. On a straight part he let me hold the handlebars and he let go. I screamed. He laughed in my ear, a laugh I will never forget. That laugh is the heart of the memory. I knew I was safe.

Back then Reza didn't have any kids.

I remember the dirt road, his laugh, the hot bike underneath me. I remember we came up to a crossroad, sand everywhere, the outline of two intersecting roads. No signs. When I see it in my mind, it is just us. Nothing else in a vast desert.

Two roads, sand.

I remember he said, "Khossie, you pick which way."

And I don't remember anything after that.

Not the direction we went.

Not the trees popping up as we approached an oasis village.

Not even a second thing Reza said.

I just remember he let me pick and that the roads led in completely opposite directions.

My mom would have probably scolded him for letting me hold the handlebars. But that's not something I kept.

If we had stayed in Iran, I think Reza would have been my number one best friend.

AND THE OTHER UNCLE memory is the time my dad and his brother-in-law (sister's husband) took me pheasant hunting when I was four. His name was Askar, but you can call him Oscar in your head if you want. The forests along the edge of Ardestan are full of foxes, owls, rabbits, and pheasants. There are also leopards, which is why I begged to go with them (and also because they were doing manly things).

I don't remember much about Askar, except that he looked like my dad, but he was half a hand shorter, half a size smaller, half as educated, and half as friendly. Looking back, my dad was like the Pokémon Askar evolved into.

But Askar lived in Ardestan every day, while my dad had moved to the city of Isfahan to be a doctor. So Askar had all the latest village gossip, and helped Baba Haji pen the goats and carry the pomegranate bushels.

Even though my dad grew up in those woods, Askar knew the best part of the woods to find pheasants.

I don't remember how the trip began, only that my mom objected.

"Akh, Masoud, he's four."

"Let him come. This is good for him."

"Madame Doktor," Askar would say, using the two most respectful words he could possibly use to honor my mother. "I will take care of them."

"We won't even leave the car," said my dad.

The next part of the memory jumps directly into my dad's gold Chevrolet.

I am seated in the back, and my mom is leaning all the way in through the window, squeezing my neck. "Be careful, my sweet mazloom boy," she says.

"Akh. Sima, he's not going to war."

She sucks her teeth, because even saying such a thing—heaven forbid. She kisses my face fifty-seven times, until I shout. Then she gives me a cardamom pound cake with slivered almonds on top. It's the size of a brick, wrapped in foil.

The memory jumps again to the Chevrolet grumbling down a dirt road, lined on both sides with beeches and mulberry trees. A mulberry wood is the kind of place the animals have names and jobs and go on storybook adventures.

My dad parked in the middle of the road. We were miles into my grandfather's land, and no one else would drive up from either direction. We watched the hedgerow and waited for pheasants to show their speckled tails.

They started talking—I have no idea what about. Grownies will talk sometimes in boring words about boring ideas to groom each other like apes, to let each other know they're pals.

Something about that early morning, the way the sun made everything bright and golden. It looked like a kid had colored the world—unafraid to use every pencil in the box. I watched and listened as closely as I could.

You could hear the hedgehogs scrabbling into their nests. My dad reached back sometimes and I gave him a chunk of the dense cake. When they saw a family of pheasants, my uncle propped a rifle out of the window of the Chevrolet and shot. The bang wasn't very loud. The trees ruffled. The other pheasants flew off. One dropped. For a while, the woods quivered. We stayed in the car until the air was still again, and the pheasants came back. Then my dad took a turn.

I asked, "Will there be leopards?"

"Maybe," said my dad. "Keep looking."

I squinted at every dappled leaf in the mulberry wood, hoping to see leopard eyes looking back. Imagine how unlikely it is for two creatures of any kind to see each other—through the shadows of the woods—eyes connecting, attention ready. For a moment like that all the universe would have to conspire to move all its pieces and line them up just so.

I think a person gets seen, really looked at, looked into, *seen* the way a leopard would see into you, maybe ten times in their entire life.

And even then, who knows what a leopard would be thinking.

After three or four pheasants had fallen into the hedges, I said, “Can I try?”

I had spotted all the ones he shot before, so I was already involved. My dad sucked his teeth. He could hear my mother, probably.

“Let him,” said my uncle.

My dad nodded. Back then, I wanted to be exactly like my dad.

I gave him the cake to hold, because we still needed a snack chief. My uncle Askar turned around and adjusted the rifle so that it rested on the shoulder of his seat, and still pointed out of his front window.

He held the barrel and the stock.

“Okay, put your finger here, but don’t pull.”

I focused my vision to the end of the barrel.

In the woods, I could hear the rustling of wings. Sometimes the pheasants would perch on the lower branches of the trees.

“Look through here,” said my uncle.

I scanned the trees. A speckled lump sat in the crook of a tree. I pulled the trigger and fell back in my seat. It was the loudest noise I’d ever heard.

The lump dropped from the branch.

My dad and uncle cheered.

“My champion!” said my dad. “One shot!”

“You earned our dinner,” said my uncle.

I know what it must sound like to you, but I was super proud. "What a son you've got," said my uncle, and my dad agreed.

Hunting isn't a sin if it's useful.

If you're feeding people—which is what good men do.

We got out of the car to collect our trophies. From the window it was just a video game on TV. Everything looked different when we got outside.

The hedgerow was thorny, and I was too small to push past it, so I ran along the gully on the side of the road and watched my uncle march into the wood. Somehow he had memorized the location of every drop. Mine was the farthest, which meant I had made the hardest shot.

"Come on, come on," I said.

When he came to the last one, I heard him stop short.

"Oh no," he said. "Masoud, over here."

"Is it a good one?" I said.

My dad picked through the patches and stopped beside my uncle. They were both looking at the ground. My dad sighed.

"Let's leave this one," he said.

I ran into the ditch and through the thorny hedge to where they stood.

At their feet was a baby owl with my bullet in it.

Its other eye was still open.

We looked at each other. Can you imagine how unlikely it is for any two creatures to cross each other in a universe as big as this one? There is no telling what it was thinking, but it looked at me as though to say, there is no eating a baby owl, that's not useful like hunting a pheasant.

On the ride home I cried in the back of the car, but quietly so the men wouldn't hear me. That's the end of that memory.

It's the only one I have of Askar—how disappointed he was, frowning at the dead bird.

Anyway, I told you all this because killing owls is no different than killing kittens. In case you thought I was putting myself above anybody. I'm not above anybody.

That was the second innocent thing I killed, if you count the bull.

And that was before I even turned five.

OKLAHOMA IS THE ONLY state in the Union where it is legal to own an anti-tank sniper rifle. It shoots bullets the size of milk cartons and if you hit a deer with it, all you leave is red mist.

OF MY GRANDPARENTS, my grandma Ellie was the least likely to kill any animals. She always had a princess quality about her, which is to say, people talked about her like she was spoiled.

I don't know what it would be like to be thirteen and married. I guess one thing it makes you is scared all the time that everyone will hurt you. Even as she got older, people said she acted like a kid—thought only about her own problems—and wasn't very mother-like.

I don't have any stories about her early life.

Nobody ever described the wedding. A little girl in a room full of grown men, wondering which one is her husband. My mom just sighs and says, "It was a different time," and he was a young man, but nobody's convinced, not even her.

What else is there to say, though?

It happened. Welcome to earth.

Arman—the pinched grandfather I told you about from the picture—her husband, was a bad husband, who was known as "the Governor," and governed mostly a bunch of affairs with other women.

Ellie took more damage than an Oklahoma trailer park in a tornado and people still blamed her for retreating into the bomb shelter of her own mind.

Those are the only facts I know. Child bride. Horrible husband. I could live a thousand years and they'd still be the only parts I know for sure.

The bones of the history are that they had four kids, grew apart, and divorced.

The rest of the story I only ever heard through the cracks of doors, as my aunts whispered it to each other over tea—years later in places like Toronto, London, and Edmond, after they had survived it all and could safely compare their experiences.

Every side of an explosion looks different.

If you're looking at a bull collapsing to the ground and I'm beside you looking at it, we're seeing two bulls die, two rivers of blood, two everything. That's why there is an infinite labyrinth of stories, even in just one family.

The story I heard was that Arman became a governor of a town near Tabriz. A little town where he was a big man.

They lived in a house with an open porch where my mom studied and where her younger brother would use a piece of broken gutter to reach the apples on the trees in the next yard and twist them from the branches so they would roll down into his bag.

My grandfather was the kind of man who had goons, bigger guys in suits that don't fit, with sweat stains up their backs. He was good-looking back then, I assume, because the only thing I ever heard about him was that women liked him. Maybe in a different version of our story, he would be the one to give me advice about how to impress Kelly J. In that version he is my grandfather the sophisticated charmer who wore silk jackets and taught me how to wink like a cool guy. One thing about being a refugee is that you lose those little lessons, and you have to teach everything to yourself.

Ellie was only twenty-something and had four kids to worry about, so she didn't even know that husbands don't take showers in their offices in the middle of the day. Or that governors don't have to work late nights.

Basically he was going out and winking at other women (and they would wink back) and no one told Ellie because he was powerful.

Ellie had a lot of sadness in her life. Sadness of the kind that makes perfectly normal people into poets. After dinners, the family would sit in the open terrace with bowls of dried apricots, and pistachios, sugar candies, and a big samovar of black tea.

Arman would be off somewhere, Ellie would write poems about the night air under the oil lanterns, and the children would sit beside the cherry tree. Her oldest daughter, Soraya, was nearly in college. Sima, my mom, was in high school. Both were straight-A students. The brother, Salim, would be in town with other boys making a kite out of butcher paper, glue, and hand-carved branches. And Sanaz, the youngest, the last daughter, at eleven years old, was the baby.

Does writing poetry make you brave? It is a good question to ask. I think making anything is a brave thing to do. Not like fighting brave, obviously. But a kind that looks at a horrible situation and doesn't crumble.

Making anything assumes there's a world worth making it for. That you'll have someplace, like a clown's pants, to hide it when people come to take it away.

I guess I'm saying making something is a hopeful thing to do.

And being hopeful in a world of pain is either brave or crazy.

Later in her life, Ellie would go crazy. She believed mysterious people were trying to kill her with alien sound wave machines, so she would sleep in a tool shed to hide herself.

But for now she was brave.

I always imagine the man she met was a librarian of the village—with a library so old it had a signature in one book from Esther in the Bible, who would go on to become a queen. But no one ever said his name or his job; it's just what I like.

The village where he lived is a real place where the houses are carved into stones that bulge out of the ground, as if a volcano had bubbled up the earth and hardened into giant pillars.

Maybe he lived in a different village.

Doesn't matter.

I'll describe the cool one.

Imagine colorful wooden doors in odd shapes and windows at wonky angles embedded into the rock. Sometimes the top of one house has a rickety bridge to the balcony of another. It's a stair-step bunch of cave homes stacked around each other. And curving along the windowsills is a little river, like a stone gutter, winding around the entire village. Sometimes it goes into the house, where you could wash your hands in the constant flow of cold mountain water. Sometimes it makes a tiny waterfall cascading next to a dirt staircase leading down to a new terrace of houses.

I imagine if you were a kid with a friend, you could make a paper boat and write a secret message on it. Then you could go to your window and set the boat in the water and watch it flow away, in the channel, past all the other homes and you could shout, "Hey, Ali! Look out!" And your friend (his name would be Ali) would run to his window just in time to retrieve the boat. And he'd get your message ("Ali is a dog's son. Wanna play ball?")

In the lumpy village of doors and windows carved out of rocks, there would be one tall pillar, like a lighthouse, with a door so narrow you could only pass through sideways, and green window shutters with irregular slats all around it. Inside would be a spiral staircase around a stone column. As you went up, carved into the column itself, would be shelves, where books were stacked by the dynasty in which they were made.

You would go backward in time, so the first floor would have the current century. That shelf would have the tea glass and the tray with paper clips and rubber bands, because literature has not been the focus of this dynasty. But you would climb up and reach the Pahlavi, then the first big shelf of American dynasty writers like Stan Lee. Then Britain (J.R.R. Tolkien), then France (Alexandre Dumas).

As you climbed the stairs around and around, the outer windows would shine colored light through their stained glass. Then finally, on the shelves for the Seljuk Turks in the thirteenth century, you'd find the poet Rumi, who said, "You are not a drop in the ocean. You are the entire ocean in a drop," and Attar, who wrote *The Conference of the Birds*.

The next shelves would have Ferdowsi of the Abbasid Empire—the father of the language in which I dream. If it wasn't for him, my dad says, we wouldn't even have Farsi. "Look at Egypt, look at Syria," he says. "They don't speak Egyptian anymore. They don't speak Syrian."

After the Muslim conquest in the years around 750 AD, they all switched to Arabic. "But not us," my father says to me over the phone. "Because we had the *Shahnameh*"—Ferdowsi's epic poem—"we had that and could hear the beauty of the Persian language. He told all the history of the Persian people, back until it blended into legends, and then myths. All of it. It's there."

Above the *Shahnameh*, near the top of the tower library, would be the shelves for Ibn Sina—the father of modern medicine. He was the guy who wrote the properties of things, like how aloe soothes skin, and ginseng gives you focus. It was like alchemy back then, but later people realized it was the first book of medicine.

This is why it was so easy for my mom and dad to become doctors like Avicenna, because your blood is a very complicated river of information inside every part of your body. And it carries things you would never believe from generation to generation.

And the last shelf, in the cramped peak of the tower, where the stairs end and a tiny window looks out onto the village and hill country beyond, are a few pages from the lost books of Persepolis, the city of kings. This was the city that was burned by Alexander the Great during the Achaemenid dynasty three hundred years before Christ.

Back then it was the richest city in the world. Now if you visit, it's a pile of stones that only museum people care about. On the stones, there's still writing that says stuff like, "I am Xerxes, king of kings, ruler of all that you see before you," as if you should be impressed, because back then you would have seen a shiny kingdom, but now you see a colossal wreck on a dirt burger.

The library was destroyed and so Persian literature doesn't go back much further than that.

They say Alexander the Great saw what his soldiers had done to the city and regretted it. But that's like breaking someone's bones and then saying you're sorry.

Anyway, in the library tower of the wibbly-wobbly village dug into the rocks, there might have been a librarian.

He's the guy I made up to fall in love with Ellie.

I guess he could have been from a city and sold motorbikes or something.

But Ellie was a poet. And she never chose her husband, and never even grew up to decide what kind of stuff she liked as an adult, or dated anybody with the same interests.

So I just imagine Kaveh the all-alone librarian of Kandovan, who was as tall and thin as his tower, and moved like a cat, and sat in the light from the window at the top of the stairs to read and remember the kings.

STAY WITH ME ON this one.

In Oklahoma they call fruit leather "Fruit Roll-Ups."

Which isn't fruit and doesn't feel like leather.

The flavors are sour blue or cough syrup.

And the shapes are Ninja Turtles.

My mom won't buy us any because she says it's nothing but sugar mixed with chemicals to make it neon colors, and it'll give you cancer.

I think it's just because we can't afford it.

In Iran the number one snack is fruit leather made by humans.

I had some at school once and Jared S. said, "Why is it so brown?"

Because dried fruit is brown.

"Not pineapple."

"If you just dry it without chemicals it turns brown."

"Not mangos."

"Yeah mangos."

"Not apricots."

I'm honestly impressed with how many fruits Jared S. can name, since he eats all of his in gummy form.

In any Persian market, you can get cherry leather, or black currant. But people make their own, and villages have special combinations like apple pomegranate, or plum lime, which is like sour blue but not blue (and not give you cancer). Tamarind is the best flavor. It is very sour, and very brown.

Jared S. says it looks like "the crap they use for catfish bait." But I am not friends with Jared S.

IN MY MIND, **KAVEH** the librarian would sit in his library with a book in his lap and a stack of fruit leather next to him like sheafs of paper. It wouldn't spill on anything, and he could keep it shelved in between the covers of a book that had no pages after an imam had torn them out for offending Allah.

On every shelf, he had one. A book with fruit leather pages.

I imagine Ellie entered on a Tuesday right after school started and people went to work. It's not gross to say she was pretty, because I'm Scheherazade and not her grandson right now.

And everyone agreed she was very pretty. And cautiously curious. And educating herself one book at a time. At that moment, Kaveh was reading a line in a poem:

The seed of a pepper—black
The mole on the lip of a lover—black
Both burn at the touch
But the first is one thing
And the other, another.

He looked up from his book, saw her at the bottom of the stairs, and said, "Oh," as if he suddenly understood.

"Welcome," he said.

"I'm looking for a book," she said.

"How can I help you," he said.

"I'm looking for a book," she said.

"Yes. Sorry. What book?" he said.

"Poetry," she said.

"Hafez? Nizami?"

"Not poems. How to *write* poetry."

"You write?" he said.

"I try," she said.

"Here's one," he said.

"How much," she said.

"One poem," he said.

She didn't say anything.

"I was only joking," he said, "This is a library."

"I thought it was a store," she said.

"Yes. I figured. You don't owe me anything. Please take it."

She took it and walked out. He said, I love you, I love you, I love you, in his head.

THE NEXT WEEK—MAYBE—she returned with a poem written on a cream-colored sheet of paper. It was not about him. It was about books. But it talked about books as if they were couples, lined up beside each other as if they were standing for wedding photos—and the only trouble was that a book is shelved with a lover on either side. And how would anyone know the right pairs?

"It's beautiful," he said.

"I think it's tragic," she said.

"Yes," he said, "but it's also true."

In Muslim Iran, it would be a scandal for a man to spend any time alone with a woman, even in a library, but Ellie was a governor's wife and not always obedient.

She would knock on the crooked door in the mornings. They would sit in the alcoves of each floor reading to each other and eating sheets from the book of fruit leather. They consumed the pages and were consumed by ideas.

Sour pomegranate. Sweet descriptions of kissing.

Sweet mulberry. Sour passages of death.

Sometimes, she would put her head on his shoulder—after a poem about birds or something—and cry inconsolable tears.

Ellie had four children, a husband, parents, cousins, and friends, but felt very alone at this time—and grown out of season.

And sometimes you fall in love that way, when you're drowning in a world of pain.

It's not a happy love.

It's just whoever manages not to hurt you all the time. You think they must be the best the world has to offer. The little window of time you aren't in pain can seem like happiness.

But I think Ellie and the librarian in the tower of stone were in real love. Somehow, in all the world, with all the people in it, in all their wonky shapes, they were shaped to fit each other. And they found each other—born in the same country, how lucky—and both loved poetry and fruit snacks—and like poetry they felt their hearts expand infinitely in all directions when they were together, so that it was possible to forget all the pain in their lives and the world, or at least to endure it as long as they could be together.

Maybe that was it.

I MADE ALL THAT UP.

The only part anyone told me was that Ellie found a lover. They decided to kill her husband, and run away together.

I AM EMBARRASSED TO ADMIT that I wrote a poem for Kelly J. for Valentine's Day—not embarrassed that I wrote it, but embarrassed that I gave it to someone so mean.

It said, if she wanted, we could read together.

I would feed her tamarind fruit leather.

And to me, she was a seed of black pepper.

Kelly J. is the kind of person who would give private letters to her friends to laugh at during our hour in the library—which doesn't have any books about any Persian stories anyway.

There is a book on animals. It has a page on Persian cats.

And there are definitely no books full of fruit leather. That is too much to ask of anyplace in the real world.

When I tell people my stories, about the hero Rostam or the size of pomegranates from the orchards on my Baba Haji's land, the villages in stone pillars, Orich candy bars, or anything that happened to me, they never believe me. There is no evidence in their library.

They think I'm one of the poor kids trying to say I used to be rich.

But I was.

I know it's crazy that the kid in Oklahoma on welfare who barely spoke English at first used to be a prince. I know.

But I did. I had a Nintendo and uncles and tons of store-bought snacks. A house that smelled like flowers all the time, with birds in the walls and a pool.

I wasn't always poor.

Other kids don't know that.

They think I'm lying.

And if you tell somebody they're lying all the time, they start to believe you a little.

They start to question their own memories.

Cause they're so different than everything happening around them. They think, maybe I was always smelly. Maybe I never had anything like a dad.

Maybe I'm going crazy, like Ellie after her exile, making up stories to feel better about myself. Maybe it would be too painful to live otherwise.

But I don't think so. I close my eyes and squeeze tight my grip on the memory of my Baba Haji, smiling, reaching to squeeze my face in his bloody hands. If you could see it like I do, how proud he was that I was his—you'd feel so good that a grandpa like that loved you—maybe you'd never cry again.

THE VERSION THEY TELL me goes:

Ellie fell in love.

Her lover had no name.

"They tried to kill her husband," my sister once whispered to me. She was talking about our grandpa.

On Tuesday nights, when international Bible studies of the University of Central Oklahoma could meet, my sister and I sat in the corners of dark church buildings. Ray was the pastor and everyone else was Korean. We were the only kids and could find crackers or candy no matter how well-hidden in the cupboards. The TVs never worked. The ping-pong tables never had balls. We wandered the halls quietly, or my mom would come out and shush us with eyes gigantic like, "Don't make him angry."

"Ellie and her lover tried to kill her husband," my sister said.

"Don't say that."

"They did."

"I mean, call him boyfriend or something."

"Ellie got him to sneak into their house to shoot him."

"Why didn't she just shoot him herself?" I said.

"Because that's a boyfriend's job."

"I wouldn't shoot anybody for a girl," I said, even though if Kelly J. asked me to, I would step on a spider.

My Baba Haji killed a bull for me, so maybe love is always measured by what you're willing to kill.

Ellie's boyfriend must have loved her a ton.

For Kelly J., I would also put out traps for mice, and catch fish for food.

"So what happened," I said.

"Grandpa Arman was a governor, so he had men to protect him."

"Goons."

Ellie was waiting at the train station with one suitcase. Everything she wanted was in it—not any of her kids, just stuff. The train station smelled like roasting pistachios from the old Turkish merchant outside, and burnt rubber from the train braking.

She must have imagined her boyfriend would come running just as the train was about to leave, and they would jump aboard and go somewhere. Maybe all she packed was books and fruit leather.

Where did they think they were going? I used to wonder.

Probably it didn't matter.

A castle in the clouds of the Caspian Sea.

A village above a lake, suspended on giant Persian rugs.

A house beside a river of rot.

They didn't care.

Escape was all that mattered. Ellie clutched her bag and refused a newspaper from a kid and watched the main entrance by the ticket counter.

She hoped Kaveh would find Arman alone. And she hoped whoever found Arman's body would be one of his goons and not one of the children.

It was almost dinnertime and people would be wondering where she was. She sat on a long wooden bench and couldn't think of any word that described her anymore.

When she looked up again from her watch, a man with a button-up shirt stretched over his belly stood in front of her. His armpits were soaked with sweat. He had a waxy bag of roasted pistachios from the old Turk outside.

"Are you Mrs. Piroozkhah?" he said. He snapped open a pistachio shell and popped the nut into his mouth.

"Yes," said Ellie.

"Arman's wife?" he said. He asked as if he already didn't believe her.

"Yes."

"I was sent to tell you he's dead," said the goony man.

"Arman?"

"No. Your other one."

Her librarian.

Ellie's mind might have broken right then. No one knows. But she was never again completely sane. She half heard the steam whistle blow, and half watched the train pull out of the station.

The man waited for her to see the last car pull away from the platform, the last hope that the story would end happily. He let the pistachio shells fall to the ground.

When it was quiet again, he said, "The boy is dead." Maybe they even burned his library, but he was definitely dead. "You'll never see his face again."

Ellie had nowhere in the entire world—at that moment—to be, and not be alone.

Even the nook of a tree can make you feel safe if you hide yourself in it.

Somewhere in some dark gully in a back corner of a village, her beloved Kaveh lay slaughtered, blood flowing from his neck for stray dogs to lick at, until it turned brown.

The goony man put his wet paw on her shoulder and she realized she had been vibrating. She jerked away from him. If he touched her again, she'd scream.

He said, "Arman Khan"—her husband—"says he won't hurt you. But you can't live here anymore."

My sister explained that what he meant was that Ellie would be exiled to England. She would have to take Sanaz, her youngest daughter, because she was eleven and Arman didn't want to be responsible for her.

"She was already packed," I pointed out to my sister.

What did Arman say when she went back to get Sanaz? What did they tell Sanaz, or the others?

No one ever told us. It was just exile. Stop talking about it.

Probably a million trains have gone back and forth on that platform since then.

"Why did she keep his name?" I asked. "If they got divorced, and if she tried to kill him, and if he banished her from Iran, why did she keep his name?"

"I dunno," said my sister. "Maybe they never got divorced."

We drank the grape juice that they used for communion from the church fridge. We could barely stay awake, it was so late. The next day was a school day and we'd tell people we watched all the shows they were watching while we were at church.

Then my sister said, "Divorce is a sin, you know."

And I spit my juice out laughing.

AT SCHOOL I DON'T tell anyone about church.

At church I don't tell anyone about home.

The neighborhood kids don't know anything about anything else.

The trick is to keep your stories to yourself, so they can't use them against you.

My best friend is really good because all he talks about are the Dolphins and video games, so we talk all the time but he doesn't even know what refugees are. I'll tell you about him later, because I think you and me are friends now.

You know every memory I have of all my grandparents and aunts and uncles and cousins. You've got them all.

You can probably count them yourself. And they're as fuzzy to you as they are to me. You won't clench them like I do, that's for sure. To you, they might even be junk.

In the movies, kids get fishing trips with their grandpas, and grandmothers give them hugs.

Maybe my memories are only worth a couple peach pits to you.

But you've got them now. All the pieces are in place for you to understand what happened and how we ended up in Oklahoma.

If you've been listening this far, then maybe you won't laugh or call me a liar. When I tell you what happens next, you'll see how everyone played their part. It's not so hard to believe if you've got the memories I've got. And only a few moments would be something you might have to call mythical.

You don't even have to believe those parts if you don't want to.

But they're all true.

So I think you should.

BECAUSE YOU AND I are friends, I will tell you a full day of my life in wondrous Edmond, Oklahoma, the jewel of the I-35 roadway.

It's always the same story but it happens a thousand different ways.

I wake up—most of the time super late, because I secretly stay up till 4 a.m., and because bus 209 has Brandon Goff in it.

So far I've missed more days of my first hour class than I've attended.

My mom works different jobs. Sometimes she won't even tell us what she's doing. For a while she was in a factory that printed business cards for people. She says a lot of people just make up degrees to put by their names. But she has a real MD and PhD and she's still stuck by a conveyor belt, cutting big stacks of cardboard.

I don't eat breakfast because I wake up so late.

My mom runs in. "Daniel. Khosrou. Wake up."

"Ugh," I say, cause my mouth is as dry as a cardboard factory from eating bread all night. Bread is the only food I can take from the kitchen at 4 a.m. because the fridge door makes a loud noise when you open it, and our pantry is full of ingredients like dried lemons, rice, and onions. The only snacks are the potato rolls my mom bakes and leaves on the counter. She puts sugar and cinnamon inside half of them for me, and those are always on top, so when I sneak into the kitchen, I don't even turn the light on.

Anyway, she says, "Akh! Daniel, pasho pasho!" which means, "Akh! Daniel, get up get up!"

I don't get up.

"You missed the bus."

I get up.

"Get up!" she says.

"Wha? Oh no. Did I miss the bus?" I say, which is a tae kwon do move called deflection.

My room has six books in it. And it has no beautiful rugs or pictures of fields, so I am no khan of flowers. The carpet is shaggy, beige, and covers everything in the apartment like dead grass. There are a couple shelves where I keep porcelain animals, and Micro Machines cars, and a La-Z-Boy chair we got when the people in the apartment next door left it outside.

In my closet are balls for sports I still don't know the rules to. A baseball glove that is hard shiny leather. I've never used it because people tell me I should spit in it and grind dirt in there to break it in. I just play soccer instead.

I get up and get my coat.

I came up with a trick in America. You can shower at night, and sleep in a set of those sweats from Sam's Club. I have five. If I wear the green sweatshirt, then I wear the green pants, so it's a fashion match, and not weird. I used to have all the same color, and Ashley said I was wearing the same thing every day, so the different colors are for Ashley's mental accounts. Then you wake up, you just need socks, and you can go to school.

My mom drives me.

I know she's worried every day. I come home sometimes with a bruise on my face from Brandon Goff, or mad cause they said my egg sandwiches smell like swamp-crotch and Ashley or Kelly or Stacey made a show of holding their noses as I walked by.

And my mom doesn't know any of the rules. She doesn't know any of these people, or what they want from us. She's just dropping her kid into some building full of strangers, hoping he doesn't come back bloody.

The office ladies don't treat her like the other parents. They look at her straight in the face and speak slow and loud, like she's a busted drive-thru.

"Yes. We understand Ms. . . ." They never say her name. They just look at a paper and cut it off. "Ms."

". . . Ms. We understand he's late. That's an absence."

"Okay. Can I . . ." She doesn't know the terms they use. "Can I clear him?"

"You mean clear him from the absence?"

"Yes."

"You can clear excused absences."

"Okay. I'd like to."

"This isn't an excused absence."

"What is it?"

"An *un*excused absence."

See what they're doing? Presenting the information in little bits so they can beat her with it. My mom tries to hold it in. Because otherwise she'd scream at the ladies in three different languages and they'd treat her like even more of an animal.

"Okay," says my mom, "how do I clear an unexcused absence?"

"You can't."

She waits. Finally, the lady sighs super loud, like it's not her job to do any of this; it's just her job to eat cookies. She rolls her eyes, "He. Needs. A. Note. From. A. Doctor."

"Yes," says my mom. "I'm his doctor."

"I'm sure you are," says the lady. "We'll need the note on official stationary."

My mom will get the note. But she'll have to beg a doctor in our Bible study for a notepad. This is ridiculous because she's a doctor, and because she works in a notepad factory. She says, "Okay. Thank you," and walks out, and the office ladies make that snort noise to each other that means, "What a pain, right?"

You should know, Mr. Knatvold doesn't care that I missed his class with unexcused absences because I have a 112 in his class, because Tanner the tongue exploder takes up most of the class hour asking if the Hulk could beat up Superman.

"No."

"But he's green."

"Doesn't matter."

"Yeah, but Superman hates green."

"He hates kryptonite."

"That's what I said. Hulk wins."

"No."

"Hey, yo, Mr. Knatvold, what's the periodic table of kryptonite?"

And then he farts at a Jennifer, and that's class. So I show up and take the tests on Fridays and on the rest of the days Tanner's got one less person to mess with. He grabs me when I'm not looking and rubs a sheet of paper on my forehead like he's giving me a noogie. And when it gets a spot on it, he waves it over his head and screams, "I struck oil! Grease in the Middle East!"

Everybody's face has oil on it.

In my other classes I make sure to answer all the questions. This is a good trick for friend-making. Don't laugh. I'm not wrong about this. It's not that I think people will admire me and be my friend.

But the trick is that in America, nobody wants to answer questions. When Mrs. Martz has a math issue, even if they know the answer, it's bad to answer. That's a nerd thing to do. Also, it's "try-hard," which is a thing that you are when you race to finish tests before everyone else. I'm not a try-hard anymore, but I answer all the questions and then smile at a Jared or a Jennifer, who is slumping in their seat like, "Don't worry, Pal, I got this one."

That's how to be "in on it." Perform a service and say it's no big deal. Then people can see how chill you are. You can even answer to get the teacher to move on, and then look around and wink, like it's an inside joke.

At lunch I stand at the back of the cafeteria line. Always in the very back. This is a different trick that has three benefits.

First, all the rich Matts, Kelly J., and Daniel W. (the Daniel who was born a Daniel and whose mother is a teacher) bring their lunches, so they start eating and they're finished by the time the line is done.

Second, if you're the last person in line, sometimes the cafeteria lady who goes to our church will give you more of the food the other kids don't want, like extra green beans, or two scoops of mashed peas.

But the third trick is that if you stand at the back of the line and realize you don't have any money, you don't have to tell anyone. You can wait. Nearby, the packed lunches trade their pudding cups for string cheese. The cafeteria trays start to come out to find seats with their friends. The steam is still rising from the gravy—it's not brown Jell-O yet.

Some kids get their tray and then realize their card is out of money when they hand it to the lady who puts it in the punch machine. And that's the worst thing to do.

They have to stop the line. The punch card lady is always the most angry. She snaps her fingers if you don't have your card ready when you're up. Her eyes are always squinting behind her glasses. And if the card is empty, she groans and then looks around and shouts, "I need an AP!" which is an assistant principal, to come and take the kid out of line.

Everybody hears it and stops to watch.

Once, it happened to Nick, who is the dirtiest kid in school, not very big, red hair. He lives in the same apartment complex as us, but his mom smokes. The assistant principal said, "Come with me, Nick. We'll get you sorted out."

And Nick followed her, but he brought the tray, so she turned and said, "Oh, you can leave that."

But Nick didn't want to.

The punch card lady glared at him. "Leave it."

Everybody in the whole cafeteria could see him. He couldn't have the food. Nick put the tray on the counter, but he snatched the bread roll. The card lady said, "Hey!"

But Nick shoved it in his mouth. He looked like a hamster. The AP took him by the elbow and all the kids watched them leave. Daniel W. knows all the teachers and grown-ups, so he was the one to say, "Thief," as Nick walked by.

I only ever got caught without money twice.

They take you to the office where the ladies give you three saltine cracker sandwiches with peanut butter in the middle. They call your mother and say, "His account is empty. You'll have to request the assistance program through the office. No. The district office. No. They only accept requests from our AP. It stands for 'assistant principal.' Just send it to us and we'll take care of it. You're welcome." And they sigh again.

The way they toss the bag of crackers at you makes you feel like the lowest thing in the world. It's against policy to make a kid go hungry, but you can tell, you're not their guest. If you were a guest you would be treated with kindness and tea and all the best food they could offer. Being generous to a guest is one of the most different things about these countries.

In Iran, when a guest comes, you tell them they may be angels, they are welcome and the whole house is filled with the joy of their presence. And the person always apologizing is the host, that they might have more to offer.

But here, it seems guests are supposed to apologize all the time that they're taking anything. It's like they think the host is burdened. I don't understand it. But I know I never want to go to the house of any of these grown-ups, who make you beg for so little. I don't want the cracker sandwiches they made with all the groaning in their hearts. I don't want to be poor.

But if I can't have that, then I don't want them to know how hungry I am.

Anyway, if you stand at the back of the lunch line and you don't have any money in your account, you can wait and wait for the whole lunch period and then just as you're about to grab a tray, ask to go to the drinking fountain.

At the fountain, you drink a ton of water until you have to pee. Then you go to the bathroom. You have to stay there for fifteen more minutes. You can wash oil off your face and fold paper towels into triangles. You can breathe on the mirrors and draw something in the mist really quickly before it fades.

Then lunch period is over and they don't know you haven't eaten anything.

If you have a friend who leaves food on his tray, you can eat that before he throws it out, but I don't recommend that because even young people here think they're doing you a favor to feed you their trash. So just forget it and get in line for recess.

Recess is the time to mention Kyle, who is my great friend. I have never been to his house. He lives in Chimney Hill with the Jennifers and Daniel W. His dad painted his room the colors of the Dolphins team and he has more games than I've ever seen in my life. Since I live in apartments, it's too dangerous for him to stay overnight with us, and my mom would be shamed if I went to his house but couldn't taroff and offer hosting him in return—so we just play at recess.

On the north grounds, we play dodgeball. On the south playground we sit on the roots of a huge tree and talk about football or *Final Fantasy* games. I break the acorns open and stuff the bitter nuts into nooks of the tree trunk so the squirrels won't go hungry. Kyle and I met because he was the new kid after me. So he didn't know anything about me before I could be nice to him.

Sometimes I'll hear a good yo' mama joke and write it in my notebook.

Sometimes Kyle will draw monsters in his notebook.

I told him once that Ifrit is a Persian monster.

"The one from *Final Fantasy*?" he said.

And I said, "Yeah. I mean, that one's a fire ifrit. There's all kinds. Like, they're genies, basically, and demons. But in our stories the demons aren't all the same. There are some they call 'the demons who believe in God,' and those are tragic figures, because they made the mistake of siding with Satan when he rebelled against God, but as soon as they were smashed down to Earth, they regretted it and believed again. But it was too late. They were already cast out. They just wander now and nobody believes that they want to be good, because they look like hairy demons. And they don't have homes in heaven or hell. They're just always stuck and disbelieved."

I realized I had been talking for like ten minutes, because if I didn't explain everything, he'd think I was making it up.

I had said in church once that there might be demons who believe in God, and that's what happened. Nobody believed me. So I shut up and went back to cracking acorns.

Kyle said, "Cool."

Which was basically like saying he believed me.

He drew the ifrit with a cross burned into its chest, and it was the coolest picture I've ever seen.

When the bells ring and everybody lines up to go back, Kyle and I get in different lines, because we have all different teachers.

We don't see each other after that.

As we go inside, I usually make sure to be as far away from Brandon Goff as possible. If he sees Meg G. first, he tells "Your mama's so fat" jokes and if he sees me, he tells "Your mama's so poor" jokes, like your mama's so poor she can't afford to pay attention!

I'm not sure why that one's even funny.

It's just true.

She can't afford to pay attention.

AFTER SCHOOL THEY HAVE CLUBS. I'm on academic team, Latin team, and cinema club. It is important to have a classroom to go to when the last bell rings, because that's when people fight the most in the halls and just behind the gym. Never be in the bathrooms when school lets out, for example.

I don't even know cinema. They're all movies from when Hollywood was called Tinseltown, and they couldn't make explosions. I asked if we could watch a van Damme movie and they said it was rated R, and also I'm just the treasurer. Then they told me it wasn't a "classic."

I just go for the popcorn and wait till the coast is clear in the halls.

Sometimes I sit with people after clubs while they wait for their parents to pick them up in their own cars. I have my notebook out to hear their jokes, like, "Yo, gimme a quarter."

That's not a joke. But I notice they don't have shame in asking each other for money, so I write it down. There is a candy machine in every hall in the school and some kids have money every day for a Coke, a pack of cookies, and either chewy candies or candy bars. All just for one kid.

When they get fruit chews, other kids usually say, "Don't be stingy. I'll get you one back tomorrow."

And the kid will give them one. I never say that, because they know I'll never "get them one back" tomorrow. But sometimes they give me a yellow or green, which are the trash flavors. I sometimes say no thanks, so they don't think I'm a "mooch."

I just say, "Nah," which is real cool, like, I don't need it.

And that wins respect so you can say yes next time.

The lemons are really good too, so it's a good move.

When their parents come, they sometimes lean over their kid and ask me, "Would you like a ride home?" because they think I live close to them in one of their neighborhoods, but I say, "Nah. Thank you. My mom's on the way."

I **WALK HOME ALONE BY** the main road so the cars will see me. Sometimes the grown-ups driving by will call the police, but it's okay because I don't do drugs or spray paints. Walking through the woods is more dangerous because there are no adults in the woods, just other kids. And kids are dangerous.

On freezing days I have to take bus 209, which is the bus that goes to the apartments, the trailer park outside of town, and all the way out in the boondocks. The farm kids on the bus are super tough and don't talk much and don't care about school at all. Meg G. is twice as big as me and knows all about saddling horses. Her hands have rope burns from when she pulls in the steers.

The Jennifers make fun of her all the time, because she has a boy's haircut, but she's not a bad person. She even hit Brandon Goff in the face once.

He was leaning over the seat of the bus laughing in her ear about her coat, which I always thought was cool. It's orange, for hunting. He kept saying she was a big bumpkin pumpkin and I don't think she would have even done anything except he kept cackling in her ear. Until finally she smacked him right in the face, really hard. It made a wet splat sound, and then she went back to being a stone.

He even swiped at her head, but she didn't flinch and he backed off, cause all his friends were laughing at him by then.

When I get on the bus, I have very good strategies.

First, I get on last. One time I got on first and took a seat by the window, and a kid named Harley crunched right on top of me and jammed my shoulder into the glass and said, "I didn't see you there."

"That's okay," I said, cause there was nothing else to say.

"You're in my seat. No one's ever in my seat, so I didn't see you there."

"I forgive you," I said.

He smashed me again.

The bus driver said, "Everything alright back there?"

We could see his eyes watching us in the big mirror above him. Harley said, "Yep," and sat next to me. Then for the rest of the ride, we both stared at the mirror. I tried to hold the driver's eyes as long as possible, but whenever he'd look down to make a turn or something, Harley would punch me on the thigh or the shoulder, until I could only feel the throbbing where I hadn't gone numb.

When we got to the trailers, he put his knuckle on my bruised leg and ground it in as he got up. I screamed and the driver looked up again, but it was too late.

Harley said, "My seat," and left.

The next day my leg was so purple it had patches of green in it.

So I get on last, and I say hello to the driver so he'll like me and look at me as much as possible.

Strategy two is that you can't sit up front, which everybody knows, because on a regular bus it would make you a dweeb, and on bus 209 it will send you to the hospital.

Once, there was a kid whose name I don't know, who sat in the front—straight up like he was first chair clarinet or something. It was like he just got to this country and didn't know any strategies.

Brandon Goff only noticed the new kid after we left school. Brandon was all the way in the back, but it was still like putting a big juicy chicken in front of a cartoon fox.

He quickly bent a paper clip in half so the two prongs stuck out—we called those "wasps." And then he opened the bus window, put the two stingers on the lip and slammed it back down, so the prongs flattened into super sharp blades—we called those "killer wasps."

The kid had no idea what was about to happen. His posture was super good. I think he was probably on the wrong bus.

Brandon shushed everybody when they giggled, as he took a thick rubber band off of his wrist. He put the killer wasp in it like a slingshot and pulled back so far I thought it would snap in half. I was in the middle of the bus looking back to front, back to front, waiting for the long seconds while Brandon aimed.

It flew so fast I didn't actually see it.

All I saw was the grin on Brandon's face.

The snap of the rubber band.

Then nothing.

Then, half a paper clip just popped out of the kid's neck. The two prongs stabbed right in.

No blood at first.

Another second for the kid to feel it.

Then he shrieked so loud that the driver slammed the brakes.

We all flew forward.

The kid clawed at the paper clip and ripped it out of his neck.

That's when the blood came from the two holes, and the driver called for help on the bus radio.

We never saw the kid again.

The image we all remember is the little spray of blood from the holes, like two little waterfalls, just before he clutched them and fell over.

THE THIRD STRATEGY IS to lean down and put your bag on your head.

The fourth is to pick up your feet so they can't grab your ankles and write on your shoes.

Five is don't sit in the very back. That's Brandon's seat.

Six is open the window in front of you for when they fart on you.

Seven is don't open the window next to you so they can't throw your notebooks out.

Eight is to cry if you have to. If they take pennies and flick them at your skull and say, "Money for the poor," and the pennies hit so hard your eyes go white, and you fall over, then it's okay to cry to make them stop.

That's all the strategies.

Meg G. and I sit next to each other, and I hope someday she leaves school and wins 4-H and doesn't ever have to be around rich people or mall people again.

WHEN YOU ENTER THE apartment complex, it feels like entering the courtyard of a dead king and his decaying cement kingdom.

You can hear people shout at each other through their windows. There is nothing breakable that isn't broken. In the open area, Dwight and his brothers play football. If they see me, I can't run straight for our door, because I'm alone and maybe they'd just push me inside and start hitting me where nobody could see and take my Nintendo.

So if they see me, I run to the gas station across the street and wait till they get hungry and go inside. The gas station has comic books, so I can pretend I'm looking at each one really close, because I'm a shopper.

I say, "Hello. Where are your comics?" so the attendant knows I'm interested and have money. He says, "Over there," and I say, "Ah! Perfect."

I don't go near the candy or the attendant will think I'm stealing and kick me out. The next closest protection is the emergency clinic, but they won't let me hang around anymore.

The greatest American hero is Logan Wolverine, who is also an immigrant (from Canada) and who can heal from anything.

If I ever get one, I'll buy his comic book first.

When Dwight and his brothers go inside, I run to our door.

My mom works in the mornings and then goes to Oklahoma University at night to get another master's degree. An American degree she can use here.

My sister has a million after-school activities so she can get into Harvard.

Ray—while they were divorced—wasn't around. Then after they got married again, he would be at work at a bank till really late.

So I turn on the lights in the kitchen, and the two bedrooms, and even the bathroom. Then it feels like people are around.

I **CAN COOK ALL KINDS** of things.

My top dishes are:

1. Eggs with stewed tomatoes and onions on pita bread
2. Tuna salad mixed with egg salad, also on pita

Most days, my mom has a carton of bean sprouts waiting for me. I get out a pan and put it on high heat. Then I put a chunk of butter in there. It has to be so hot the butter melts right away. I let it bubble, then drop the whole carton of bean sprouts.

They make a giant sizzle. I can move the pan back and forth like a chef so the sprouts turn without a spatula, so I do that.

When the sprouts are starting to shrivel, I pour in a bunch of soy sauce. It sizzles again, then turns the sprouts brown.

That's my specialty.

It might be a Japanese dish. I don't know.

I eat a whole bowl of sprouts and watch TV for three hours until people get home.

My mom comes home exhausted every night.

I have never seen her not exhausted.

And also, I have never seen her not working.

People in Oklahoma think this must be how refugees are—never sitting, never sleeping, like they have no knees and no dreams. Maybe people think that's just the way my mom talks, kinda panicky and chipper at the same time, like someone scared who doesn't want you to think she's scared—even maybe like you're the one she's scared of.

She is only as tall as a house plant.

Her eyes are almond-shaped, which is the Persian shape for eyes.

She comes home and goes straight into the kitchen. I don't mean that she comes home, goes to her room to change clothes, wanders into the bathroom, picks through mail, and then finally arrives at the refrigerator.

I mean she walks through the door, drops her bags and coat on the chair by the door without stopping on her way straight into the kitchen to start cooking.

She's probably the best mom in my whole school. Sometimes I walk out of my room and don't even know she was there.

She says, "Hi baby joon. Did you do your homeworks?"

I say yes, even though I do all my homework in the time at the beginning of class while the teacher takes attendance and tries to get everyone to be quiet.

Then we eat a big feast.

My sister will be home by then too, and we get plates of buttery rice with beef chunks and kidney beans stewed in green onions, mint, and parsley.

My mom takes the yogurt she makes herself and cuts cucumbers into it with salt and pepper. And she bakes bread—real bread to dip into it. And she has jars of mixed pickles.

And she grows radishes.

And for dessert she has fried dough balls in rosewater syrup, and baklava, and saffron cookies stuffed with cinnamon, sugar, and walnuts—all of it she baked over the weekends.

And she brews black tea.

And none of it is from cans or anything.

We eat as if we're the shahs of Oklahoma City.

She asks if school is fine, and it's easy to say yeah with a mouthful of cookie. This is the best part of the day, and the only time I think my mom is happy.

We leave the table when Ray gets home and pretend it's so we can do homework. My sister works on her business plan, and I play *Final Fantasy.* If they get loud in the kitchen, I turn the volume up.

If Ray isn't mad, he'll put on a van Damme movie and show me kicks.

Or everyone goes to bed and I hide under my blanket reading *The Hobbit*. I stay up as long as I possibly can, so I can be alone. I stay up until my eyes hurt.

The second I close my eyes, it all starts over again.

I hate waking up.

I stay up so late that I always sleep past the alarm clock and miss the bus.

And that's it.

That's a whole day.

If you're a kid who's counting the memories of your grandpa's hands, and your dad's laugh, and a whole country full of different flower smells, and birds you woke up to, and your grandma's craggy face—geez, you could barely even picture it—and all the words to a language people think you made up, then all the days you spent getting beat up in Oklahoma aren't even worth collecting.

So you can keep this one if you want to.

OKLAHOMA IS BEAUTIFUL SOMETIMES. People who are kind and feed poor kids are always beautiful. It depends on how you imagine the state shape.

Either it's a soup pot sitting on a fire with cozy steam lines coming from it, from the soup that someone in church will share with you, like this:

Or if you draw the lines straight, suddenly it looks like a cleaver cutting into something soft like this:

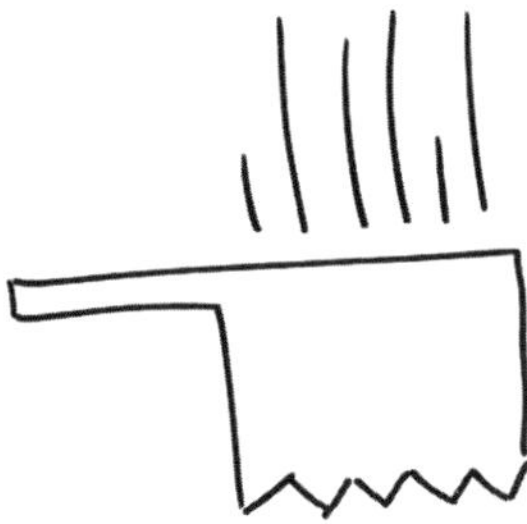

In the maps, they don't draw the extra lines, so you don't know which Oklahoma is which.

BUT FIRST THERE'S THIS poem from Rumi that my dad says sometimes. It's important. It goes:

That fly
Sailing
On a leaf

Of hay
On a sea
Of donkey piss
Raised his head
A sea captain.

Obviously the best thing to be in that story is the donkey. But if not that, then the fly who is an adventurer of new lands and not a refugee. But definitely don't be the pee river. And definitely don't be the leaf wallowing in it.

OKAY, THIS IS THE STORY of how my Lionheart mom got a Death Warrant on her head and had Nowhere to Run for a while. Those were all van Damme movies, by the way, where lots of people die. Get yourself ready. Go poop now if you have to, cause I won't pause the movie if you have to go in the middle.

IT STARTED WHEN ELLIE moved to London and decided to become English. She colored her hair to be lighter and never spoke about Arman and drank tea with her pinky up. And she didn't say their names.

But just cause they don't have something in English doesn't mean they don't have it in England, know what I mean?

I mean she couldn't escape the memories, and maybe never left her seat in the train station for the next forty years.

IT GOES LIKE THIS:

By the time my aunt Sanaz turned nineteen, she spoke English like a proper Disney Princess Diana. If you can express yourself super well, show people who you really are—that you're just like them—then they might love you. So Sanaz met an English guy who was so handsome and clean that Grandma Ellie cringed when he shook hands with my dad, who, at that time, was just out of prison for buying enough opium to give to an entire village of sad people.

When this happens, I am three years old. My sister is six. We both have Orich strategies for each other already. My mom and dad were both out of medical school and had already moved to Isfahan, to the house I told you about with the jasmine garden and the birds in the walls.

Sanaz and Charles are finigonzon and finigonz.

They wanted to get married.

We bought plane tickets.

England was the first time I tasted peanut butter. My sister almost lost a finger. And my mom met Jesus. All three were life-changing.

First, I will tell you about the peanut butter.

London was a cold city, paved with wet stones. When we arrived at Ellie's apartment she opened her door, said, "Khossie!" and squeezed my cheeks into paste.

Everyone screamed and hugged.

My dad was wearing a long overcoat he bought in the airport of England (because he had never needed a coat that thick before) with a wad of cash as thick as a peanut butter jar. He carried the giant suitcases into the entryway of the apartment, plopped them on the ground, and said to Ellie, "Where do you keep the knives?"

THIS IS WHAT HAPPENED: My dad approached the suitcase like his dad approached the bull. My mom said, "Massoud, what are you doing?"

No answer.

The suitcases, I should tell you, were a set from one of those expensive fashion stores that Oklahoma rich people drive to Dallas to shop at.

In the airports, the attendant had lifted them and said, "Wow. Beautiful."

When we got to my grandma Ellie's, my dad took the big suitcase to her bedroom. The suitcase was big enough for me and my sister to fit in it. He unzipped the top. Inside were all my mom's clothes and things for a three-month visit.

"Massoud," she said.

"Hold on."

Dad picked up the suitcase and turned it over on the bed. Everything fell out in a pile. My mom sucked her teeth because that would be such an annoying thing to do.

Then my dad took the knife and stabbed it into the suitcase. He cut all the way around, then ripped open the inner lining. Underneath it was a hidden compartment. My dad turned the suitcase over again and poured out a bunch of brick-shaped things, wrapped in red plastic bags.

He did this with the entire suitcase set. Something like a few thousand dollars worth of luggage.

Cut them all into bits.

Poured out a whole river of red bricks.

Apparently he'd paid a tailor in Isfahan to sew them into the lining of the super expensive suitcases so the guards at the airport wouldn't think to inspect them.

The red bricks were drugs, I found out later, when my sister told me this story.

In fact, I don't even know if I was there—because I don't remember what happened to the suitcases once they were destroyed. I guess they threw them out.

The only part I actually remember with my own eyes is standing in a really nice German suitcase store in London as my dad shopped for a new set.

I was really scared, I remember, and my mom wasn't there. Maybe they had a fight when she found out he'd smuggled drugs into the country.

I just remember being scared.

The shop had marble floors. Huge glass doors, with suitcases displayed like sports cars. The attendants all wore black and pointed their noses at the vaulted ceiling.

My dad barely spoke English, but walked into places as if he was returning to his castle. He nodded to the doorman and shook his hand. The doorman nodded back.

And suddenly everyone wanted to talk to him. My memory is the back of his coat. And a young German saleswoman laughing at every joke.

At some point before the memory, he must have said, "Wait here, Khossie."

I remember standing in the entryway next to a row of suitcases. I poked one of them and it rolled on freshly oiled wheels.

"Oh no no no," said the attendant, lunging at the suitcase before it moved two inches. "No touching," she said, smiling but not smiling.

But I had nothing else to do. And the attendant—maybe her name was Gertrude—realized I was just going to be in the way. "Would you like a treat?" said Gert.

I looked at my dad.

Back then, I wasn't poor, so I could take things if people offered them.

My dad nodded. You have to understand, when he nodded to me or the doorman, it felt like everything was okay and you were a good person and you deserved good things to happen.

So I said, "Yeth pleeth."

Gert said something in German or English—I didn't know either language except for "yeth pleeth"—and a different person ran into the back of the store.

The other one returned and gave Gert a package.

Gert handed it to me. Her face was still in my face. She was kneeling.

"Tantu," I said.

She stretched her lips into a smile again and got up.

"It's peanut butter," she said. I don't think she had kids or knew what to do with them. What she gave me was a sandwich cookie with peanut butter cream in the middle.

I already told you I'd never tasted peanut butter before.

It was the taste in my mouth when my dad said, "I take this set, yes?"

And he handed Gert a stack of money as thick as a novel. It was so much that Gert laughed at it, and put a hand on my dad's arm like she had to touch him.

He didn't even care what color luggage he got.

The peanut butter was super sticky.

I realized it's for keeping kids busy, and their mouths shut.

I watched Gert skip behind the counter to stuff the money someplace.

Her helper went into the back to get boxes.

And a little river started to flow along the marble floor toward my dad.

He turned around to say, "Khossie, you ready to go?"

His mustache was turned up, but when he saw me it fell.

"Khossie!" he said.

Gert looked up and saw the river moving toward her luggage.

It was pee.

Cause I'd peed myself.

It just spread across the store looking for something to soak.

Gert ran toward the nearest luggage set and pushed it away. The rolling bags scattered like pool balls. But they dragged pee with them and painted the floor with more of it. Everybody started scrambling to move suitcases as the pee river chased them around the shop.

Gert shouted for the helper. He doesn't need a name. None of these people need names. I never saw them again. They were all furious. They said stuff in German or English.

My dad picked me up. He was embarrassed, I could tell. All the laughing was over. I still had half my peanut butter cookie in my hand, but I dropped it. He held me away from his coat. He pointed at the wet luggage and said, "I take this too, yes?"

It's a funny story when he tells it.

Everybody laughs and it ends with two sets of luggage and a hilarious trip shopping for pants before we got back to Ellie's place.

My dad always walked into every door carrying a mountain of gifts.

And even when some of them were soaked in pee, everybody would be happy.

NEXT I WILL TELL you how my sister almost lost her finger. This was two years before we both lost our dad.

By the time we got to Oklahoma, my sister had become hard and sharp, but in London she was still soft clay, and we were still friends.

I would spend all the hours she was gone asking for her, and saving half of my cookies on a plate in Ellie's kitchen, for when she got back.

Back then, I thought she was the smartest person I had ever met.

Now I know she's the smartest person *anyone* has ever met.

Trust me on this. I saw her when she was five—she could recite twenty pages of the Persian history books our dad gave her.

People thought she had a photographic memory—real grown-ups, not her family. She learned English, no problem. They put her in two schools at once in Oklahoma, just so they'd have classes hard enough. I've never seen her struggle to understand anything. Sometimes I would stare at her and I knew I could see more inside her than anyone else, and all I could see was the whirring light complex of a supercomputer.

Have you ever looked at the inside of a computer?

With the boards and the boxes like miniature cities?

You can't *see* them working. There's nothing moving.

You can't understand it by looking. It's too complicated.

Anyway, that's my sister.

She was a person too, but more and more she hid that part. She loved our dad more than anybody. I'm not sure she ever liked me at all for being born.

When we went to England, we planned to stay for months. She was six so they had to find something to do with her.

Everyone was busy. My mom helped with the wedding and went to Ellie's church and learned about Christianity. My dad went around the city meeting friends and giving them gifts in red bags. If anyone asked about him, my mom or Ellie would say, "He's a powerful man, with many friends. Lots of obligations." I don't know what that means. My mom once said he was just meeting other addicts and wasting himself.

I went to parks with Ellie.

And my sister—they put her in a daycare so she'd have something to do. Otherwise she'd destroy stuff. She was cheeky like our dad, and when grown-ups were around, she'd say things no six-year-old could possibly know and they'd all laugh. But you couldn't leave her alone or her brain would overload and I would end up crying.

So they had her in daycare in a neighborhood in London that didn't like new people. Looking back, they probably thought we were Muslim immigrants who were going to cram into Ellie's little apartment and cook smelly food and act unEnglish or something.

One little kid at daycare would hit her a lot.

Like, my sister would be sitting at a round table, coloring, and he'd smack her in the head with a crayon. But when she'd cry about it, everybody was awkward, because the kid's parents didn't really care (and didn't want people like us in their kid's class), and the teacher was a bashful British lady who wasn't going to take sides. So people told my sister the kid probably liked her and that she should be nice to him, even though she should have pinned him down and made him eat the crayons.

Till one day, the kid said, "Ay! Brownie. C'mere."

They were in the schoolyard and he was standing by the door to the kitchen. I should mention, my sister is a genius, but socially—definitely not a genius. She walked over thinking the kid was finally going to be friends with her.

He said, "I got a secret. Wanna hear it?"

She nodded.

He said, "Put your finger here. It's special."

Don't ever listen to anyone who randomly says, "It's special," instead of a real reason. My sister was suspicious, so she only put her pinky finger in the little space in the hinge between the door and the doorjamb.

The little boy ran over to the other side, as if he was going to hand her a secret note or something.

I think about my sister in that exact moment a lot.

She's just six.

Brand-new place. She doesn't speak the language exactly.

She's alone at a school.

Some kid pelts her with crayons.

And everybody has given her bad information: Be nice, he likes you.

But he doesn't.

He hated her. Even in his brand-new kid heart, he'd found the hate spot.

And she's just standing there with a tiny delicate finger placed in the hinge of a big wooden door.

The kid is probably giggling like a villain.

He's giving every sign that he's going to hurt her.

And she is genuinely hoping he's going to play with her.

It's beautiful.

How badly we all want love.

It's tragic.

How bad we are at searching for it.

"Closer," said the kid.

My sister leaned forward.

The kid slammed the heavy door in her face, like, "Not welcome."

It didn't even slow down.

The hinge clamped shut and cut her pinky in half.

She didn't even have time to scream.

The noise of the door slamming was the only part that got the teacher's attention.

She looked over from across the yard.

My sister's pinky was dangling by a thin string of skin. A little river of blood poured down her arm, over her dress, and onto her leg.

My mom says that by the time she arrived, the only thing the teacher had managed was to put my sister's pinky parts in a mug of ice.

My mom says my sister was standing by herself, shivering. The kid was back playing with all the other kids, who got an extra long recess, because of what he did to my sister.

At that moment, if you looked in her eyes, past the tears, I bet you wouldn't even see the pain of a severed finger, but the shock of how cruel people can be. And how stupid it was to put her finger in a doorjamb, hoping for the best in somebody.

And if you think my sister would ever fall for anything like that again—now that we're here in Oklahoma and lots of boys have that same way of showing they like you—then you'd be dead wrong.

AS MY MOM RUSHED her to a hospital to have her finger sewn back on, my sister hardened her expectations for the world into a tight ball.

She cried most when she saw the needle that would sew it back on.

My mom told her she'd never have to go back to the school.

When my dad got back from wherever he was, he took her for ice cream. And then they all came back to Ellie's apartment.

I remember that my sister went straight into the bedroom to sleep and my mom cried as she told Ellie what happened.

That's how my sister almost lost her finger.

But I didn't just tell you the story for no reason. I told you because it was the start of everything that would come later. It was the first step of how we ended up in Oklahoma.

And it wasn't even the weirdest thing that happened that day.

I wonder sometimes, if I had looked at the space under the door to the bedroom, where my sister was sleeping, whether I would see beams of magic light shining from inside.

Because when my sister opened the door and walked out a few hours later, she was suddenly happy again, as if everything was going to be alright.

And when they asked her what happened, she said she'd met an angel.

BELIEVE ME, I KNOW how it sounds. But imagine you're six and you came home every day crying, begging not to go back to school. And the grown-ups just pat you on the head and say, "There there. It'll get better." But it doesn't get better. Only worse.

Until today, you got your finger chopped off in a door and everyone realized they should have let you stay home.

If that was you, would you walk out two hours later into the living room—where the adults are sitting at the table having tea and biscuits and kicking themselves—and would you tell them everything was fine, or would you milk it a little?

The answer is you'd milk it so hard it would turn into butter.

There is no reason to come out and say you're fine.

But that's what she did. She said she was lying in Ellie's bed. By the door was a rolled-up Persian rug that we had brought with us for Ellie. When my sister woke up, she saw a man sitting on the rug. She didn't know him, but she wasn't scared.

When she described him—kind eyes, brown hair, a glow like a TV in a dark room, white robes—Ellie gasped and said, "Oh my God, you saw Jesus."

And my sister said, "Yeah," even though she had no idea who Jesus was or what he looked like, because we didn't have pictures of him in Iran.

He only said four words, "It will be okay," which is funny, because that's what all the grown-ups said, and it wasn't.

Ellie was the happiest I have ever seen her.

Maybe because it meant there would be another exile.

"Your daughter's a Christian," she said to my mom, who was furious.

"Yeah!" said my sister, "I'm a Christian!"

Because she saw it made my mom twitch.

That was the moment that everything started to blow up.

It wasn't the bang.

Maybe it wasn't even the lit fuse.

But it was definitely the struck match.

The flash and the spark that sent us flying across the world.

And it was mostly absurd.

Miracles are absurd by definition.

If they weren't, they'd just be odd things that happened. Improbable things.

But while miracles are impossible, they aren't coincidences. They're knives that cut into our reality. And they're messy and weird.

So all of a sudden my mom had a six-year-old saying she was a Christian, which—if you didn't know—was a crime in Iran.

Not a regular one either, a capital crime. The kind where if you're found guilty, they kill you.

I SUPPOSE IF YOU DON'T want to believe it, all you have to do is say my sister wanted to be like Ellie, or she wanted to harass my mom. Both of which are true.

Or she was dreaming.

Or the pain medication for her finger made her brain wibbly.

Miracles are easy to explain away.

It doesn't really matter what you believe.

Because the point is that Sima (that's my mom's name) was forced at that moment to pay attention.

She came to England unwilling to hear Ellie's (or Sanaz's) conversion story. When they arrived in England, they found a church that welcomed them. That made them Christians.

Sima was a committed Shiite Muslim at that time, which meant—

You know what, you're not ready for this.

You kinda have to know the history of Islam—which Sima knew—and compare it to her experience in England as she heard about Christianity. Then you can compare the claims they make about Truth and Reality that we all share but also mostly ignore in different parts. Which is why we can see the same things but come to different conclusions about how to heal all our broken hearts.

Which we all have.

Which is such a big part of our lives that we don't even notice the pain of it.

We're completely numb to it, because it's constant.

It's so true it's boring.

Which is really our brains, terrified, hoping to ignore the fact that we have giant holes in our chests.

That's why everyone is distracted with TV shows and no one likes to talk about it.

Our broken hearts problem.

But we're going to have to talk about it soon, so gird your loins, reader.

For now, here's a poop story to make you feel better. Or if not better, then at least distracted.

IF YOU WANNA KNOW how rich somebody is, just look at what they eat and how they poop. Everybody does both, so it's not like comparing cars.

Those are two things you can even compare with animals—so for instance, you could see some dude grab up a bunch of taco salad with his hands and shove it in his mouth like a bear and then go off into a porta-potty on a construction site and you know that guy is probably dirtier than the bear.

Or you see people in Edmond who buy boxed cereal and bottled water, and you don't even know where they poop. Probably every bedroom in their house has a bathroom with candles and potpourri and stuff. They don't even have to smell themselves. And if you're a king, you don't even have to wipe.

Poor people don't get to choose what they eat, and they don't get to hide where they poop—that's why we think of them as animals.

So there's one aspect of pooping—being rich or not.

But you can tell a lot about cultures too, by how they handle pooping, cause it's the other half of their cuisine.

Korean food is the tastiest but makes the smelliest poops.

English food is pretty much the same in both directions.

South Indian food is so spicy it burns on the way out, but it's worth it.

Oklahoma BBQ takes its time and sits heavy in your belly for more than a day.

Oklahoma Tex-Mex is some of the best food in the world, but the poops are soupy.

Italy has a great taste-to-poop ratio, which is probably why so many people like it best.

And I don't want to brag, but Persian food is the perfect balance of tastiness and on-time firm poops.

That's because Persians are one of the oldest cultures in the world and we make really nice rugs. So we had to make good strategies, or spills (both kinds) would be bad for the rugs.

The bathrooms in Iran are so different that when I told Mrs. Miller's class about them, it was a disaster.

Here's what I said: You walk into a room in your house and everything is stone or tile.

"What about your precious rugs?" said Jared M.

"No rugs," I said.

"What do the rooms look like?" said Kelly J.

"Normal," I said. Some people put flowers by the sink, or framed pictures on the walls. Just like Oklahomans so far.

The difference is we don't have the chairs.

"What chairs?" said Jared M.

"The chairs in American bathrooms."

"We don't have chairs," he said.

"The chairs, the chairs," I said. "The ones you go in."

"You mean poop," said Kelly J.

"Yeah, the poop chairs," I said.

"Toilets," said Mrs. Miller. And then she spelled it on the chalkboard. I know how to spell it. I'm not a second grader.

I just didn't remember the word. It's even the same word in Farsi. I just forgot cause everybody was staring at me.

"Wait," said Jared. "You don't have toilets?"

"Ew," said Kelly J.

"We have toilets," I said. "They're just not chair shape."

We have toilet bowls set into the tile floors.

"So a hole in the ground."

You squat over them. They even have really nice inlay steps for your feet, so you don't slip.

"Do they flush?"

Of course they flush everything away. We've had running water longer than the United States has existed. But you don't sit in the uncomfortable position where it feels like nothing will ever come out because your butt is squeezed together. Squatting is way better for you, with less chance you'll get hemorrhoids.

"I'd rather get hemorrhoids than poop on the floor," said Jared.

I should repeat, it's not *on* the floor. The toilet pan is just set at ground level. Rich people have lots of colorful stonework tiles around it, like you're pooping into a little babbling river in a field of flowers.

"Sounds dirty," said Kelly J.

"Yeah, gross," said a different Kelly. "Can we stop talking about this?"

No one really believed that bathrooms like that could be nice and I couldn't find any pictures, so I dropped it.

I didn't even tell the Kellies that the dirtiest thing I can think of is sitting on a chair that clogs all the time and wiping butts with dry toilet paper. There is zero chance all the poop has come off with that method.

Think about it. If you got a bunch of peanut butter and jelly on your hands—like, you squeezed a whole handful and now you're sticky—do you use a series of disintegrating tissues and pretend all the residue magically wipes away, even though your skin is basically a sponge with a billion pores all packed with peanut butter, or do you just wash them with hot water?

Cause it seems pretty obvious to me that all the butts in Mrs. Miller's class are poop-smeared and grosser than gross.

But I hadn't said any of this when Jared said, "Wait. So do you wipe with leaves?" And I was so busy thinking about how ridiculous it is to have a basket of leaves in a bathroom that I said, "No."

"You don't wipe?"

"Class!" said Mrs. Miller, cause everyone turned into howler monkeys. "Class! Quiet down."

"We wash," I said, "with soap."

"And your hands?" said Kelly.

Of course with our hands. How do you shower?

"Yes," I said.

"That is disgusting." Everybody agreed.

"It's like a bidet," said Mrs. Miller. "It's just a nozzle that sprays water. It's very hygienic."

I said, "They do it in France."

People like France, so that ended the conversation, even though the French kings pooped right in the hallways of their castles.

I READ THIS AT THE library one Saturday.

Imagine you're a rich French person. Your dad had an oil company or something. You have a giant house somewhere in fancy France. One day you get a fancy invitation to the palace for a party to celebrate the king's new jacket or something.

So you go. You put on your best outfit and make sure you smell great and you pull up in front of the palace looking creamy.

The party is like a party in the movies.

Everything is a fairy tale.

All the best food served by servants from other countries.

Flowers everywhere.

Then the clock strikes twelve and the king yawns. He summons his minions to carry him to bed. People start to clear out.

You practically float down the hall to the entryway. You turn a corner and—don't forget you've got your fanciest shoes on—you step into a steaming pile of fudgy French poop.

Right in the middle of a palace that looks like a museum. A big pile that only a person or a Great Dane could have made.

It's all over your shoe.

When you lift your foot, it makes a shlorpy sound.

Some other party people walk past, but they don't even care. It's just you standing there with the poop. You're the only one who cares about it.

Then the smell hits you.

You'll never smell flowers, or anything nice, ever again.

Thanks for coming.

Hope you had a nice night.

THAT'S HOW SIMA FELT in England as her daughter claimed to be a Christian just days before they went back to Iran.

Because she knew no one else was going to stop to help. She had to deal with it herself before she went back home. Scrape it off her shoe or just keep going with it hanging on.

Because if they found out—the Komiteh, if the Komiteh found out—they would cut my mother's throat.

She had to deal with it, even in the middle of her sister's wedding, in the middle of a vacation, when it was the last thing she wanted to do.

The "it" I'm talking about is Christianity.

And she was a very serious Muslim at that time, so she knew what I'm about to tell you.

And she knew it was crap news.

A HISTORY LESSON:

When the Prophet Muhammad died in the seventh century, after he'd taken over most of the world, it was kind of a surprise to everybody. Suddenly, the messenger of Islam is dead. He's just dolloped there in his best robes, and everyone's huddled over his breathless body, hoping he'll give some sign of what they should do in case he dies.

And the problem is, Who's going to take over? The known world is at stake and Muhammad hasn't left instructions on who will inherit all the goats and the yogurt and the servants and the countries.

His sons are all dead, so that's out.

The other two possibilities are his cousin Ali, and his right-hand man, Abu Bakr.

You can imagine. It could have gone a thousand different ways.

They're eyeing each other over his corpse and fingering their scimitars like it's high noon in an Oklahoma boomtown, except in the desert. Blood relatives versus the second-in-command.

A tumbleweed whorls across a dune.

The rigor mortis of the Prophet whistles a gunslinger tune.

The fate of the world shivers in a dry saloon.

The gulf between them was big enough for a whole religion to fit into.

Burying him was the last thing the two factions would do together.

The pushing and shoving would start even before the wailing of the wives came down from the almond trees.

Here's the issue. Islam was the third kid in the family.

Judaism was the oldest.

Christianity was the middle child.

Then Islam.

So the two groups were basically fighting over which sibling to act like.

The Shiites were the ones who wanted Ali—the cousin—to take over, because they said we should be like the Jews. The magic is in the blood. The people. So if the Prophet had blood relatives, they were special.

The Sunnis said, No, no, the new thing to do is like the Christians. Jesus didn't appoint cousins. He had the apostles and then later, the popes. Popes were elected. They were the best person for the job.

So the Sunnis followed Abu Bakr, because he'd been Muhammad's best advisor.

It was a fight between siblings. But if you know anything about fights, the ones in a family are way worse than the ones between strangers.

The Sunnis and the Shiites went to war for hundreds of years.

Until the Shiites—the ones who thought God wanted a bloodline—lost for good in the tenth century. But they didn't go away. They stewed about it. They knew they were right. For years they would go underground, rise up for a few fights, then go back into hiding.

It's no mystery why minorities have to hide, and harden themselves.

The smaller the army, the more it has to whip itself up into a frenzy. If there's only one of you, you have to hole up just to keep the world at bay. So the Shiites hid. They even pretended to be Sunnis if they had to.

Nowadays the Muslims who live in Iran and Afghanistan are the Shiites, and in Oklahoma, they call them the fundamentalists.

This is all important, I promise.

The main thing to remember is the magic. When people believe something, you can ask them, How does the magic happen?

And what you're really asking is, What can I do to be happy?

For the Shiites, there's magic in the bloodline of the Prophet. You still have to submit to the rules of Islam, but it's sure nice to be family.

The word for those people is "sayyed."

It means "master," or "holy one." And people who are sayyed have these lists that go, "Muhammad begat this dude, who begat another dude, who begat so and so . . ."

So they prove they were begotten by the Prophet. They're closer to God because they pray to their great-great-great-granddad. They're pure.

They get invited to all the best parties.

Technically, sayyedi are entitled to a tenth of your money. But how many Christians do you know who give a tenth to the church?

And *very* technically, sayyedi are the only ones allowed to be presidents—you can tell cause they wear the green turbans. But, of course, in the real world, if you're powerful you can just say you're sayyed and no one will say anything.

Like if a big guy says he's good at video games, even though you know you'd gank him, you just keep your mouth shut.

People lie, basically.

But who begat you is a question with an answer only someone else can tell you.

You're born, and when you're old enough to understand, they tell you whose child you are. You get claimed. That's when you're born again into something—not the world, but the word, the family name.

It's the most important thing about you, whose you are. It's more important than your race or religion. It's more important than what shows you like. It's the part of you that talks to itself so late at night that you're not even sure you're awake.

It's the concentrated you, collected in a pool of genetic fluids, creative juice, carbonic goo, passions, past mistakes, memories of other people, opinions about sweets, the intense desire to visit Italy, habits, the smell of your fart—all together in a thick maple syrup of your human situation. Your blood. That's you. The truest thing about you.

To the Shiite Muslims of Iran, the sayyed were religiously important because the blood in their veins was Muhammad's, and the blood in his was God's.

This is why it's unthinkable that a sayyed would turn away from Islam.

My mom, Sima, is a sayyed.

So is my dad.

I DON'T THINK EITHER OF them was lying.

My dad has a goat skin with all the family tree on it. He jokes that it goes all the way back to Shem. That's Noah's son. He laughs when he says it.

When I was really little, I remember old people would come to our door to have me touch them, like I could give them a blessing or something. Cause I was a double sayyed. Really, it was one lady this one time. I don't even know what it was about. I was playing video games when my mom called me to the door.

The old lady standing there was little, with a crooked back and a black chador framing her face, so you couldn't even tell if she had hair. Her face was craggy like my Baba Haji and in my memory she reaches out to cup my face in her hands.

Just like him, she stared into my eyes and smiled.

I just remember that one thing. I never knew if either of them got what they wanted from me.

I realize maybe those aren't even two different memories. Maybe I gave the memory of the stranger to my grandpa so he'd have a good one. Or just blurred them a little into each other.

I don't know.

I don't know.

Knowing about yourself, about your family, knowing the name of a grandpa and saying it out loud so he can hear it. It's probably the thing kids in Oklahoma treasure most. They hide it, of course, the way you should hide your most valuable thing. But I bet they walk around with a treasure chest full of clear memories. And the chest has their family name engraved on it. And the chest is their chest. The memories are in their heart. Their hearts are full. I bet. Full of something that isn't dripping away into nothing.

A patchwork memory is the shame of a refugee.

I don't even know if the strange old lady at the door was a relative or something. All I have is her touching my face. The rest is flushed and gone.

ANYWAY, HERE'S ANOTHER POOP STORY.

I got invited to Kyle's house!

First I had him over for my birthday. My mom made a giant feast, but we also got chips for party snacks.

His dad dropped him off and stood around the parking lot for a while, talking to Ray. Ever since he came to America, Ray has been in Oklahoma, so he knows how to "shoot the breeze."

He said, "Is that the new Ford Explorer?"

That's the nice car Kyle's dad had.

Kyle wanted to go inside, but I stood around to watch. Kyle's dad said, "Sure is. Will the boys be alright with just the sleeping bags?"

"They'll be great," said Ray.

"Should I give him some money for anything?"

I winced, because Ray would be super insulted if Kyle's dad took out any money.

"Oh, we'll be fine. Thanks for bringing him over."

"You sure? In case they decide they want to go mini golf or something?"

Ray was smiling at this point, but I could see his pivot foot was grinding into the concrete. "If they do, it's my treat," he said.

I'm not sure if Kyle's dad even realized how mad Ray was, how much danger he was in. I think he really thought if the boys wanted to go mini golfing, it was as simple as getting in a nice car and going. Or maybe he wanted to know what the plan was—like, were we going to stay inside and not go wandering around the apartment complex. Probably, he thought it was dangerous to do that.

Anyway, Kyle's dad thought about it with an innocent look on his face. He was a serious dad and everything, but he was standing in range for a spinning wheel kick without even knowing it. "Okay," he said. "Thanks again."

Ray relaxed. Then Kyle's dad said, "C'mere," to Kyle and gave him a hug. He kissed his head and told him to behave. I think if I ever hugged Ray, he would flinch. Not that I ever would.

Anyway, Kyle ate the chips, but the dinner didn't work.

My mom made fesenjoon—which you probably haven't had, but it's delicious.

"What is that?" said Kyle, when she put it down.

"It's chicken stewed in pomegranate juice and pureed walnuts," she said.

"It's chicken," I said again.

Kyle only eats chicken. His dad makes him chicken tenders three days a week. I told that to my mom, so that's what she made.

"Why does it look like that?" he said.

The stew is kind of a brown blob on a bed of rice. But it tastes amazing, I promise.

"It's really good," I said.

But he wasn't going to eat it. He tried to eat the bits of rice that hadn't touched the stew, but there were only six or seven of those. My mom said, "Do you want the chicken if I wipe off the sauce?" and he said, "No, thanks."

I said, "What do we do?" to my mom in Farsi.

And she looked at me like she was ashamed. She's the best cook in the whole world. Nobody has ever disliked her food. I couldn't eat if our guest wasn't eating. But guests never refuse food either.

In Dubai, once, my mom helped a poor lady and she gave us frog to eat, and I had to chew it with my eyes closed. But you couldn't say no.

And anyway, fesenjoon is no frog. Even rich people eat it. If you get a chance, you should really try it. It's sweet and tangy and the rice is buttery. Kyle cringed at it and said, "Smells like poop," which is untrue.

It only *looks* like poop.

But wait, that wasn't even the poop story.

My mom ran out to the gas station and bought a box of mac and cheese. She made it for him and he ate that, and we played Nintendo all night. So that was my birthday, but it meant I got to go to his house a few weeks later.

In Oklahoma, rich people have nice things.

In Iran, they have nice spaces.

Courtyards and fountain streams versus sports cars and mounted screens.

Kyle's house had TVs in every room, even the bathroom, and they all had cable. I didn't need to be dropped off, cause I could just ride the bus home with him. He rides bus 34, where everybody plays Game Boy or trades cards until they get home.

At this time, my poop situation was stable.

I probably wasn't even thinking about how a stomach is a balloon full of stew, gurgling around behind your belly button.

I was staring out the window at the tall oak trees as we drove by. In Edmond, the rich neighborhoods have all the old trees.

There are a lot of Kellys on bus 34, by the way. I watched one of them get off in front of a house with two garage doors. A mom was getting out of a car with shopping bags from the kind of store that gives big square shopping bags. Kelly's mom looked exactly like Kelly if she spent the next fifteen years crumpling the skin of her face and smoothing it out again like a sheet of paper.

I still followed all the strategies for buses, so I stayed down and held my ankles off the floor, while Kyle told me where he was in *Final Fantasy*. We never talked about our families, ever. Like, his parents were divorced, but his mom would come down from California and live with them on some weekends. But we never talked about that. That's what made us friends.

Only when we got off the bus and walked up the brick walkway to his door did I remember.

"What?" said Kyle.

"Nothing," I said. He opened the door and went inside. What I was thinking was I didn't have a sleeping bag. It's not that I forgot it. I just didn't have one. But you were supposed to have them, I think, at sleepovers. I thought, If I could wait till he falls asleep first, then maybe it wouldn't be a big deal.

Around then, my stomach started to feel swampy.

But Kyle wanted to play basketball, so he called his dad to move the car.

Kyle only had to ask once, and his dad came out of the house to do it.

After that, his dad stood around with us. He put a hand on Kyle's shoulder.

"How're you boys liking your classes?" he said.

I said, "I'm getting straight As," so he'd know I'm a good influence.

Kyle's dad showed us how to make our jump shots go far. Then he went inside.

I guess none of this matters to the poop story. I just thought it was so weird to be outside in the daytime with a grown-up. He seemed so unhurried. His work was over and he didn't have more work.

Anyway, we went inside for dinner.

Kyle's mom got home from the mall and showed us her haircut. Her hair was short and black and shiny. She had blue eyes and knew all the shows we watched. She even had her own Game Boy. I had never met a mom who caught her own Pokémon. Total finigonzon.

When she walked into the kitchen, we were setting the table. She dropped her bags on the big island and said, "What's this?"

Kyle's dad said, "Dinner."

She pretended to breathe it in and fluttered her eyelashes, "Sounds good. I'll have that."

And both Kyle and his brother laughed, but I didn't get it.

"So Daniel," she said, "how's your mom?"

"Uh, good," I said.

Conversation is painful when you're trying to hide. When we sat down, Kyle's dad put a plate in front of me that had an open bun topped with a giant dome of hamburger chili.

"Have you had sloppy joes?" he said. "They're Kyle's favorite."

I shook my head, no. But here's the thing, sloppy joes look exactly like steaming loose poop if you're not used to them. In fact, if you took the brown chunky chili and poured it over rice instead of bread, it would look a lot like fesenjoon. Pretty much identical, because most food is brown. But what was I gonna do, stand up and say, "May the shame that you heaped at my feet be returned unto your head thricefold!

And unto the heads of your family, and animals, for truly truly your own favorite food is poop-like!"

No.

You can't say that.

That would be the least Persian thing to do. To us, being polite is way more important than telling the truth. So I tarof, which is good manners, pick up the sloppy sandwich, and smile and go, "Mmm, that's good. Really tasty." Looks a little like fesenjoon too, which is a positive trait . . . fesenjoon.

The dish we had at my house with the chicken and walnuts and pomegranates. They look similar's all I'm saying. Of course they taste different.

Both wonderful and worth trying.

Anyway, that isn't even the poop story.

We had the sloppy joes and Kyle's dad started to make ice cream sundaes with store-bought fudge and by then my stomach situation was a broken washing machine tumbling a bunch of sleeping bags full of mud.

"May I be excused?" I said.

And Kyle's mom said, "Of course. Is everything okay?"

"Yes, very much so," I said. "I just want to wash my hands."

"Sloppy Dan!" said Kyle, which was a funny inside joke we all had over the dinner where we'd call everything sloppy.

So I got up.

Kyle's dad moved aside as I passed and I realized there was a sink right there at the kitchen island.

I said, "Uh, I'll get the other soap."

The bar soap.

So I scooted out of the kitchen, but not so fast that my legs separated too much, cause I was feeling super lumpy.

I heard his mom say, "The bathroom is to your right."

And it was. The door was right outside the kitchen. I shouted back, "Thanks!" but kept scooting, because no way was that bathroom far enough for them not to hear.

I pinched all the way up the stairs to Kyle's bathroom and closed the door and that's when I remembered the problem.

Remember when I described the differences between Oklahoma toilets and the ones in Iran and how obviously better they are because squatting is good for flow and washing is good for hygiene? The truth is that I never actually changed my poop strategy when I got here. The whole time I was in America, I never went number two anywhere but home.

At home, you can put bricks on either side of a toilet and squat over it.

Standing on a toilet seat is harder than it looks.

They jostle.

I was trying to balance myself when I heard a knock on the door.

"Daniel?"

Kyle's mom.

The last mom you would ever want knowing you don't know how to poop. "Are you alright in there?"

"Yep!" I said, hoping the volume would blow her away like a gust of wind. "I'm great," I said.

"We have a bathroom downstairs," she said.

"Okay," I said.

The noise of the toilet seat clacking on the bowl made it sound like I was trying to skateboard or something. I tried to explain myself. "Uh, I'm just washing my shirt. I got some sauce on it."

She said, "Okay, just shout if you need anything."

I tried to hold it until she walked away. If you ever try to squat on top of a toilet, you'll probably realize that aim becomes a major issue, along with balance and not breaking the hinges of the seat. Almost everything becomes an issue, because it's a super hard thing to do.

But I did it, finally.

I should say again that dry wiping is disgusting, so that wasn't an option. And I'm not an animal, so washing in the sink would be impossible. I tried to roll up a bunch of toilet paper and soak it under the faucet, but they dissolved into bits.

Time was running out.

My ice cream sundae was probably melted.

She probably thought I was washing all my clothes or something.

I had one option.

I took off my socks (pants were already off) and turned on the faucet in the bathtub. This is how I handle it at home, but always before a shower, so a bunch of soap and shampoo will go after it and keep everything clean.

The bath at Kyle's house was so loud it sounded like Niagara Falls. The water slammed into the tub. The pipes sounded like engines turning on.

I caught the water in my hands to check the temperature and also hopefully to make it quieter. It was still cold when, *knock-knock*!

I screamed, "Agh!"

"Daniel are you . . . are you taking a shower?"

Kyle's mom again.

"No! No! Um, I'm washing my feet."

"Did you get sloppy joe on your feet?"

"Haha!" I said. I don't think I was sounding normal at this point. "No."

"Did Brie wet the floor in there again?"

Brie was their little Pomeranian dog, who wet the floor sometimes.

"Yes!" I said. "Yes. Maybe. My sock is wet, so I just wanted to be sure."

As I said this, I wet my sock so I wasn't lying.

"Okay," she said. "I'll just put your sundae in the freezer till you're ready."

When the water warmed up, I got in and washed. Then I realized I didn't have a towel here and said a very bad word. I dried with toilet paper, which I flushed.

And then I cleaned their tub with the cleaner under the sink.

And then I put my pants back on.

I bunched my wet socks into my pocket, which immediately wetted my pants.

And finally, I left.

Brie was waiting outside.

I petted her head. She licked my hand.

It was clean, but it didn't feel clean. Even though dogs lick their butts. I leaned down and let her lick my nose. "Thanks, Brie," I said.

So anyway I'm good at sleepovers now, and can have a best friend.

You just have to tell them Brie wet the floor every time.

THAT WAS THE POOP STORY.

My mom was a sayyed from the bloodline of the Prophet (which you know about now). In Iran, if you convert from Islam to Christianity or Judaism, it's a capital crime.

That means if they find you guilty in religious court, they kill you. But if you convert to something else, like Buddhism or something, then it's not so bad. Probably because Judaism, Christianity, and Islam are sister religions, and you always have the worst fights with your sister.

And probably nothing happens if you're just a six-year-old. Except if you say, "I'm a Christian now," in your school, chances are the Committee will hear about it and raid your house, because if you're a Christian now, then so are your parents probably. And the Committee does stuff way worse than killing you.

When my sister walked out of her room and said she'd met Jesus, my mom knew all that.

And here is the part that gets hard to believe: Sima, my mom, read about him and became a Christian too. Not just a regular one, who keeps it in their pocket. She fell in love. She wanted everybody to have what she had, to be free, to realize that in other religions you have rules and codes and obligations to follow to earn good things, but all you had to do with Jesus was believe he was the one who died for you.

And she believed.

When I tell the story in Oklahoma, this is the part where the grown-ups always interrupt me. They say, "Okay, but *why* did she convert?"

Cause up to that point, I've told them about the house with the birds in the walls, all the villages my grandfather owned, all the gold, my mom's own medical practice—all the amazing things she had that we don't have anymore because she became a Christian.

All the money she gave up, so we're poor now.

But I don't have an answer for them.

How can you explain why you believe anything? So I just say what my mom says when people ask her. She looks them in the eye with the begging hope that they'll hear her and she says, "Because it's true."

Why else would she believe it?

It's true and it's more valuable than seven million dollars in gold coins, and thousands of acres of Persian countryside, and ten years of education to get a medical degree, and all your family, and a home, and the best cream puffs of Jolfa, and even maybe your life.

My mom wouldn't have made the trade otherwise.

If you believe it's true, that there is a God and He wants you to believe in Him and He sent His Son to die for you—then it has to take over your life. It has to be worth more than everything else, because heaven's waiting on the other side.

That or Sima is insane.

There's no middle. You can't say it's a quirky thing she thinks sometimes, cause she went all the way with it.

If it's not true, she made a giant mistake.

But she doesn't think so.

She had all that wealth, the love of all those people she helped in her clinic. They treated her like a queen. She was a sayyed.

And she's poor now.

People spit on her on buses. She's a refugee in places people hate refugees, with a husband who hits harder than a second-degree black belt because he's a third-degree black belt. And she'll tell you—it's worth it. Jesus is better.

It's true.

We can keep talking about it, keep grinding our teeth on why Sima converted, since it turned the fate of everybody in the story. It's why we're here hiding in Oklahoma.

We can wonder and question and disagree. You can be certain she's dead wrong.

But you can't make Sima agree with you.

It's true.

Christ has died. Christ is risen. Christ will come again.

This whole story hinges on it.

Sima—who was such a fierce Muslim that she marched for the Revolution, who studied the Quran the way very few people do—read the Bible and knew in her heart that it was true.

We accept it like a yo' mama joke.

If someone says, "Yo' mama's so dumb she sold her car for gas money," you don't say, "Yeah, but why? Was she properly aware of the long-term consequences?"

You just accept the premise that yo' mama is dumb and we move on from there. Maybe you lay down some facts about his mama.

My mama is not dumb, by the way. So when you're evaluating whether she's sincere in her belief or a lunatic, you should know she's got more degrees, speaks more languages, and has seen more of the world than most people you know.

And how do you know anything for certain anyway?

Maybe don't be so certain all the time.

HERE'S SOMETHING ELSE YOU need to understand: Sayyeds don't convert. That's why I told you all that stuff, so you'd understand how mad everybody got.

Being a sayyed meant you were rich. But the blessing wasn't just in your pocket. It was in your *blood.*

For Muhammad's kids to go against the family, for my mom to reject her own blood, another conversion has to happen—from sayyed to najis.

A "najis" thing is a "vile" thing.

It means "ritually impure," "unclean on a cellular and cosmic level." The halal food laws exist so Muslims avoid eating najis things. Young boys throw stones at dogs because they are najis and shouldn't be touched. Najis people can give you their uncleanness just by touch. Old ladies would rather die than have you so much as breathe your stench on their teacups.

To the Supreme Leader of Iran at that time, a najis sayyed would be a loathsome thing, a God-hater, a spoiled child, an insult to the Holy Prophet, someone whose badness it's not even said what to do with. The Supreme Leader would simply write a fatwa—a law—to have you killed and buried someplace far away and cold.

I TRIED TO EXPLAIN BEING najis to Kyle and he said, "Oh, like cooties."

"No," I said. "Almost nothing like cooties."

"Because there isn't a cootie shot for nuggles."

"And because they don't kill you if you have cooties."

"Okay, that's two things. But the rest is like cooties."

And he's right. Besides those two things.

SIMA WAS BAPTIZED JUST a few days after the wedding of Sanaz, her youngest sister, Ellie's youngest daughter.

Ellie is the exile, if you remember.

My dad wasn't paying much attention, because he was busy tearing open luggage, removing the drugs, and buying new luggage.

And my sister was getting her finger cut.

And I was eating cat food.

But if my dad had been paying attention, he would have been against the whole thing.

In Oklahoma, on the phone, he'll tell me, "We should never have gone."

"To the wedding?" I say.

"No. It would be horrible to miss the wedding. The church."

"The wedding was in the church."

"Akh! You know what I mean."

I don't, but I don't say anything.

He thinks it was religion that ruined everything.

"It was like waking up and your wife is a completely different person. Jesus this. Jesus that. And suddenly she takes my children and goes across the world."

These are the parts of the conversation that feel like a video game. He's jumping around the topic—religion bad, ruined his life—and throwing a billion fireballs—Why do governments tell people what they can believe? Why would she take his children?—and all the while, the giant lizard on the screen he's trying to avoid is my one question: Why didn't you come with us?

IF THERE'S ONE THING to know about my mom, it's that she doesn't stop.

And if you don't stop, you're unstoppable.

As soon as we got back to Iran, after the wedding, she joined a secret church with a missionary named Pastor Pike, who would one day—three years later—get his throat cut in the street like he was a mad bull.

It was the Committee who did it.

The Komiteh.

The secret police of the Supreme Leader of the new government.

In our city of Isfahan, they were the shadows on every wall. The invisible claw of the Supreme Leader. They could do anything. Their sudden raids on homes would make families disappear. They tortured people to get information about who was breaking Islamic law.

And anyone could be helping them.

If the old lady across the street saw a satellite dish on your roof, or a picture of the old king in your kitchen—you'd make eye contact with her on the way to your trash can, and you'd realize she had a hammer over your head. She could tell the Committee and you'd disappear.

People suspected their own cousins and dreaded their own children. In the middle of assignments, teachers would hold up a picture of a whiskey bottle and ask if anyone recognized it. An eager six-year-old might raise her hand, and come home to find a ransacked house and Daddy gone.

You couldn't tell the Committee members by sight.

You couldn't smell the blood on their shoes.

To be stared at too long at the market meant you were suspected.

And so, in turn, you suspected *them*.

The Committee was the Supreme Leader's best idea.

It curdled society in its own fear.

One day, they would catch my mom and kill Pastor Pike. But for now, they were lurking behind the curtains of every bathtub.

I WILL TELL YOU THREE stories of my mother, the unstoppable:

1. The time she fixed my bloody nose in the secret church
2. The time she got a bunch of threats
3. The time she got caught

It goes like this. We got back. The birds of my aviary had all waited for me and they listened to my stories about all the different candy they had in England. The jasmine plants were still the smell of the entire city of Isfahan to me, but that's only because I mostly played in our backyard.

Sima, the daughter of an exile, and the granddaughter of an exile, came home already knowing her fate.

At the time, I told you, it was illegal for Muslims to become Christian, and more illegal for Christians to preach to Muslims. So she went to Jolfa, the city within the city of Isfahan where the Armenians make cream puffs. They were excused to be Christian, because Shah Abbas said so in 1606.

That's where my mother met Pastor Pike. Pike was a missionary from the United States, so he had to hide in a room in our house. It was as if Sima brought home a stray cat and said, "Can we keep him?" and my dad said, "If the Committee finds out they'll kill all of us." And my mom said, "Then we'd go to heaven telling people about the truth and saving their souls." And he said, "Akh!"

And you can kinda see it from both their sides.

My mom had the enthusiasm of somebody who just played *Chrono Trigger* for the first time and has to tell everybody about it.

The members of the secret church would meet in abandoned buildings.

It was just a small group of them, maybe thirty people. Everybody was careful about how they spoke, even to each other, because anyone could be with the Committee. They would pray together about other things, but also that the secret police wouldn't kick the doors down at any moment and arrest all of them while they prayed.

My sister and I would play in the parking lots outside the little doors to the basements of the abandoned buildings. It was like the Bible studies in Oklahoma. There was nothing ever for us to do.

I was a climber and a jumper. She was a finder and an explainer. We hated waiting for grownies to talk about eternity. It seemed so obvious that everything was already eternal. That something made all of it. Something that loved and was beautiful and was cosmically and royally ticked off with what everyone was up to.

We never walked straight into one of the buildings where we met, because it would look suspicious. So my mom would take us to the local grocer at the corner to seem like we were walking around the neighborhood doing chores. The grocers had gunny sacks of dates and almonds next to stacks of fruit leather, not Orich bars or anything like that. We got little bags of puffed rice, hemp seeds, and roasted chickpeas. If you picked each rice puff by itself and sucked the salt from it and waited till it dissolved in your mouth, then the Bible study would be almost over by the time you finished the bag. I never ate the chickpeas, because they were as hard as cherry stones.

At this point, I should also tell you I picked my nose a lot back then.

Not with oily, salty fingers. I would lick them before.

My sister would say, "You are disgusting."

I would also lick them after.

Anyway.

One day, I was rolling a chickpea in between my fingers.

They were almost done. They'd all walk out—not together—at different times without looking at us so it didn't catch attention.

My sister had already tried to swap her chickpeas for my fruit leather, which was a scam. Now we were walking on a narrow garden wall. She said, "You can't tell anyone, you know."

"I know."

"If you tell anyone, they'll kill Mom."

"I know," I said again.

I picked at an itch in my nose with my thumb. That's when I noticed the chickpea fit right inside my nostril. It was snug and if I blew out, it made a pleasant pop sound and flew off. I stuck another one in and shot it at a yellow flower sprouting from the rock wall.

"You won't even get to see her. They'll just grab her and probably Baba too, and we'll go live with grandpa Arman." That was my mom's dad, the stern governor who would never have taken us.

"Why not Baba Haji?" My dad's dad, the poet farmer, the love of my other grandmother's life.

"Because," said my sister. "Just don't tell anybody."

That's when I knew she was lying. If anything happened, of course we'd go to Baba Haji and Maman Massey in Ardestan. She just wanted me to stay quiet.

I tried to shoot out another chickpea, but it didn't come out.

I breathed in by accident.

It went up.

"They could run in there with guns right now."

I put my pinky finger up there cause it's the smallest, but it didn't fit behind the chickpea. It just pushed it up farther.

I stopped walking.

"If we see a black van, we have to run inside and tell them."

The chickpea was so high up my nose, it was between my eyes. I scratched at it, but all it did was turn.

When my sister turned around, she screamed. For a second, I thought maybe there was a black van behind me. But she was looking at me. That's when I saw my booger finger was covered in blood. Not a little blood.

The way my mom describes it, the grown-ups were all huddled together in prayer when the door of the basement slammed open and little Khossie ran inside, weeping with a river of blood pouring from his nose.

Everyone startled like a flock of birds on a sidewalk.

They thought for sure the Committee men were right behind me with guns and vicious hearts and fists willing to hit a five-year-old.

Except my mom. She ran toward me and scooped me up. I was too old to be held, but that didn't stop her.

"What. What. What," she said. "What happened."

And I remember this part, because even though it was hurting now, and the blood was rushing out, I was so embarrassed to admit in front of everybody that I'd stuck a chickpea up my nose. She pinched the bridge of my nose and closed my other nostril and said, "Blow."

And then, "Blow," again.

On the third blow, a glob of blood and mucus and chickpea went flying out and hit the floor in front of Pastor Pike.

Everyone laughed the way you do in a scary movie, because they were still imagining the Committee men.

A couple people stopped coming after that.

But no matter how many times her husband lashed Sima with a belt, she believed. You can't make someone stop believing something. In fact, she hung a little cross necklace from the rearview mirror of her car, which was probably a reckless thing to do. But you know, in Oklahoma, after the hundredth time I rode bus 209 and got cut with something or Brandon

Goff ripped my hair out, I understood it. They can't break you. You stick your chin out, like, Go ahead, hit me if you're going to hit me.

My mom was like that. One day after work, she went to her car and there was a note stuck to the windshield. It said, "Madame Doktor. If we see this cross again, we'll kill you."

To my dad, this is the kind of story that proves his point. That Sima was picking a fight. That she could have lived quietly and saved everyone the heartaches that would come. If she had kept her head down. If she stopped telling people. If she pretended just a few holidays a year, that nothing had changed. She could still have everything.

Sima took the cross down that day.

Then she got a cross so big it blocked half the windshield, and she put it up. Why should anybody live with their head down? Besides, the only way to stop believing something is to deny it yourself. To hide it. To act as if it hasn't changed your life.

Another way to say it is that everybody is dying and going to die of something. And if you're not spending your life on the stuff you believe, then what are you even doing? What is the point of the whole thing?

It's a tough question, because most people haven't picked anything worthwhile.

A few weeks after that, Sima was in a market buying pomegranates, and tea, and saffron, when a black van pulled up onto the sidewalk.

The Committee men, who looked like regular men, got out and grabbed her up. Nobody in the market said anything. The van drove away and disappeared like a bad memory. The grocer probably put back the pomegranates and the tea and the saffron, so that someone else could buy them.

YOU PROBABLY DON'T KNOW THIS, but Oklahoma is called Tornado Alley, and also the Buckle of the Bible Belt, which means it's a great place to hide.

You are surrounded by as many Christians in Oklahoma as Muslims in Iran. Cars practically come with the crosses attached.

But also, Oklahoma gets more tornadoes than anywhere in the world. Except it isn't spread out over all 365 days of a year. They happen in the summer, almost every night, sometimes three or four at a time. Huge tunnels of wind that claw the earth. Like if God was scratching His belly, just above the belt buckle, each finger would be a tornado.

Sometimes they erase entire towns off the map. Suddenly your grandpa's house is as gone to you as mine is to me.

When you see a tornado rip swimming pools out of the ground, you realize something Oklahomans already know. People aren't very big. In fact, if you stand in the wide flat expanse of an Oklahoma field you can watch a rain cloud roll in from miles and miles away, pulling a curtain of rain across the prairie toward you and your little body will collide with less than a trillionth of it. The rain won't ever notice.

Men who make Committees and go around stealing mothers and hurting them, they're just red ants killing black ants in a giant universe that has tornadoes bigger than the biggest thing we have ever built.

And that's a nice thought.

It's nice to be unimportant.

THERE'S A SONG HERE that goes:

Oklahoma ditches run Oklahoma red
When Oklahoma rivers have been overfed
With Oklahoma rain, from Oklahoma skies
And I've still got Oklahoma dirt in my eyes.

I think it means we need more than rain to clean us.

NOBODY EVER EVER SPEAKS about what happened to my mom when the secret police took her.

I don't think they realize that I have seen more than seven rated-R van Damme movies and my imagination is probably worse than what happened. I mean. I don't know. Maybe it isn't.

Scheherazade never had this problem, because she made everything up and she didn't love anyone in her tales. To her, this would be the moment that a young woman—nameless, no kids—was caught up in the lair of a vile djinn. Or, if she's lucky, a demon who believes in God. But she isn't lucky and so we hear the clicking of the monster's teeth, and the clacking of his boots.

But this is my mom we're talking about.

I asked her once about it, while she was cooking, so I knew she couldn't go anywhere. She said, "Akh. Why do you want to know?"

Ray wasn't around, so she could be herself.

I said, "I just do."

Which got me nowhere, so I added, "It's for school."

She didn't believe me.

She kept chopping a mound of herbs the size of a basketball.

I went for plan C. "C'mon, c'mon. Please. Just tell me. I can handle it. Did they have bazookas?"

"What's a bazooka?"

"A rocket launcher."

"Khosrou," she said, clicking her tongue. "Of course not."

"Guns?"

"The ones in the van did, but they didn't want to be so obvious."

The word she used also means "rude," like Persians are so polite that even the secret police who go around killing people don't want to be so rude as to scare the kids in a market.

"So they had badges? How did you know they were the Committee?"

She finished with the herbs, scooped them in both hands and dropped them into the stock pot. All the leaves wilted and shrank until they all disappeared into the broth.

She was looking into the pot, but had gone back to that day in Isfahan—you could tell—and was remembering whatever answer there was.

"We just knew. They looked completely normal. Men in corduroy pants and knit caps like your uncle wore. I thought I recognized one of them. And in the van, the one in the front seat turned around and said, 'I'm sorry, Madame Doktor.'"

"You knew him?"

"He knew me. Maybe I treated his mother or something."

"Then what?"

She didn't say anything.

I used the same trick again, where I'd say something so ridiculous she had to correct me. "Did you go to prison?"

"No."

"The torture prison."

"Evin."

"Evin Prison. Did they take you?"

"No."

"Is that where Dad went?"

"Khosrou!"

She shushed me, like she was embarrassed even though there wasn't anybody around. And besides, he only went for a short time. At first, the government thought he was a big-time dealer since he'd bought more than any person could use for themselves in a year. But really, the giant stash was to throw a party for a whole town—which is so perfectly *him*. He was just being a good host.

"Then where?" I said. "Was there a different prison?"

"It wasn't a prison," she said.

"Then what?" I say.

Do you see how frustrating this is, by the way?

They were all like this. My mom, my dad, even Ray. They hid stories that explained what we were even doing in Oklahoma. Maybe just from me. I don't know. If you're the only person everyone else is keeping from a secret, then you don't know what you don't know.

"They had houses all over Isfahan," she said.

The houses were unmarked and sat in the rows of tense neighborhoods like uncracked knuckles. "They lived together?" I said.

"No. No. They lived with their families. Maybe just a few houses down. They used the houses to hold people, to interrogate them . . ."

"Is that what they did?"

It occurred to me at this point that I didn't want to hear this anymore.

"The one who knew me looked just like your uncle Reza. He had a red beard. He was still very young, very respectful."

"Why didn't you scream when they took you from the van to the house?"

"No one would do anything. They would pretend they didn't hear. Everyone was scared." She paused. "And who would they call anyway? This was the police."

So they took her into the house where evil happened—next door to all the sweet families. "What did it look like?"

"Akh. Khosrou. I'm working."

"I'll help."

"It's okay. The house was normal."

"Did it have a TV?"

"No. No. There was no furniture. He took me to an empty room with just one chair in it."

"Did you sit in it?"

"Eventually."

"They left you alone?"

"For a while."

"What did you do?"

"I cried. I prayed. I waited."

"So it was completely empty? Why didn't you jump out of a window?"

"There were no windows."

"It was just a box? What about the floor, could you pull up the floor boards?"

"It's not a Vam Bam movie. The floor was cement," she said.

"Damme."

"Don't say bad words, Khosrou."

"That his name. Van Damme."

"I don't like it. Taste this. It's roasted eggplant with lemon and garlic."

"Good," I say.

"When you say bad words, they think you're uneducated."

"Okay."

"I sat and waited."

"What were you thinking?" I said.

"I stared at the grate in the floor. The whole room was tilted like a bathtub to a metal drain in the middle."

I didn't ask her what it was for, because I knew.

But in case you don't know, it was for blood.

THE THING IS THAT Scheherazade was telling her stories to a king in the language they both spoke as babies. So she never had to explain the demons who believe in God, or what was rude. She just showed it in the story. But the shame of refugees is that we have to constantly explain ourselves. It makes the stories patchworks, not beautiful rugs.

Anyway in Iran when you go to someone's house, they put out a spread with tea and sweets on a rug, and you sit together and the host should offer you the best stuff.

The only offering in front of Sima was the drain and the threat of a little river of blood winding its way across the floor toward it. That was why the Committee men left her alone in there to look at it. It was like bringing someone a tray of tea and putting a gun on the table next to it.

I didn't say anything for a while, because she was melting a little butter in the microwave in a mug, adding saffron, and then pouring it over the steaming rice.

And because I was thinking this is the same person as the one in the story. It's no myth. And she's so small.

The legend of my mom is that she can't be stopped. Not when you hit her. Not when a whole country full of goons puts her in a cage. Not even if you make her poor and try to kill her slowly in the little-by-little poison of sadness.

And the legend is true.

I think because she's fixed her eyes on something beyond the rivers of blood, to a beautiful place on the other side.

How else would anybody do it?

The dinner was finished, and she hadn't told me everything that happened.

I said, "So how did you get out?"

She closed the oven and put the back of her wrist on her forehead and closed her eyes, like she was checking her own temperature. She said, "The one who knew me came in finally and said, 'You can go now.'"

"That's it?" I said.

"They had already asked me to tell them the names of everyone in the underground church."

"Did you?"

"No."

"So they let you go?"

"He said, 'Please, Madame Doktor, they'll kill you and your kids if you don't tell them.'"

"And then they let you go?"

She nodded.

"Did he say anything else?"

"That I had one week to think about it."

"And then you just walked out the door? Nobody saw you?"

"They saw me."

"You just walked home."

"I ran to the market."

"To get the car?"

"And groceries. We needed dinner."

KING OR QUEEN READER, this is a good place in the story to hold our breath—with Sima in the demons' clutches, running through Isfahan, toward a home she knows she can never live in again—and ask a question that relates to this: Would you rather a god who listens or a god who speaks?

Be careful with the answer.

It's as important as every word from Scheherazade's mouth that saved her life.

And everybody's got an answer.

A god who listens is like your best friend, who lets you tell him about all the people you don't like.

A god who speaks is like your best teacher, who tells Brandon Goff he has to leave the room if he's going to call people falafel monkeys.

A god who listens is your mom who lets you sit in a kitchen and tell her stories about castles in the mountains.

A god who speaks is your dad who calls on the phone with advice for your life in America.

There are gods all over the world who just want you to express yourself. Look inside and find whatever you think you are and that's all it takes to be good. And there are gods who are so alien to us, with minds so clear, the only thing to do would be to sit at their feet and wait for them to speak, to tell us what is good.

A god who listens is love.

A god who speaks is law.

At their worst, the people who want a god who listens are self-centered. They just want to live in the land of do-as-you-please. And the ones who want a god who speaks are cruel. They just want laws and justice to crush everything.

I don't have an answer for you. This is the kind of thing you live your whole life thinking about probably.

Love is empty without justice.

Justice is cruel without love.

And sometimes, like Sima, you get neither.

OH, AND IN CASE IT wasn't obvious, the answer is both.

God should be both.

If a god isn't, that is no God.

HERE'S WHAT I KNOW about our escape from Iran.

Sima had one week to "think about it," which meant she had one week to tell the Committee men the names of all the people in the underground church. All those people I scared when I ran in with the bloody nose—all dead if the Committee got to them.

She had one week or they would snatch her again.

And they would kill us—my sister and me.

She had one week to choose.

And it wasn't like she could go anywhere. The Committee was everywhere. In vans all over the city. Neighbors. The daughters of pistachio vendors. The sons of pharmacists.

I was in kindergarten, remember.

I only have a vague picture of a room, lying down on a carpet in rows with other kids like me for a nap time. And I remember once sitting at a table for school lunch, and hearing my teacher say, "Ooh!" like a happy bird and looking back and seeing my dad in a big coat. He bought kebab for the whole school. Maybe it was my birthday? I don't remember that part. But even the teachers got some—the best kebab in Isfahan, with buttered rice and roasted tomatoes. We all got to eat it. Nobody was too poor or anything like that.

My dad would pick me up from school in his gold Chevrolet. That day we got home and my mom was flying around the house like a bird in a panic. My dad thought she had finally gone crazy. She was shouting things we couldn't understand, stripping pictures out of a photo album and throwing them into a suitcase. When my dad grabbed her by the shoulders, she looked at him like a scared bull, like he was a Committee man. And he let go like she was on fire. He said, "Tell me."

And I don't remember more, because they spoke in the bedroom.

I went to my room and got Mr. Sheep Sheep. If we had to go anywhere, he would be my first choice, because I was his shepherd, and he was my number one friend. After that, I stuffed my pockets full of the Orich bars from the toy clown's pants on my desk (remember, there were more in the bus-shaped cushion, but I thought I would save those for when we came back). And then I remembered my Atari, which was my number one toy.

I am told that from here on out in the story, my grandpa Arman (the severe) was present, but like I told you, I don't remember him there. Maybe, like a djinn, he found little corners of the story to hide in. I don't know.

The story goes that we all got in the car and drove to the airport, even though we would probably be followed by the Committee men, and the moment we gave our passports to the soldier at the gate, a giant red alarm would go off, and everybody would be arrested.

"Don't you have to have papers and stuff?" I once asked when we were safe in Oklahoma. And my mom said, "We did."

"That same day?"

"No. A couple days later."

I imagined it all in one day. One big chase scene. But my mom says I went to sleep that night in my own bed, holding Mr. Sheep Sheep, until my grandpa Arman could come to help.

When my mom describes it all, she skips over the interrogation and the panic and says it was a time of three miracles—three things that couldn't have happened without the intervention of angels. This is the part that the pastors of Oklahoma churches love the best, and ask her to repeat as often as possible for their congregations. And when I told it to Mrs. Miller's class, I did the same as her, because this is her story. And if she says it was miracles, then it was miracles.

"That's crazy," said Jared.

"Jared," said Mrs. Miller.

"He's just making it all up," said Jared.

But why would I make up miracles about paperwork?

Why wouldn't I tell you it was like Faranak taking Fereydun into the Alborz Mountains?

That's a real proper legend that everybody knows. And they'd think I was cool, if I was like that.

If you're going to make it all up, you'd make it so you were the hero.

I'd be like, "Yo, this part of the story, I was the hero Fereydun. Put your hand down, Jared. I'm not taking questions right now."

And people would be like, "That's cool."

Because it *is* cool. Fereydun was a stud finigonz, who was so cool that the evil king dreamed he was walking toward him with a hammer to destroy him. So the king tried to kill Fereydun while he was just a kid. Fereydun's mom had to take him out of the country.

And for a while, she gave him to a rainbow-colored cow to give him super milk while she was away. Then he grew up into a man with shoulders so broad, and a brain so fast, that he could only ever be a king.

And in fact, in Persia, they would say King Fereydun shined with the light of greatness and wisdom, and people would have to cover their eyes when they saw him.

Which is where salutes come from.

And Jared—always Jared—he'd say, "Like military salutes?"

And I'd say, "Yes, the salute is a Persian symbol for shielding your eyes from the light of greatness when a boss comes in the room."

Then Kelly would say, "Your story is kinda like that. Since you had to escape with your mother from an angry king."

And I would nod and say, "Except for the rainbow-cow part, yes."

And the whole class would stand up and give me a salute. And I would salute them back. We would all salute, and then play together at recess.

That's how you know I'm telling the truth, because I *didn't* get the salutes for telling a good-sounding version. I just said what happened, which is that my mom says we saw three full-on miracles.

And even though everybody was willing to believe a rainbow-cow story, for some reason they won't believe miracles when they happen in offices and airports.

Anyway, the miracles were these:

1. The papers
2. The police
3. The plane

It was New Year's, which is a two-week holiday, and nobody could get the papers to leave the country. And even if they could, *we* couldn't because the secret police would have stopped it.

So even though my mom had panic-packed a suitcase, and screamed at my dad, who had insisted there was nothing wrong and it would all blow over, even though she said it *wouldn't* blow over unless she gave the names of the church, and he'd said, "So, maybe—" and she'd growled something, and he'd given up.

Even with all that, they still couldn't do anything, because they didn't have the papers. We were all dead.

The end.

Oklahoma never happened.

Except!

That afternoon, my dad got a call. A dental emergency. A miracle tooth!

I told you already, he was the best dentist in Isfahan.

Well it just so happened that a minister of immigration, a mullah, a boss man in the government, had taken an eager bite of a peach and broken his left front tooth on the stone. The sticky juice was still in his beard as my dad reached in to fix it.

It was like the story of the mouse pulling a thorn from the paw of the lion. Except my dad is the lion and the mullah is a toad. But we lived in the land of the toads and needed toad papers.

That's how we got them. If it had gone any other way, we'd be dead.

The mullah goes for a pomegranate, we're dead.

My dad is the second favorite dentist in the city, we're dead.

But everything went alright and we all piled into the car. I imagine my mom as she crossed the street with her suitcase, looking in both directions for an unmarked van parked somewhere. I didn't know we'd never see our birds again, or I would have said good-bye. I would have maybe gotten a sprig of jasmine from the yard and kept it in my pocket. I dunno. Maybe I'd have gotten one of my dad's shirts. Anything.

But I had Mr. Sheep Sheep and a pocket full of Orich bars.

In the car, my dad drove like a mouse, scurrying down side streets to avoid any people we knew. He said, "Is there any food?"

No one said anything, so I held out an Orich bar.

"My son," he said, which was like saying, "My great son, thank you."

My sister hit my elbow and said, "I want one."

So I gave her one. And another for my mom, because at this time, she was my favorite and she'd feel left out.

I ate the last one, and that was the last Orich bar I ever tasted.

IF YOU WANT A god who listens, maybe all you want is pity for losing your only friend, like Mr. Sheep Sheep.

If you want a god who speaks, maybe all you want is revenge.

I'LL GET TO THE other two miracles. For now, we're standing in a brush field beside a parking lot: my mom, my sister, my dad, and me. I'm standing a little farther out and staring. I'm staring nervously at the tall grass swaying above my head and holding Mr. Sheep Sheep.

There are no trees in the field. In the distance the airplanes come and go. There is no place to hide for a baby sheep.

The grownies are staring at me, then looking at each other in code. I'm standing a bit away from them. I take another step back, clutching my friend tighter. I'm wearing my corduroy pants and plaid shirt. That's what shepherds wear.

My dad is wringing sweat from his mustache. He clicks his tongue to hurry this ceremony along. My sister—who never loved sheep—sighs.

My mom doesn't want to force me.

She kneels down and looks in my eyes. Her eyes are big and black and very very sad.

"Baby joon," she says to me. "It's time to set him free."

I don't think any shepherd has done this kind of thing before.

But Mr. Sheep Sheep is a sheep. Am I the only one who can see he's a *sheep*?

You don't set sheep free. They're your friends.

It's unthinkable.

Little sheep, left in the wild, are carcasses. Every story tells us so.

Baby sheep, lost in the woods, must immediately search for their mothers—no distractions from strangers.

Sheep wandering around alone in parking lots, like this one, would die. They would lose their *lives*. Wolves walking down the mountains, into the dry thinning scalp of the middle of Iran, would be looking for juicy sheep. For the long journey across the drylands, Allah would provide, they would think.

And they'd pounce when they saw him.

They'd crunch all the buttons of his eyes for the nutrients.

They'd slurp all the stitching thread of his mouth and nose.

I don't want to do this.

My mom's eyes dart to every vehicle in the distance. "And we're not coming back for him?" I say.

"No," she says.

I remember looking at my dad and realizing this is news to him too. That we're never coming back. His eyes grow wide and begful. His mustache becomes a red unhappy cut across his mouth. This is the look of sadness that I imagine on his face when we speak on the phone.

My sister is reciting fairy tales and patriotic songs since the grown-ups haven't been paying her attention. Our dad picks her up and she stops.

"Let's go," she says.

But we can't go until we free Mr. Sheep Sheep.

If we went into the airport with him, they would take him at the security checkpoint and cut him open with a knife.

I didn't know this at the time, but they told me in Oklahoma.

They would cut his throat and look inside the stuffing for illegal drugs.

Which is a cruel and ridiculous thing to do.

If my family wanted to smuggle anything, we'd just make custom linings for a luggage set. If they cut Mr. Sheep Sheep, like the bull, there would be no river of blood except for the one pouring from a small exploded heart in my chest. If you can believe a little kid like me could just fall over dead, then believe it here.

So we can't go into the airport. And we can't stay outside, because the Committee men would be following us. Any second they might peek through the window of our house, see nobody home, and realize what happened.

We stand in the tall grass and I clutch my stuffed friend.

My dad eyes a van driving slowly across the lot and says, "We have to go."

The Committee men would have killed us in the field if they found us.

I look at my sister. She smiles at me the reassuring smile of an older sibling. Then she drags her thumb across her throat and points at Mr. Sheep Sheep, the same smile stitched on her face.

I wrench my eyes upward, without tilting my head—my strategy for holding back tears. My pupils roll back. My mom's shaking her head, saying absolutely not. "It will break his heart," my mom says.

I don't know what she's talking about, only that after being friends with him my whole life, I am supposed to leave Mr. Sheep Sheep to die.

My mom has the one suitcase. There are no toys in it.

Maybe we could hide him somehow?

I am crying at this point and have no idea why the world has to be like this.

And then I realize something. Something I hadn't noticed.

My dad doesn't have a bag with him.

He's leaving me at the airport.

I'm his Mr. Sheep Sheep and he's going to send me somewhere I don't even know, without him.

I put down Mr. Sheep Sheep. He props up on the dirt on a flat-panel bottom. His stubby round legs poke out in front of him. His arms reach out for a hug.

I look in his black button eyes.

They beg.

I turn my back and my mom sweeps me up in her arms.

My chin bounces on her shoulder as she begins to run. I wave good-bye to my friend.

He won't live past sundown, I think.

That was the third creature I ever killed.

THE OTHER TWO MIRACLES were later at the airport, but I don't remember them firsthand, so here's what my dad said when I asked him one Sunday from Oklahoma.

"Is that what she told you?"

"Yeah."

"They weren't miracles," he said.

"Tell me anyway."

"There's no such thing as miracles, Khosrou."

"Okay, whatever."

"Only science. Only poetry. Only the mind."

"So, at the airport . . ."

"And the mind can do anything. It can create anything. It is God, Khosrou. The mind is God."

"That's blasphemy, Dad."

"So what? So I'm blasphemous. What more can happen?"

"People could be listening." You can hear them sometimes, the American secret police, the CIA, tapping into our calls to listen. Sometimes we hear them cough.

"Let them listen," he says. "Let them hear how all this talk of God ruined my life and took my family."

He's crying now. I think it's probably midnight in Isfahan. He's sitting in the dark empty house. The birds in the walls are probably asleep. Or maybe he opened the windows and let them free a long time ago. I don't know.

I wait for him to finish.

Here in Oklahoma, the sun is up. We're not even looking at the same sky or anything cheesy like that. We're in different worlds. He's calling from the land of stories and genies. I'm in the land of concrete and weathermen. Or maybe I'm in the new world, free and full of adventure. And he is in the dying city, crumbling into dust like an elemental fiend. It doesn't matter. They're far apart.

"How did we get past security?" I ask. "Why didn't the Committee put big red flags on our passports?"

"Accident," he says.

"Accident," I say.

"Complete accident. We would have set off all the alarms. Big red lights the second he scanned the passports. Your mom was praying the whole time."

"What were you doing?"

"Slipping money in between the papers."

"How much."

"Enough to buy an Orich factory."

"So you just paid off the guard."

"No. That wouldn't be an accident. That's how the world works every day. We got to the front of the line. Your mother was mumbling. The guard had a mullah's beard."

"So?"

"So he was religious. Everybody was insane but me. He wouldn't take any amount of money."

"Did you take out the cash, so he wouldn't be insulted?"

"I tried. If he saw it, he'd be furious."

"And then what?"

"I nudged your mother forward so I could sneak it out. She was so scared. It was a terrible week for her. She just said, 'Please—'"

"Then what?" I said.

"Akh. Wait a minute. I'm telling you. She said, 'Please—' and then your grandfather, Arman, came running, holding your sister. He said, 'Sima. Sima! Your son is missing.'"

"Me?"

"You, you son of a dog. Arman told us he took you into the duty-free shop. The toys were over on the other side of the security gate, and so you must have wandered over there."

“I was probably looking for Mr. Sheep Sheep.”

“Yeah,” said my dad. He thought the story was cute, I should say. He liked to tell stories about how difficult I was, peeing in luggage stores and running off in airports, because that’s what dads who get to be with their sons every day do. They complain about it, instead of begging God to bring them back and pretending they were little angels.

“You were off being a little goat pellet. But your mother heard this and started sobbing. She almost fell, but we caught her. And the guard said, ‘Go, go find your son.’ And so he waved us through. If he hadn’t, we’d all be dead.”

“Did it take long to find me?”

“You? No. You were right in front of the candy shop. The woman gave you a chocolate and you followed her around like a piglet. We scooped you up and ran to the terminals.”

It’s weird. I even asked my mom if her dad had made it all up, but she said no. He would never embarrass himself like that. It was as if I disappeared for ten minutes.

“What was the third miracle,” I asked my dad.

“There weren’t any planes. We didn’t have any tickets.”

“Did you find tickets on the floor or something?”

“One flight going to Dubai had some kind of leak, so they landed in Iran first for repairs. Totally unscheduled.”

“How did we get in?”

“Money.”

“But it was totally random that the plane was there?”

“Yep.”

“Wow.”

"Yeah," he said, kinda dumbfounded about it.

"It's really nuts," I said.

"Your mom's had more miracles than I've had hot food."

Then we didn't say anything for a while.

I mean, you don't have to believe any of it and I wouldn't blame you. But if they were accidents, then it was like putting a jigsaw puzzle into a tumble dryer and having it come out with all the pieces in the right place.

YOU KNOW WHY I told you all those poop stories. Because food and poop are the truest things about you. I walked past the bathroom once when Kelly J. was walking out and the smell was so foul and sour it was like she could never hide her rotten insides, no matter how pretty she is.

Jared S. is rich, but his mom feeds him bread I wouldn't give to the ducks and meat they color pink with chemicals, like he isn't even welcome in his own house—so I feel bad for him. We all have our own pain.

You can't trick people when it comes to food or poop. If you give them bad food, they get sick. If they have blood in their toilets, something is wrong. They have a disease or somebody kicked them in the stomach a lot.

If you give them sugar, they get excited and then crash. Their bodies expose the lie. There are no myths or legends that can trick you by the time you've put something in your mouth and you're digesting it.

Even though people tell me I'm poor, my mom makes the best food in the world. And they tell me I smell, but I saw after gym class that they have "skid marks" on their underwear, which is poop that didn't wipe away with the dry paper. They soil themselves every day instead of washing.

Anyway, I also told you all that because I don't want you to think I'm some dingleberry weakstick whose mama is so gross that people don't even want to eat next to me.

And I have a food and poop story about Ray. First the food story.

One night really late—so late it was early—I was reading the part where Sam the hobbit sees Gandalf come back and it's like seeing his grandpa return from the land of death and memories. And his grandpa laughed, and it says it sounded like "water in a parched land." I could imagine exactly what the feeling must have been like, but not what it was. Does that make sense?

And Sam thinks maybe all the sad parts of the adventure will come untrue, now that this one has. And the beautiful part is that they do.

Outside my room, the rain and hail were smashing into our windows. In Oklahoma rain can sound like the gallop of horses come to your rescue, or the laughter of darkness. It was late summer, when tornadoes ride up and down the state every night like wraiths, and sometimes attack the towns looking for hobbits, who are really just kids.

I had a koloocheh—which is a bready cookie stuffed with cinnamon and walnut, which is exactly like the lembas bread that the Elves make, which means maybe J.R.R. Tolkien had Persian friends.

If you ever read the books, that really is the best part.

Ray opened the door without knocking.

"Daniel, get up," he said.

"Why are you wearing a trash bag?" I said.

"Your mom thinks it's safer. Why are you crying?"

"I'm not." I wiped my eyes anyway. "I was reading. My eyes are red."

"It's two in the morning."

I didn't tell him I was at the best part. Do you know how much I would have had to explain about hobbits and lembas bread and wizards who hold your cheeks in their hands and pour love into you?

A lot. And what would he care? The only dad he ever had tied him to a tree. He threw a black trash bag at me and said, "Come on. Put on your shoes."

I followed him through the dark house. My mom was waiting by the door. She helped me pull the trash bag over my head after I tore holes in it so I could wear it like a poncho. "Be careful," she said. Ray sucked his teeth, like she was babying me.

I put on my shoes. Outside, the hail sounded like clacking teeth. Before he opened the door, Ray turned around and handed me a box of three-inch nails.

"Don't drop these."

There's a sarcastic phrase in Farsi that goes, "Good thing you told me, cause I would have done it otherwise."

I didn't say it, but it would have been the moment to say it. Why would I choose to drop them?

Stepping outside during a tornado, or even a storm on the outskirts of a tornado, is a pig idiot thing to do that no real Oklahoman would do. Tornadoes are tunnels of wind half a mile wide that pick up cars and fling them three towns over. If you have a barn, and it's still standing in the morning, it'll have rocks and keys and bolts embedded in the wood like they were shot from cannon.

Every kid knows you run inside when a tornado comes, find the thickest pipe that goes the deepest underground—like the one in your bathtub—get in, put a blanket over you, and pray to a god that listens.

We know this because Oklahoma has more tornadoes than anywhere on Earth. If you're keeping up, that means they don't just have a god who listens or a god who speaks, but a god who puts his finger in the dirt and swirls it.

Anyway, if the tornadoes don't suck the air out of your lungs and toss you like a rag doll, and if the swarm of nails doesn't go through you like shotgun pellets, there's still the sheet lightning.

As I followed Ray outside, a giant web of lightning appeared in the sky like a crack in a glass, and lit up the neighborhood as bright as daytime for half a second. I didn't even have time to start counting before the thunder exploded over our heads.

Another bad move is to go climbing a tall metal ladder in the middle of a thunderstorm when lightning is looking for just two kinds of things to strike: tall things and metal things.

I don't know if Ray had to shout because of the hail, or because he didn't think I was listening. "Take this!" He shoved a hammer into my chest. "And hit the corners. Watch what I do."

I still didn't know what he was talking about. I had been in a hobbit glade like three minutes ago. So he probably thought I was scared. "Don't be weak," he said.

Then he ran out from under the front door, into the storm.

I followed.

Immediately, everything about me was soaked. The poncho was useless.

Ray ran to a ladder propped against the house and started climbing.

I stuffed the hammer in my sweatpants pocket and followed him up. The wind was waiting for me to clear the roof line. When I did, it smashed into me and almost sent me sailing backward.

Ray grabbed me by the poncho and shirt and chest skin, and pulled me down so I wasn't such a big target. It's hard to look around in rain and hail that punches at you sideways when you're on your hands and knees. It's not weak to squint your eyes.

The storm was ripping the roof tiles clean off the house. There was nothing to hold on to. I played a sumo game with the wind. The only light was lightning.

"Go!" said Ray. "If it gets under the shingles, it'll flood the house."

He grabbed some nails from the box I was holding and started pounding them into the corners of the tiles. I put the box beside me and took a nail. You have to do a bunch of things with your hands if you're trying to nail shingles down in the middle of a tornado:

1. Hold down the flapping corner of the shingle.
2. Hold the nail on the right part.
3. Hit the nail with the hammer.

That's already three and you only have two hands. And don't forget you have to hang on to the roof for dear life.

So I pounded the nail in (in four hits, which isn't great, but not bad), and went to get another nail. At the same time, Ray reached out for more nails. I told you already, I put the box beside me. In case you ever do something like this, don't put anything down beside you.

The box had slid off.

Ray said, "Good thing I told you not to drop them," in Farsi, which is when I remembered the phrase is for when you warn someone about something and they do it anyway. That was when I realized I had to write down the memories and myths and the legends—and even the phrases and jokes. Or I'd lose everything. Maybe even the recipes.

But first I had to climb back down the ladder.

My mom stuck her head out the window and said, "Be careful!"

I dug the nails out of the bushes and went back up. Ray had another box of nails anyway. He just wanted to keep it closed so he could return it to the store if we didn't use it.

I pounded nails into flappy shingles for another half hour and didn't talk to Ray.

I thought, My grandfather's house is six hundred years old and made of stone.

I cried.

Dear reader, you have to understand the point of all these stories. What they add up to. Scheherazade was trying to make the king human again. She made him love life by showing him all of it, the funny parts about poop, the dangerous parts with demons, even the boring parts about what makes marriages last.

Little by little, he began to feel the joy and sadness of others.

He became less immune, less numb, because of the stories.

And what about you?

You might feel what I felt on the roof that night. I was ashamed of being so weak, angry at Ray for everything he'd done, tired of being poor, and afraid of the thunder and lightning crashing all around me. I thought of my Baba Haji as I braced against the roof of the house.

I prayed to God I would see him again.

It won't be in this life, so it has to be wherever God puts us.

I prayed that even though I was Christian and he was whatever he was, I prayed that God would still let him hold me once we're both dead.

Reader, I think He heard me.

I think He's a God who listens as if we are his most important children, and I think He speaks to tell us so.

I looked up.

The hail felt like nails.

It didn't matter.

I opened my mouth.

Ray said something I don't know what.

I was busy eating the tornado.

THE NEXT DAY IN CLASS, Mrs. Miller didn't even ask us what we did during the storm, because Oklahoma people know that you shouldn't do anything. Instead she said, "Today I want you to write about the strongest smell you ever experienced."

But I already told the class about the wall of jasmine flowers in the garden of the house with the birds in the walls. So when it was my turn, I read aloud, "The strongest smell I ever smelled was last summer when I dug out a poop trench."

She sighed.

"What's a poop trench?" said Jared S.

"That is so gross," said Kelly J. "I can't—I can't be here."

I said, "Our toilet was broken so my stepdad made me dig trenches in the backyard to find where the pipes had split open."

"Sit down, Kelly," said Mrs. Miller.

"I have to go," said Kelly. "Can I be excused?"

"How much did he pay you?" said Jared.

"He didn't."

"I would've told him no," said Jared.

I doubt it, Jared.

One day, Ray told me to come outside and I thought he was going to yell at me for mowing too close to the house and cutting the tulips. But he gave me the shovel and said, "Dig."

"Why?"

"Don't ask why."

"How big?"

"Till I tell you."

I put the tip of the shovel into the grass and stomped on the lip. It only went in about a quarter of the way. Ray sucked his teeth. But digging is the kind of thing you can't do when people are watching. I kicked again and the shovel got half-way down. When I pulled it back, the grass made a tearing sound, and underneath was a clump of red Oklahoma dirt.

I was going too slow, so Ray grabbed another shovel and punched it into the dirt in front of mine. He stomped it in with one try. "Like this," he said, which was worse than not helping at all.

We both dug, with him going double fast to embarrass me into doing it better, till we had a hole big enough to fit a cocker spaniel.

Then he stopped and said, "That's not it. Start one over there."

Around the fifth hole, I got to the same level deep and when I stomped, the shovel slipped all the way in, and my foot sank a bit into mud. But it wasn't mud. And the smell rose up with it, of about five months' worth of flushes for our whole family.

I pulled my shoe out with a shlorpy sound.

How can I help you understand the smell?

What myth do we share that I can reference to make you feel the power?

Have you ever walked into an overloaded porta-potty? Have you ever felt your tongue retreat back into your mouth? Do you know why it does that?

Because all smell is particulate.

That means little bits of poop wafting in the air have gone into your nose and down your throat, and your body is telling you whatever you do, don't eat any more.

So you gag.

Your mouth opens and you get a real heave going, and swallow another wave of rancid smell, and that's when I bent over and puked right into the trench.

Ray goes, "Akh! Come on!"

And he jumped away.

About five feet under the trench, the pipe going to our house must have burst and turned all the surrounding dirt into sewage. Ray threw down his shovel and said, "Clear out around the pipe," and he left.

The trench he wanted me to dig had to be big enough to fit a refrigerator.

I threw up two more times and shoveled my puke out as I went. When I finished, it was almost sundown, and Ray reached down to lift me out of the hole. But I didn't take his hand, even though I had to put my own hand in the slop to hoist myself up. I wasn't mad. I just didn't want his help.

To know the truth about yourself, you have to know if you can eat tornadoes for food and shovel a mountain of poop. So when Kelly J. sees your lunch and says it smells gross, or Brandon Goff calls you a dirty monkey, then you can think, "You don't know anything about what food is and where poop goes."

That may not sound like a lot. But it's a true thing in a world without many true things. The only lie was that the poop trench wasn't the strongest smell I ever smelled. It wasn't even the worst smell.

A worse smell than all of that is opium.

OPIUM IS A SMELL I can't and won't describe.

Instead, imagine the smell of flowers but sweeter, and with broken glass in it. That's my next memory after Mr. Sheep Sheep, because I don't remember the airport or sneaking into the plane. When I say we snuck into a plane, you probably conjure up whatever plane you saw last.

Maybe you imagine a dude from the grounds crew with a mustache and those orange ear protectors counting a wad of cash at the bottom of the stairs. Then you see a little Persian woman with two scared kids stepping into the narrow cabin in the back.

Maybe the lady making announcements scowls at them, because she's no smuggler, or because there are no seats, and they'll have to stand in the back where they make coffee.

I don't even remember the moment my dad left us, or let us go—however you wanna say it. I don't have a picture for him kneeling down and looking me in the eye. Or a hug. I don't know, wouldn't you cry if you lost your family? I wasn't ugly then, and no one thought I smelled weird. I was his son. And maybe he was all torn up about it. It's the not-remembering that makes it one giant hole in the middle of a rug. Like somebody didn't even care to address it.

On one line you've got a dad who laughs and brings you candy bars and checks your teeth, and on the next line

____________.

Maybe it was all in a hurry, on the run from the Committee men, and he had to push us onto the plane without much ceremony.

I don't know.

I don't know.

That's the point.

When you ask, they never quite tell you. Like in the legend of Zal. When he says to his dad, "How can you contemplate leaving me? Of the world's flowers, my share is only thorns." His father gives the most Persian answer in the world. He says, "It's good to express your heart."

And then starts talking about his own troubles.

That's me. That's how it goes.

Anyway.

My next memory is the dark street in Dubai at midnight, where we didn't have a home, or know anybody, or speak the language.

Behind us was the airport.

We had the one German suitcase, my mom, my sister, and I. We didn't know where to go, because this wasn't a vacation. We hadn't even known we would be in this particular country until just before we got on the plane.

My mom said, "Don't be scared," which was the first time I thought, Maybe I should be scared.

The street, I remember, was completely deserted. Everyone from the plane had jumped into a car and driven off. We walked and continued to walk until we had left the lights of the airport behind. I feel like I should tell you that it was a very clean street, like a street in a video game, brand-new. No cracks in the sidewalk. No litter anywhere. If you ever see someplace like that, it's very noticeable, because everybody is used to a bit of dirt or candy wrappers or something.

But this street was dark, and quiet, and brand-new.

I think my mom was hoping there would be a hotel.

I remember saying, "Where are we going?"

And my mom saying, "I don't know."

And that was the second time I thought, I should be scared.

We didn't have anyplace to sleep. We were homeless I guess.

But then—and this is a miraculous part—we're walking down the cartoon street when a light approaches behind us. We turn around and see the biggest stretch limousine you can imagine. So big I don't even know how it turned onto the street.

"Stay close," said my mom.

The limo drove up beside us.

The door opened and a giant with one cycloptic eyebrow stepped out. He was so big his mama must have worn hula-hoops for bracelets. Under one arm, he had a rifle. I'm not a little kid anymore, so I know it was an AK-47. Oh, and he had sunglasses at night.

He got out and stood by the open door of the limo. We stood frozen in front of him, because of obvious reasons. There was still nobody in the dark street. Like it was all a dream where you forget to fill out the background. Or in *Final Fantasy* where the whole world recedes and it's just you and the bad guy in a space like an empty page.

We didn't know if he was a bad guy.

"Get in," he said.

We got in.

I REALIZE, BECAUSE JARED S. said so, that I never "explained Dubai," which is like saying, "explain Canada," but whatever I'll try.

Of course, then everybody says my reports are boring, or they don't say it, they just sigh like a Jennifer. Even though it's kinda like if you went to Iran and tried to explain Oklahoma football and the people said, "Wait, what's Oklahoma," and you said, "A state," and the other people said, "What's a state?" and you never even got to the football part.

But I'll be quick.

Dubai is a city in the United Arab Emirates.

That's a country on the Persian Gulf.

It's actually made of seven emirates, which are like states, but more like principalities, because they're owned by seven princes called emirs. That's why they're called emirates.

All seven emirates are only as big as half of Oklahoma, but the UAE is one of the richest countries in the world.

They have a mall that sells nothing but gold—every store, floor to ceiling, gold. It's so hot there that swimming pools boil, so one emir built himself an indoor ski resort. It's a giant building with a ski slope covered in snow, and giant fans on full blast to keep the air cold.

They have castles like in the movie *Aladdin*. The streets are so clean because the fine for littering is a ton of money and a flogging. The whole country is a prince's private property.

I mention that because when we got into the limo, the giant with the gun closed the door and went to sit in the front, and we found ourselves sitting across from a man with a thin black beard, smoking a hookah pipe with long fingers laced with gold rings. He seemed far away and mild, the way you might imagine a king would be if he had nothing to worry about.

My mom spoke to him in a bunch of languages till they found one they both liked. On the tray next to his pipe was a plate of pistachio cookies. My sister whispered to me, "He's the prince."

I thought those must be good cookies, then.

I reached for one, but my mom said, "Khosrou," and I sat back.

The prince laughed.

You might be wondering why he found us in the street and invited us into his limo. Well, remember those friends of my dad's I mentioned? The ones he visited in London? Legend has it that my dad knew these people, and nobody knew that he knew these people. He called a great prince of Dubai with his mythic charm and told him our situation. So here the prince came, like the eagles in *The Hobbit*, swooping in at the darkest hour to save us.

That's what I thought, anyway, as we rode in the sweet-smelling car, through the garden estate of the emir, past marble beds full of black tulips, to his castle by the sea. I hadn't seen *Aladdin* yet, but when I got to Oklahoma years later, it was the reference I had to explain this part to people. The palace towers weren't so round as the ones in the movie, and the real castle had helicopters. But it was all close enough.

We stepped out of the limo in the moonlit courtyard. The dry heat felt like a school bus passing by your face. The giant led us into a door along the side. The prince went somewhere else. At this time, I remember thinking, "Are we rich now?"

I was just a kid, remember. We entered the kind of room they only have in museums—vaulted ceilings, paintings on the walls. But even I knew the most valuable thing there—maybe the most valuable thing I've ever even heard of—was the one massive Persian rug, the size of half a football field, laid out along the floor. It was so big I couldn't even imagine the loom that must have made it.

I imagined the carpet hanging, like the sail of a ship, from two wooden masts, and my grandma slowly making each knot. It would take as long as she was alive, I thought. I realized at that moment I would never see her again. For me she would forever be a mythic weaver in the basement of an ancient house in Ardestan.

She's there now. I'm here in Oklahoma where rugs don't matter to anybody. That's the end of it. There are no magic rugs to fly me to her. There are only shag carpets for rich Oklahomans, and million-dollar rugs for princes. And the refugees are lucky if they get quilted toilet paper. Believe me, even when I thought we were going to live in the marble palace, I would have given it up to sit on that basement dirt floor again.

But anyway, it was a grand ballroom. About twenty women in black burkas swept back and forth, placing trays of food, enough to cover the rug and feed a thousand people. They didn't say anything to us, or to each other. The trays were piled high with saffron rice with grilled tomatoes, ground beef kebabs, filet kebabs, chicken and lamb, yogurt with cucumber and dill, fresh spring onions, purple basil, radishes, pickled vegetables, and a whole grilled fish with garlic.

Imagine half a football field of food.

And there was more coming.

Until the prince entered the room and the women in the burkas shuffled out in silence. They kept their heads down and wouldn't look at us.

"Aren't they going to eat?" I said.

"Shh," said my sister.

"Sit, please," said the prince.

We sat at the far corner of the carpet and put some food on our plates from the trays closest to us. The prince sat on the opposite end.

My mom and the prince spoke some more, but we didn't hear it.

I asked, "What are they saying?"

"Don't spill anything," said my sister.

"What happens to the food," I said.

"His wives eat it after, in a different room."

If you want to know the truth, that was all the information I got before the prince stood up, put his hand on his heart as a kind gesture to us, bowed a little to my mom, and excused himself.

We were alone with all the food and the rug in the palace.

"What happened?" I said.

"Nothing," said my mom, trying to smile. "Eat."

I didn't know at the time what had happened. But it was clear that we were no longer welcome in the palace.

I stuffed more kebab into my mouth, some yogurt mixed with rice, and a pickled cauliflower, and used the basil to shove it all in with my fingers.

"Are we staying here?" said my sister.

"No."

Then we left.

An hour later we were back on the street, homeless again.

HERE IN OKLAHOMA, WHERE RAY is the star of nightmares and the international Bible study, there is a Persian man who owns a rug store in the rich part of Tulsa. His name is Abbas. He has to call them Turkish rugs, because it's illegal in America to do business with Iran. But really the rugs are from Iran, and they just ship them from Turkey, because Mr. Abbas is a man who takes pride in his work.

Only Oklahoma oil families can afford the rugs. And even then, Mr. Abbas has to explain that every village in Iran has its own colors and patterns they're famous for. Mr. Abbas always shows the red field designs from Kashan, which look like a field of wild flowers. He points out the diamond-shape medallion in the center, since they're named after Shah Abbas, which is also his name.

Rugs from Qom always use a bit of turquoise, and the ones from Naein are ivory with light blue branches. So if you get one of those, they're extra valuable. Some rugs from Isfahan even have silk and gold thread in the paisley designs.

Here's another fact about rugs, and then I'll get back to the story. They are graded by how many knots they have crammed in every square centimeter. So if it only has sixty knots in one centimeter of carpet, then you'd see that rug on the floor of a tea house in the bazaar, and you'd be welcome to step on it. But some rugs have 400 knots in one centimeter, and if you owned one as small as a pillowcase, you'd still be rich.

But no matter which grade or pattern—no matter even if the greatest grandmother in the whole world wove it—every rug has a Persian flaw.

The artisans of Kashan and Isfahan and Tabriz and Mashad all knew that only God was perfect—the only one who could listen to and speak the perfect truth. To remind themselves, and to show their humility, they would purposefully include one missed knot in every rug, one imperfection.

I think it's pretty funny that people would mistake themselves for perfect if they didn't include a hole in a rug.

But that's the whole point of the Persian flaw—it's there to remind you of all the other flaws, and even the flaw that makes you unable to see them in the first place.

It's like the game Oklahoma kids play called "two truths and a lie," which was made to remind them that this world is full of deceit and misunderstanding.

The Persian flaw in Mr. Abbas was that he underestimated my sister. And the one in us was ambition.

It went like this: One day in the summer, we went up to Mr. Abbas after Bible study to show him our mug rugs.

"What are mug rugs?" he said.

They're coasters for mugs, but we made them like little rugs. Not even the real Persian way on a loom. My sister walked us to the craft store and we bought square plastic grids and wrapped yarn around them. On the edges we made yarn tassels. The designs were basic colors like Easter eggs that no one in Tabriz would know. But Mr. Abbas said, "They're so cute."

Our mom was over by the refreshments table, retrieving her dishes, and Ray was standing nearby to make sure we didn't insult Mr. Abbas.

"Let's go," said Ray, but my sister ignored him.

"You could sell them in your stores," she said.

Mr. Abbas laughed. There were other grownies around, so he might have felt obligated to be kingly, to pat us on the head. He was short and waddled like most kings. He said, "That's true. We could be real business partners. How much do you think we could charge?"

The other grownies giggled, probably because he was jokingly taking her seriously. But when my sister landed in Oklahoma, and the first grownie bent down and said, "What do you want to be when you grow up, young lady?" she said, "What's the number one college in America?" and Pastor Hamond said, "Harvard, I suppose," and she said, "There. I want to go there."

So when Mr. Abbas asked about the prices, she said, "Ten dollars each."

"Ten dollars," said Mr. Abbas.

"They're handmade Persian rugs," she said.

"Are they?" he said.

"Okay, Persian-made hand-woven rugs. We could sell to you for five each, and you'd make one hundred percent profit."

At this point, Mr. Abbas must have realized that he was completely entrapped. Five dollars is not too much for a king. He said, "I could probably give them to my customers as promotional cards."

And that's how Mr. Abbas agreed to pay my sister five dollars for every mug rug she gave him at the next Bible study, which was after the summer.

The next morning was a Saturday, and it was our first summer in Oklahoma, so we didn't know that kids went to camps, and soccer leagues, and vacations, and stuff. Everybody just disappeared and we were left.

My sister had a system where we each picked what to watch on TV every thirty minutes, but she timed it so I got all the slots where we agreed on shows, and she got the ones where we didn't.

So we were watching a show about high school kids on a volleyball team, instead of a cartoon about a duck detective. But then she turned it to a court show about people who steal air conditioners from their grandparents.

I made a grunty noise, cause I had cereal in my mouth.

"What? This is what I wanna watch," she said. Her smile was a warning.

"Change it back," I said.

"No. I want to see what the judge says."

The judge screamed at them and gave them a fine. Up next, a girlfriend who stole radios.

"You know," said my sister, "I'd give you all my time slots if you helped make mug rugs."

"All summer?"

"Only while you're making mug rugs."

"Do I get paid?"

"I'll give you fifty cents a rug."

"You make five bucks."

"Four-fifty," she said, "after your cut, and I only make about the same after all the costs," which I found out later was completely untrue. But I didn't know then. I still believed the things she told me. So I agreed, and she put me to work.

Every day, we would wake up and our mom would already be gone. Cereal has to be eaten in a specific way, so we did that first. Then we each took a plastic grid and started weaving. She was afraid Mr. Abbas would go back on the deal, so she said, "Make them all perfect." But I would hide a Persian flaw in each one, which was hard because mug rugs aren't very big and have about seven knots per inch. I would move them around, because if you put a little hole in the same spot of every rug, then it's not a flaw anymore, it's the design.

Sometimes, I would go outside, but I didn't have a bike and the closest park to our apartment was past a creek where a couple of kids had died once. Kyle had gone to his mom's house in California, so I didn't really have anything to do outside.

I am now an expert weaver of mug rugs.

My sister and I never talked much, because I only picked riveting shows about duck detectives and mouse detectives so we were riveted. But once, during the afternoon shows about grownies kissing, I said, "Remember that huge rug in the castle of the Prince of Dubai?"

And she said, "He wasn't the Prince of Dubai."

"Yes he was."

"No, you're dumb."

"You told me he was the Prince. *You're* dumb."

"I said he was *a* prince."

She was right. Or, I didn't remember if she was, but it was how every conversation ended. I didn't say anything, because there's no reason to talk to people who are just waiting to pounce on your flaws and put their fingers in the holes.

She said, "Oh come on. I remember the rug. What about it?"

Nothing about the rug. I was just counting the memories. Sometimes you just want somebody to look at a thing with you and say, "Yes. That is a thing you're looking at. You haven't lied to yourself."

But anyway, I just wove another mug rug until she said, "He wanted to marry me, you know."

"Who?"

"The rich guy in Dubai."

"No."

"He did. That's what they were talking about."

"How do you know?"

"I heard Mom tell Ray. The prince said we could stay at his palace and we'd be safe. But it would be weird if we weren't family, so he'd marry me."

This was just about the grossest thing you could possibly imagine—to think of your sister as a finigonzon. I didn't want to know any more. I always wondered about that moment, though, about the dinner in the palace and then a year of being homeless again, living in the back of a free clinic for poor people, which was a nice place with a nice family. But I'll get to that.

In all our lives, my sister only told me her stories twice. We never compared our memories, ever. I think because where they were the same, they were painful and obvious. And where they were different—even just a little—they were so important to each of us, that we hated each other for not remembering them as we did. For years, we couldn't forgive each other for misremembering even the color of our grandmother's scarf.

I said, "So why did he let us go?"

"Because we refused, duh. He had thirty wives already. Didn't you know those women were his wives?"

"I knew that," I said.

"And I was eight," she said. "That's disgusting."

"I know," I said. "I meant how did we leave without insulting him."

"Oh. Mom said we were Christians."

"He was okay with that?"

"He wouldn't want one anyway."

"He seemed nice," I said.

"He was on opium," she said.

In my head we were back on the street, wandering. We found an outdoor bazaar with lights on and walked around. If you want to know the truth, the only other part I remember is that I couldn't hold it anymore and went in my pants. It was all the kebab from the palace. I had begun holding it days at a time, and couldn't, with all the walking that night. When my sister smelled it, she said, "Mom! He pooped himself."

I said, "Shh," cause people would look.

I remember my mom asking people for a bathroom for what must have been an hour. And finally getting into a water closet that smelled. And my mom trying to open our suitcase on her knee, and stuff falling out. And my sister complaining, because we didn't know anybody and it wouldn't be safe for her to wait outside. And when we peeled off my clothes, it had gotten onto the pants and everywhere. My mom finally exploded and cried when she realized we didn't even have a plastic bag and couldn't afford to throw away the pants. She cried and said, "I can't. I can't." And she hit her forehead on the bathroom mirror as she washed the soiled pants in the sink without soap, because there wasn't any.

I stood in the corner with my bare feet on top of my shoes and no pants and wondered if the glass would break. We were both scared that she'd never stop crying. But when she did, she gave me my sweatpants from the suitcase, and we just carried the wet pants for the rest of the night.

It's actually kind of funny that years later, I would have to dig poop trenches in Oklahoma. Like I had been practicing for wallowing in it my whole life. Maybe we get the endings we deserve. Or maybe the endings we practice.

At the end of the summer, my sister presented two hundred mug rugs to Mr. Abbas with a bill she wrote up for one thousand dollars. And that was when he saw the flaw in his plan, which was that we'd forget or let go of a chance to be less poor. But Mr. Abbas wasn't a refugee. And he was in front of everyone, so he wrote her a check, which she deposited into her college fund. She never mentioned it, and I never asked for my money, which if you do the math is a lot.

But that's okay. That summer was the most time we ever spent together voluntarily. She taught me how to play rummy, which is a card game Americans play at summer camps. And we watched mostly cartoons. And besides, nobody should have to sit there with grown-ups deciding whether to sell her into slave marriage.

That's what I did all summer.

Plus we tasted root-beer floats.

THE TRUTH IS, IN THE real world there's no such thing as a Persian flaw, because that assumes you could have a thing that has only one thing wrong with it.

One disaster always begets another, and another. Your dad disappears in Azerbaijan, and your uncles sell you off, and your daughter gets set up with a mean man, and their daughter gets a warrant on her head, and a million other tragedies play out on every side. The story goes on, and you can't pretend that dropping one knot in a rug is the only mistake keeping it from perfection. The truth is that everything has a hundred thousand flaws.

But it's pretty to think that we can make perfect things and scratch them a little to keep from being gods. It's comforting, the way in myths the heroes are all one personality flaw from perfection. If only Rostam was more humble. If only Zal's dad listened.

The closer you get to history, it's like the closer you get to the weave of a rug. You see a thousand thousand complications. Like this part of the story, which I remember too well. There is no counting the memories anymore.

Before, when you were in the parlor of my mind, I only had one or two things to offer. My Baba Haji's craggy smile, my uncle on the motorcycle. It was like I only had one kind of treat in the pantry, and I offered it up.

But now, in Dubai and after that, we sit together and my pantry is full of memories about every boring detail. It's like an Oklahoma grocery store. There is a whole aisle for snack cakes, and I could offer all of them. But maybe back when I only had one snack, maybe that was cream puffs from Akh Tamar, and maybe now all I've got is a dozen flavors of junk cookie.

Will it be alright, reader, if I choose just the good ones? By the way, Mrs. Miller says I'm not allowed to write about poop for class assignments anymore.

Which is fine, because I only have three or four more of those. But it's also a little silly, because in the *Nights*, Scheherazade tells about all kinds of grownie stuff that would make the demons blush.

I know Mrs. Miller would say, "These are not the *Arabian Nights*, Mr. Nayeri; they're writing assignments."

And I would say to that, "O wise and merciful Mrs. Miller, every story is nestled somewhere within another story."

And she'd say, "Please stick to the prompts or I will have to give you an incomplete grade."

Ah. See? Another Persian flaw.

I'd have a hundred in her class otherwise.

THE TWO MEMORIES OF our time in Dubai that I have chosen are titled, "Blood or Ketchup?"

Because one has a bunch of ketchup, and the other has a bunch of blood. But both have some of both.

The first is after we spent a few months in Dubai. I mentioned already that we found an Australian doctor couple who were missionaries. They started a clinic for people who couldn't afford clinics and they lived in a small house in the back. When they met my mom, they said we could share it with them. So we all crammed into the little house. They were kind people with specific features, like a man with a blond beard, or a woman with a band of freckles across her nose and different-colored eyes. But they were Christians so I won't describe them to you, or I could get them killed.

We didn't have toys in Dubai, so we made kites out of sticks and butcher paper. There was not a lot of wind where we lived with buildings in the way. So they never flew. One day, my mom was working in the clinic and Jim, the Australian doctor, said, "Your father's coming to visit."

"Mine?" I said.

"You weren't supposed to know," said my sister to me.

"Sorry," said Jim.

"Why wasn't I supposed to know?" I said.

"Cause everyone thinks you're traumatized, and if it doesn't happen then you'll freak out."

But I wasn't traumatized. I just hated Western toilets and never used them till I had accidents. And I would sleep under my bed because I thought the Committee men would find us any minute. I'd cry that they would kill our mom and we'd be orphans. I know that sounds like I was a coward, but—I don't know, maybe I was a coward.

It was in those days that my mom noticed that nobody could say my name, Khosrou. The Australians, the Americans at the embassy where she would sit all day to beg them to let us into their country, nobody.

I was watching a Japanese cartoon about a kid who drives a robot when she decided to solve the problem. She said, "Daniel, it's time to eat."

I look back now and I think this was not the best way to solve the problem. "Daniel," she said, "Come eat, Daniel."

I had never heard the name Daniel before, and there was no one in the room but us. I thought, Maybe she was on the phone. I kept watching. The kid's robot was turning into a gold superbot.

"Daniel," she said.

I finally looked up. She was looking straight at me. "Come eat, Daniel."

It was like my mom had forgotten my name. Or they had had some meeting about me and decided Khosrou was too traumatized to save, so they threw him away, and started over with Daniel.

I stared at her, hoping she'd recognize me.

"He doesn't get it," said my sister. "Your name is Daniel now."

My eyes didn't even go up to the ceiling that time. I just burst into tears and scrambled under the bed the three of us shared.

"Can we eat now?" said my sister.

My mom had to get down and explain everything, that she always liked Daniel cause he was in the Bible, and that people couldn't say Khosrou. At that moment I remember thinking, Maybe names don't even matter and this is something like stuffed animals that you just leave in a field and never think about again.

That was the day I decided Daniel would be ten times tougher than Khosrou—like the superbot version or something—so tough he could take any kind of damage and be unstoppable.

HERE'S A NEW KIND of damage: My dad came to Dubai just a few days later and they told us they were getting a divorce and my dad was already married again.

This would be the last time I saw my dad for a long time, so I wanted to remember everything. But for instance I don't even remember the address of his hotel. I do remember that morning, I lost my tooth. I was eating a piece of flatbread—nothing too hard or chewy. But my tooth just bent back, the one on the bottom row in front, with a sharp stab at the gum. I reached in and pulled it out. There was blood on my hand. I wasn't supposed to be eating, because we were going to eat with my dad, so I ran out of the kitchen and found my mom in the bathroom.

"My tooth fell out," I said.

She gave me some tissue to bite on so the bleeding would stop. "You can show your dad," she said. "He'll be happy."

My dad is a dentist, remember, and had more opinions about my teeth than anything else. I put it in my pocket to show him.

We took a bus to the ocean where all the skyrise hotels stuck out of the sand like a row of white teeth. In his room, we ordered breakfast. I don't remember what he smelled like, but probably cologne to cover the smoking smell. I think my mom was already mad.

When parents fight they sometimes pretend the kids don't understand or they speak in super obvious code and expect the kids to pretend with them.

"So this is it, then."

"Doesn't have to be."

"Yes it does, you married her."

And I'd say, "Can we get eggs?" even though I don't want eggs, just to push back the obviousness of the situation, to make it more normal-sounding.

"No," said my mom, and then back at my dad, "We don't have birth certificates."

"I'll find them."

It was like that. My sister and I didn't look at each other. Half of it was boring, the other half horrible.

We sat in the hotel room, at the foot of the bed, around a tray of flatbread, cheese, honey, cucumbers, and tea. There was another tray with salt, pepper, and ketchup in case we had ordered the Western breakfast.

They fought through all of it.

For every bite.

If you're a kid reading this, there isn't anything you can do about it, but grownies can at least remember—when you fight in front of kids, what you're really doing.

To us, parents are like blankets. Or parachutes, in a world that is otherwise full of snakes, and leopards, and Committee men, tornadoes, bullies, and death. And as a kid, you're looking out and seeing all this with a near constant spike of adrenaline—always a second from panic—because you understand you can't do much. You're a little ball of soft meat with no shell or escape skills or battle strategies. You're a milk drinker with milk teeth that fall out and you bleed.

The only protection is those two distracted grown-ups, fighting and scratching at each other. It's like looking up and seeing the material of your parachute fray and flutter. And you think, "I'm going to die. They're going to split apart and I will free-fall into brambles where the demons hide, into their waiting claws. The whole world will tear me open."

My mom was shouting something about divorce, when she finally looked over and saw me pouring ketchup on my flatbread and taking a bite.

"Khosrou! What are you doing?"

I was trying not to cry. And I wanted them to stop. So I put ketchup on flatbread and ate it until they noticed. It only took three pieces, which isn't great, but who cares? Ketchup's fine on anything.

My dad tried to laugh it off. "Silly boy."

"Why are you eating that?" said my mom.

"Gross," said my sister. (It isn't. There are a million grosser things. It's just weird.)

I shrugged at all of them. I didn't have a lot of words back then, except for the ones in the language I had made up, that no one else knew. But now that I'm bigger, I would have just told them that it wasn't the time to fight.

Instead I said, "My tooth hurts."

It was such a weird thing to do that breakfast ended. We knew after that that my mom and dad would file for a divorce. That my dad had a new wife, and that he would stay in Iran with her, that our house with the birds in the walls was hers now, along with my secret stash of Orich bars.

We were truly homeless now in the world. The conversion from royal and pure (sayyed) to unclean and outcast (najis) was complete. And the insult was so great that the Committee would stay after us. If they found us anywhere in the world, we would be killed.

Our only hope was asylum in places like England or America, which meant we were refugees, begging for them to protect us.

We needed papers we didn't have.

So my dad would go back, start his new life, and mail the papers secretly to the clinic. Could he send my toys? I asked. No.

What about Orich bars? Also no.

WHEN BREAKFAST WAS OVER, I thought, Maybe if he liked us enough, we could get him to stay. I was his champion son, you will remember. His new wife had not had any children yet (I asked), so there was no reason he would pick her over us. Maybe he had forgotten that we were very fun to be friends with, and that we would bring him lots of honor by winning straight As in school, along with prizes.

We weren't in school at that time, so I decided to show him other champion-like skills. (This is the second story that has more blood than ketchup in it.)

My dad's hotel in Dubai had a pool surrounded by date trees, under a sun so bright hot and white that it bleached everything. It was in view of the ocean. The pool was fed by waterfalls from other smaller pools. There were islands in the middle of the water, little floating restaurants where grown-ups could order Turkish coffee while their legs were still in the pool. They had a water slide and lily pads in a kids' pool, but I didn't go there, because it was out of sight of where my dad was sitting and I had a plan.

My plan was to show him my greatness and fill him with the desire to be our dad until at least I turned eight. He sat under a giant umbrella. Already, he had a favorite waiter who knew if he paid my dad extra attention, if the drinks were always on the way, discreet and cold, the ashtray always clean, then the tip would be prosperous.

He sat and nodded off in the sun, reading the poetry of Hafez, and sighing. My mom was on the phone somewhere, starting the maze of paperwork and office appointments to get us to safety.

My sister had found some other kids, on vacation from Turkey, a girl and a boy. My sister and the girl wanted to be left alone, but also wanted me and the boy to want to play with them, so they spurred us to do tricks that they would judge. The boy could do flips without a diving board, which probably brought a ton of honor to his dad.

For me, the game was to do something great, but also to be *seen* doing something great by my dad. I would jump and twist in the air, and when I came up from the water, I'd say, "Did you see me?"

My dad would nod, "Yes, yes," but kept his eyes on his book. He had a plate of French fries. Sometimes he'd spare a look as he dipped one in ketchup. "Good," he'd say.

But then I found the ultimate super move. We were in the shallow end of the pool. Along one edge, a set of cement stairs descended into the water. If you jumped in on that side, you'd crunch your bones on the stairs that were only a few inches underwater. But if you ran extra fast and dove headfirst at a super shallow angle, then your face would skim across the edge of the stairs and you'd cut into the water like the prince of the ocean.

If you did it wrong, you could probably die. But it also looked super cool. So it seemed like the thing to do.

I did it first, because I came up with it. Then the other kid. The girls had to admit it was amazing, and clapped from the other side of the pool. I did it three more times and became exactly like a dolphin, grazing the sharp reef of pool steps. I could probably take our family name to the Olympics. I ran up to my dad and said, "Baba, you have to see this."

"Okay," he said.

"No. Really this time," I said.

"Okay," he said.

"Okay, put the book down."

"Akh. Khosrou."

"You have to see this."

He put his book down. I imagined I would come up from the water and the entire world would change. Everyone would cheer and salute. My dad would be enthralled by me more than any country, or obligation to his parents, or drugs, or new wives. More than the good or the bad reasons to stay, even more than his love for his son, would be the gravitational pull of someone so very interesting. If I could entertain and entrance, I would be like a drug, compelling him to follow us. Like when cartoon skunks smell a pie on a windowsill and float uncontrollably toward it.

I took off. I could sprint on wet cement in bare feet no problem. I was my own circus show. I sprinted toward the stairs in the shallow end of the pool.

"Khosrou!" said my dad.

I dove.

I flew.

I descended.

Do you know those times when you've been practicing something and you've got it perfect, like juggling eggs or riding a bike with no hands; you've done it right a thousand times, and you say, "Mom! Look what I can do! Look at me!" and that's when you drop all three eggs on her kitchen floor or hit a rock and eat dirt?

Maybe that's the universe weaving a Persian flaw into your otherwise perfect plan. I dove at the pool and crunched my head into the corner of the first step. Three inches of water did nothing to slow me down. I hit the step and flipped over into the pool as I blacked out for a second.

I stayed under the water as long as I could, with my eyes closed. I knew when I stood up, the girls would be laughing, and my dad would be back to his reading. I could have cried enough to overflow the pool, but I didn't. Because there is nothing interesting about a crybaby boy.

I stood up. The sun in Dubai made the water so warm. Nobody was laughing. But everyone was looking at me. Even my dad. He had taken off his sunglasses and he was staring directly at me.

"Khosrou," he said. "Are you okay?"

I was embarrassed. I didn't say anything. I wiped the water from my face. My hand came away red. Red like my Baba Haji's hands. I looked down. The warm water on my chest was a stream of blood, flowing into the pool around me.

That's when my sister screamed, "Daniel, get out!"

I took a step, but suddenly felt dizzy, and the warm water kept pouring down my face.

IN THE **EDMOND, OKLAHOMA,** First Baptist Hospital, where we go if Ray hits my mom, or someone pulls my thumb out of the socket—and where my mom works as a custodian because her medical degrees don't matter here—they have candy machines in the waiting room.

Stay with me.

There are other things, like kids' magazines in the lobby, and pictures of kittens hanging from windowsills that let you know that kids will be in the area. And if they're scared, maybe they can do a word search or get a Snickers and they'll feel like they can "Hang in there," like the kitten. I think because in polite American society, they care more if you seem happy than if you're well.

Or I dunno, but the emergency room in Dubai—the one my dad rushed me to—was the exact opposite. Imagine the room in the Committee safe house. A square made of cement. A row of fluorescent bulbs hanging from the ceiling. A metal table in the middle of the room. A drain in the middle of the floor. That is all I remember.

Honestly, I don't even know if it was a hospital. My dad was carrying me. It was the only time he has ever done that. I thought, Maybe Khosrou will die here and no one will ever have to say his name wrong. Maybe this was my punishment for leaving Mr. Sheep Sheep. In the stories, the shepherd who abandons his duty is a villain. I knew that.

But I didn't want to die.

I know I've been acting tough-stuff so far, but it won't make sense if I don't tell you, I was scared.

A nurse in green long-sleeve pajamas met us at the metal slab. She didn't smile at me or even look me in the eye. I think she might have been scared too. I don't know. No one talked to me.

My dad said some medical stuff like, "We gave him eight hundred milligrams of boppity-boop-boop in the car."

She nodded.

He put me down on the metal slab. It was freezing on the back of my legs. I was still just in swim trunks, but they had blood on them now.

A doctor, an older man half my dad's size with a bald head and a short, trimmed beard walked in like he was already late for a tennis class.

And then the doctor put his hands on my shoulders and started to push me down on the table. I made my own noise. My dad said, "It's okay."

But the nurse was bringing over a tray of bandages and needles and nobody was saying anything in words I knew. I tried to look the doctor in the eye, to make him see me, like if he knew I was a hurt animal and not a practice dummy or something, he'd be nice to me. But he never looked me in the eye. He took a needle—like a sewing needle—from the metal tray. The nurse walked around him, behind me, and tried to pull my shoulders down so I would lie down. But the metal was so cold and no one would say anything to me, and there was still so much blood.

I jerked away from the nurse's hands.

She tried to dig her fingers in, but I was still a champion son. Disgraced and injured, but still.

The doctor sighed. He said, "Zeep! Creep!"

And a guy whose name was maybe Zeep Creep came in wearing the same green pajamas as the nurse but twelve sizes bigger.

My dad kept saying panicky stuff in other languages. Then he realized I only spoke Farsi and said, "It's okay. They're going to help."

But Zeep Creep and the nurse were obviously annoyed and planned to pin me to the table. The nurse grabbed the meat on my collarbone and yanked me down. Zeep Creep had huge hairy hands. I looked at him cause I couldn't see the nurse and said, "Please don't. No. Don't," but he didn't listen. He grabbed my ankles and the two of them stretched me out on the metal table.

The metal was so cold on my back that it burned. My whole body felt cold. I'd lost so much blood.

I saw the doctor's face hover over me.

He held up a needle, threaded with stitching line.

I think he thought he was making me feel better by showing me what was about to happen. I was just a kid then. But I thought, Aren't they going to numb the area? Aren't they going to give me candy? Aren't they going to give me a towel?

Reader, have you ever felt the layers of difference between the bone of your skull and the skin stretched over it?

The needle entered the skin and I screamed.

I wrenched my right foot out of Zeep Creep's grip and kicked him directly in his meaty face. I think he cursed in Arabic. He grabbed my foot again and ground both my ankles together. The nurse put all her weight onto my shoulders.

My dad grabbed my left arm (because I was flailing). I could feel the needle dangling from my head. Zeep Creep shouted for someone else, who came out and held my right arm. I was crying and screaming by then.

I remember the exact moment the doctor pulled the needle through the skin, dragged the line behind it, poked it into the skin on the other side of the wound and pulled again.

The line made a scraping sound somewhere deep in my skull and I felt the skin dragging across the bone to cinch together. When it met, he tugged the line two times to make a tight seal.

I felt every stitch.

Zeep Creep's grip would leave bruises.

So would the nurse's.

The thing I remember most is the friction of the thread as it tunneled through my skin. And the feeling that maybe I shouldn't have made it so difficult. Or cried so much.

It was the last day I would see my dad and he'd remember me as a weakling. And I remember thinking this is what it's like to be the one begging. My eyes must have looked like the big black eyes of the bull, begging my dad to save me.

That's what I thought then, but I'm older now.

Even if I had made the dive across the pool stairs and qualified for greatness, he still would have left the next day.

MRS. MILLER SAYS WE LIVED in Dubai for a year and I can't just tell the food, poop, and bloody parts, so I will tell you what life looked like for us.

But I did tell her the thing I said before, that food and poop are the truest parts and she said, "That's interesting." And then she leaned down to look at me over her glasses—so our eyes would have nothing between them. And she said, "Then how come when you die, those are the first things you expel?"

This was a good point and I did not know enough about dead bodies to answer.

"And how come when we tell stories of Scheherazade, we talk about all sorts of things besides what she ate and where she pooped?"

She had me on that one too. I shrugged again.

I said, "Fine. I'll write the emotional parts."

The bell had already rung, so I got up to leave.

"Last question, Mr. Nayeri," she said. "At the beginning of the year you said the truest thing about a person was whose blood they had in their heart. Do you remember that?"

I nodded, but honestly, I didn't remember till she said so.

"What happened?" she said.

I MEAN, WHAT WAS I going to say? That Ray married my mom a third time—or that she married him because, according to my sister, she thinks I need a dad so badly. And there is no returning, it'll never happen—there is no returning to the house with the birds in the walls, because the birds are all dead by now, and there is no chance I'll see my Baba Haji again. The feasting is done. He wouldn't even recognize me with my new name, and I'll never belong to either place or even have memories I can count on—that I'm the flaw in the story, the exception in her classroom, and I'm sorry.

OUR DAYS IN DUBAI were spent in the waiting rooms of the United Nations embassy, hoping they would see us, look through our mountains of paperwork, and help us find somewhere to go.

The chairs were bolted down. The pens were on chains at the desks. We didn't have any books.

I became an expert at counting.

Also an expert at watching agents behind glass to read their expressions. Sometimes one of them would spend ten minutes looking through a family's papers. She'd have thick glasses and pursed lips. She'd lick a finger to turn every single page. The family would sit with their hands in their laps and quiet the kids if they started playing a game or something, so it wouldn't bother her.

Everything would be going smoothly.

Then the agent would come to a page. Her finger would stop at her mouth. She'd flip back to check something, then forward again, then back.

A sigh.

Out of the little hole in the bulletproof glass, the whole waiting room would hear as she shouted at them, "Where is the 533-C form?"

And the dad, who barely spoke English, would say, "The what?"

"The 533-C form, sir."

"C form?"

"Yes. The 533-C form."

The kids would start to get agitated. The agent's glare would go right through bulletproof glass. The dad would rifle through the files in his lap, but the panic was already in his hands.

"If you can't find it, please go to the back and take a number to see another agent."

But that meant hours more of waiting, so he'd say, "No, no, please."

Everybody knew he wouldn't find it.

"Sir. I won't ask again."

The agent could call security and the whole family would be kicked out, so nobody wanted to get them mad. And if the family before you even irritated the agent a little, it would affect you, so people in the waiting area would start to grumble.

Finally, the man would have to admit to himself that his whole family had wasted the day—and for some of them, they had no homes or way to eat, so it was a big deal. He'd look up from the papers and say, "What is 533-C form?"

This would really tick off the agent, because they assumed refugees were liars. But you have to understand, there were hundreds of forms to fill out, and nobody knew English all that well, and the rules changed all the time, and the agents hated talking to us.

She would say, "Sir, please find the form and return when you've completed it."

She wouldn't even give it to him. The man's wife would usually put her hand on his arm and say something in their language to calm him down. His whole ribcage would deflate.

They would take their papers and walk off. The man would try to ask the armed guard where he could find the 533-C form, but the guard wouldn't speak. If they weren't poor, they could go outside and pay one of the translators who made small businesses out of having copies of all the forms and sitting with the families to translate everything from English. But most people couldn't afford that, and the translators had reputations for being fast-talkers.

My sister and I would make a game of guessing which agent we would get. And we would watch their temper over the course of the day like farmers in Oklahoma watch rain clouds. When we reached the agent, we would wait for the same moment. It happened every time. Here is a completely made-up example.

"Where is the certificate of important information?"

I didn't have one.

My mom would say, "He doesn't have one, but—"

"You need a certificate of important information."

"Yes, but—"

"You can't apply for asylum without important information."

"Okay, yes, but—"

"You can only do that with a certificate of important information."

"I understand."

"Please return when you have a certificate of important information."

"Wait. Just one moment, please, just a moment."

The agent would sigh. My mom would jump on the opportunity to explain.

"We have his birth certificate."

"That only proves he was born, ma'am."

"But I'm his mother and you can see my certificate of important information."

"Under the law he belongs to his father, ma'am."

"Yes, that's why I included the letter from his father."

"If you have compliance from the father, you can apply for a certificate of important information."

"No, they're trying to kill us. They won't give us documents to escape. We can't get the documents from the government that has fatwas on our heads."

"If you don't have a certificate of important information, you'll need to fill out an appeal for special circumstance form."

"Okay."

"Please return when you've filled out an appeal for special circumstance form."

Finally, my mother's ribcage would deflate and we would stand up to leave.

She would spend the next few weeks tracking down the new form, filling it out with all the required documentation, and having it officiated and notarized. Then we would wait again in the embassy waiting room.

You have to understand, by the fifteenth time we did this, I stopped paying attention to the names of the forms or the faces of the agents. None of the document names mattered; none of the agents acted human at any point in the story. It was like sticking a wrinkly dollar into a candy machine over and over and having it spit the dollar out over and over, for a year, with a gun to your head.

Here in Oklahoma, I understand why—why humans would sit behind a glass window and look in the faces of families running away from danger and dead sheep, and not feel anything.

They think we're bad people who will come and take their stuff.

Like when I won the tetherball tournament at recess against Trevor and I wouldn't have if I hadn't been there at all.

ONCE YOU PROVE TO the UN that you're a refugee in danger, a country has to raise its hand to take you. And they're hoping you're one of the good ones who have educations with kids who start small businesses. Or sometimes they just put you in refugee holding areas until they can sort you out. That's how we left the UAE after a year, and went to a refugee camp in Italy. I remember that plane ride because I left my kite behind—it was too big. But I kept my book by Richard Scarry called *What Do Western Animals Do All Day?* which was how I learned English words—for instance, if a pig enters a gymnasium, he will lift barbells, and then go to the butcher to purchase cured meats. I don't know what meats they eat in animal town. Maybe it's people.

And I packed four Micro Machine cars, because we still only had the one suitcase, but my pockets were my own.

And so we arrived on the outskirts of a town on the outskirts of Rome called Mentana, at a place people called Hotel Barba.

INTERRUPTION! INTERRUPTION!

Stop the story.

Stop, Scheherazade.

Stop counting the memories.

Stop, reader.

I have news.

MY FATHER, MASOUD EBNE JAMSHID NAYERI is coming to America to visit.

"Oh yeah?" said Jared S. when I told Mrs. Miller's class for my reading assignment. "Is he gonna fly on a carpet?"

"No," I said.

"Is he going to bring saffron?" said Kelly J.

"Nobody here likes saffron," I said.

But I was missing the joke. The joke was that to my seventh grade English class, I had made my father a myth, like djinns, like Rostam, or like Mike Maguffy's girlfriend from summer camp that nobody else knows.

How could the man who drove a golden chariot across the kingdoms of Ardestan, who laughs like a lion laughs—friend of the highest emirs and lowest dervishes, poet of his own religion, and master of the house with the birds in the walls—how could he ever travel to the real world of Edmond, Oklahoma?

"Why are we even letting them come here, when we're at war?" said Jared S.

I had learned to avoid this topic, but Mrs. Miller said, "We're not at war with Iran."

"We have soldiers over there," said Jared. Everyone knew his uncle was one of them.

"We don't have soldiers in Iran," said Mrs. Miller.

"We should bring them home first."

"Is he coming to stay here?" said Jessica.

Jared jumped in, "Yeah, that's how they do it. They come over without any papers."

"They don't even let you in without papers," I said.

"People just walk over the border and stay."

Suddenly the whole class was very worried about the possibility of someone without papers. They had all become little agents behind glass evaluating who got to check into the Economy Lodge Motel of Edmond.

I told them he only had a two-week visa. That he was a very important dentist and was needed in Isfahan.

But I knew that no one really believed anything I said. Kelly didn't even look up from drawing her bubble letters on a note to Stacy as she asked, "So is he going to come to class?"

I said, "Yes. Yes he is," so I could prove I had a dad who cared about me and was real. My mom could make cream puffs and it would amaze everybody. No one was going to make fun of him to his face. And it was all going to go exactly as I hoped.

THE HOTEL BARBA, WHERE we lived in Italy, was a cement building plopped on a hill. It wasn't beautiful. But on the hill, you could see beautiful things, like the peach orchards of the nearby farms, and the terra-cotta roofs of the town center in the distance. At the foot of the hotel was the parking lot. In the back was a little landfill—a skirt of garbage that flowed down halfway to the nearest farm.

When you walked in, there was a reception desk where nobody sat. Most of the first floor was a cafeteria, like one in a school, that had nothing you could steal or break. The stairs were concrete. The halls of each floor were windowless and narrow. The rooms were one square, one window, one sink, one toilet, one shower. Finito.

It was the kind of place that made a lot of people cry at night.

I'm telling all this because even though it wasn't an emir's palace or anything, it was still fine. When I say, "refugee camp," people sometimes imagine tents and kids who can't speak English. But at this time, I was seven, and knew more than a hundred English words.

It was a refugee camp in other ways, though.

We were the only Iranians. The rest were homeless people from Slovenia, Ukraine, Serbia, Yugoslavia, and a bunch of other places. Nobody knew who was who.

The Italian staff whispered that some of them wandered over the Alps and had no paperwork at all. They just walked over the mountains and showed up to sleep in the town squares of Italian villages, washing their clothes in the fountains and begging up and down the porticoes.

The refugees could barely speak to each other. The old women sat in the parking lot in front of Hotel Barba (which never had any cars and was just a flat cement courtyard) and exchanged gossip. One would say something in Czech and another would translate into Russian, and another would translate into something else. It was like a giant game of telephone just to figure out where they could go to get cheap photos taken for their documents, or which of the camp administrators to avoid.

No one ever went to town.

It was a long hike down the hill and up two more. And we were unwelcome anyway. But my mom loved the walk along the narrow lanes of the farms. It reminded her a little of Ardestan. Of all the refugees, we visited the town the most. Sometimes, I'd play soccer with the Italian kids in the square. Anytime the ball rolled over to the tables of an outdoor café, the old men would pick it up and kick it back. I spoke Italian. I knew how to say "little help" and "thanks."

Once, one of the old men held the ball and waved us all in. I looked around for my mom. She was buying more erasers in the stationery store, so I ran over with the other kids. I didn't know any of their names. The old man—he was like Baba Haji's age—leaned down and said, "Listen. If you ever see those gypsies walking toward the town, you run back and shout, 'The gypsies are coming! The gypsies are coming!' and we'll take care of it. Understand?"

The other kids nodded.

I raised my hand. "Do you mean the people in Hotel Barba?"

"Hotel Barba," he said, like he was spitting it. "Yeah them," he said.

"Okay," I said. "Them."

I didn't understand until I realized they all thought I was one of the Italian kids. I looked Italian, kinda. I didn't talk as much as the kid who played keeper. They didn't know I lived with the gypsies. The old man handed back the ball, and we all ran back to our game.

I wondered *how* the men would "take care of it." Would they stand in the way and demand papers or something? And if one of the gypsy mothers really needed something, if she gathered the courage to say, "What papers?" would they just make something up?

"The 533-C form of Mentana," they'd say and puff out their chests. And if the mom was *really* mad, like she'd been treated like garbage for years and all she needed was something from the pharmacy that she had saved up to pay for—if she said, "The 533-C form of Mentana doesn't exist," would the men just say, "Yeah"?

And what then? Punches? Kicks? A 360 back kick?

Maybe that was why Ray insisted on learning tae kwon do as soon as he could. And why he taught me.

Maybe I should thank him for showing me that any power of one person over another is built on the threat of violence.

But there must be some middle step when people disagree, before they try to rip each other apart. Right? I mean, this isn't a kindness commercial for grown-ups to shove at kids. This is my memory of real life. So the gypsies and the old men never came to any understanding. There was only the threat of violence. So the people of Hotel Barba waited till no one was watching and snuck into town one at a time. They caught the bus, or bought stamps, as quickly as they could, and never loafed around the café or the fountain.

I MET ALI SHEKARI AT the Hotel Barba. He was my best friend in the whole world, and he's probably king of Australia by now. Back then, he was seventeen, and I was seven, but we were both very good at soccer, so we respected each other like men. He was alone, and we were alone, because no one else spoke the languages we spoke. Luckily, he also spoke Persian.

Most of the hotel courtyard was taken up by circles of old men or women sitting on cinder blocks. The old women were Russian and the only Persian they spoke was the pinching of cheeks. Otherwise, they looked like babushka nesting dolls with red and yellow scarves around sad faces. They sat and probably talked about wherever they had escaped. The old men played a version of backgammon that I didn't understand and they didn't explain. They tapped the pieces onto the wooden board so fast it sounded like clattering teeth.

Hotel Barba was limbo. It was the middle waiting area between whatever hellish situation people had come from and whatever free paradise they imagined on the other side. For some of them, their kids were grown and had already made it to a free country. They dreamed of reaching them. For others, they had nobody and it was just two sides of the same bloody river.

No one thought of Hotel Barba as home.

I don't know why there were so few kids at the Hotel Barba. Maybe kids slow you down. It was just us, some kids who never left their parents because the parents never let them, and Ali Shekari, who my sister said was beautiful, except for the pockmarks all over his face and body.

I met him in the cafeteria on hot-dog day, which was the worst day of any week. I will explain, because you must be thinking that hot dogs are the best food and this Khosrou is a lying fool.

But I am not a lying fool and these hot dogs were not the juicy frankfurters you are probably imagining. They were boiled, bland, and bun-less. Also, no ketchup. And they were served every Wednesday, even though they cost more than to serve everybody's favorite, penne pasta.

You have to understand, the worst penne pasta in Italy, the tubs of it they would give refugees, was still better than the Oklahoma City Olive Garden. It was that good. The tomato sauce was rich and creamy with leaves of fresh basil, not dried. With parmesan cheese on the pasta, that was all you needed and you could eat three bowls and still crave more.

I didn't know Ali Shekari yet, because this was only our second week, but I had seen him cause he was a seventeen-year-old dude and had a denim jacket with patches. So I made sure I was next to him in line. That way I could be his bud if he needed one.

The staff at Hotel Barba were from the town and everyone knew which staff to ask for things—like if you needed help translating a form. The one who wanted to be a doctor was a nice lady. The one who always looked mad would call one of the men to back her up as she screamed at you. Most things were against the rules, so when one old lady across the hall from us fell in her shower, we couldn't do anything but steal cinder blocks from the courtyard and arrange them in her bathroom so she could sit as she washed.

In situations like that, God doesn't mind stealing.

Or maybe he does, but you get more positive points for helping the old lady who was so happy she cried and kissed my cheeks so hard she rubbed tears all over them.

Or wait, okay, actually, I think the point is that above all other laws is the law of love. I forgot that one for a second.

Anyway, the staff was mostly nice, but had rules we broke sometimes. And sometimes they'd punish us.

So back in line with Ali Shekari, we had our plates out and the Zuppa Guy (the guy who shouted, "Zuppa!" on soup night) put a couple hot dogs on Ali's plate with some potatoes that had been fried once upon a time.

Again, no ketchup.

I know this sounds ungrateful, because they were feeding us. But people are people and I'm just telling you how it happened.

Ali Shekari said, "What's this?"

And Zuppa Guy, who was usually really funny, and pretended to dance romantically with the babushkas so everyone would laugh together in all the languages, said, "This? This is American food."

Ali Shekari had a great laugh. And long, flowy black hair. If not for the marks, he'd look like the Italian soccer stars. And he was the only man in Hotel Barba who could beat up anybody, so he had to be careful to seem weak, or the staff might kick him out. But even so, he said, "Doesn't it cost more to make American food than to make pasta?"

And the Zuppa Guy said, "Yes, but you must get used to food from where you go."

Ali Shekari walked to his seat and did his laugh.

The Zuppa Guy added, "You don't stay here. So you don't get used to pasta."

When we sat down, I noticed Ali Shekari wouldn't eat his hot dogs. I already had two in my mouth at once. He didn't know any of us. We were all just strangers who lived together. But I could tell he was furious. He pulled up his jacket sleeves and scratched at his arms. They had marks too. It was like somebody had taken bucket of glue and splashed it on him. Wherever the glue splattered, it was a white splotch of skin, even up his neck, on his face, and under his hair.

He waited till meal time was over and threw away the full plate. He said, "They spend extra money just to tell us we're not welcome."

THAT MADE ALI SHEKARI the ultimate hero. A champion of champions who would not eat frankfurters or fries from the hand of a begrudging host. He was Rostam the Unbeggar, and I followed him every day from then on.

My mom would apologize to him, but I pretended not to hear and would say, "What do you want to play, Ali Shekari?" He was a hero, remember, so he would play with little kids, no problem.

When we played soccer in the yard, the babushkas would suck their teeth, because Ali Shekari was a high-flying acrobat with the ball. It would miss their teacups by the width of a mustache hair. Ali Shekari would chase it, and sometimes even speak to them in their languages. He could probably speak all the languages. And he was growing a mustache.

Sometimes he would take me to the orchards on the next hill. Since he did not eat at the Hotel Barba, he was always hungry.

It was Ali Shekari who taught me how to jump a fence, how to climb a tree to toss down peaches, and how to run in zigzags when the farmers would shout and shoot their guns (probably in the air only to scare us, but just in case).

We were peach thieves, I guess.

Now that we are in Oklahoma, I wish I could skip telling you that part, because it makes us seem like villains. And maybe the Zuppa Guy was right not to want us. But I promised the truth, and the truth is Ali Shekari never hit anyone, but he stole peaches, and that was enough for me.

The rest of the truth is that he was my only friend for a very short time, and it's my fault that I don't know where he is—if he's a king in Australia, or married to a princess, or dead.

If you had been there, hiking down the Italian hills between the stone walls, and seen the trees, hundreds of them shining, and climbed the stone fences, and picked a ripe couple peaches for yourself—if you bit into them and the juice overran your mouth and tasted better than anything you'd eaten in months, and if you heard the shouting from behind the hedges like a wild djinn coming to kill you, and you ran and you heard a hero running next to you laughing and batting branches aside, and it smelled like fresh grass and wet dirt, and the sun was warm, the wind cool, and you had nowhere else in the world to go—it might have felt like an adventure from the myth of your life.

I know it was wrong.

I just wanted you to remember it like I do.

HERE ARE THE TIMES I lied and stole.

I stole peaches. I told that to you already.

The time I lied was here in Oklahoma when Mrs. Miller found me in the library during lunch. She said, "This is the lunch hour, Daniel."

Which we both knew.

"I just wanted a book," I said. Not exactly a lie. I want lots of things.

"Do you have a lunch?"

"For my dad," I said. "To explain American football."

Notice I didn't lie about the lunch, either.

"We can ask Ms. Ivey about it when she gets back."

Ms. Ivey was the librarian.

"Oh. She's not here? Okay."

This is also not a lie, technically, even though I knew Ms. Ivey was out during lunch. But I didn't say a lie. I just asked a question I already knew the answer to.

Mrs. Miller had a son at Tinker Air Force Base in Midwest City, Oklahoma. His picture was the only one on her desk. He wasn't in Iraq or anything, but he could be. So it was important that she didn't think every Middle Eastern person is a liar, or she might tell her son, and he might one day disbelieve a good one of us and die. She lifted her glasses and rubbed the part of her nose where they sat.

"Would you like some peanut butter and crackers?" she said. "I was just walking to the office myself."

I shook my head no. Ali Shekari would have been proud.

"I've eaten," I said, which is true because I *have* eaten in the past. But I walked out anyway. It was almost time for recess. And I started to get nervous that even though I wasn't lying, she *thought* I was.

"I can find the book later," I said.

Mrs. Miller said, "Will he be able to read it? Does your dad speak English?"

I was already walking out, but I wasn't far enough out to pretend I couldn't hear, so I said, "Uh-huh!" like my dad could speak English.

And I ran down the hall.

That was the lie.

I'm telling you now.

But Mrs. Miller would find out soon enough, because he was coming to class. So I don't know why I did that. I mean, he speaks a *little*. Maybe enough to trick everybody. I don't know. I haven't seen him in five years.

Anyway, that was really bad.

I'm afraid she thinks we're all liars now.

THE LAST DAY I ever saw Ali Shekari was also the first day I attended school in two years.

It was only sort of a school.

Since we'd left home, my mom had been so worried that we'd fall behind—or worse, stop caring about our education—that she sent letters, talked to churches, and looked around until finally she found an American couple who were teaching their kids American things. They had a girl my sister's age and a boy my age, so their books were the ones we needed.

That first morning, my mom walked us down the hill after what happened with Ali Shekari, which I'll explain in a second. I was crying the whole way and not admiring nature. We snuck past the café, where the old men hadn't arrived yet, to a stationery store where my mom bought six big pink erasers and two pencils. She had packed her dinner from the night before, so our bag was full. We waited for a bus.

The bus took us to Rome, to a train station where they said gangs of gypsy men roamed at night. Another bus took us another hour to the other side of the city. Nobody spoke on the bus. I was still acting like a baby and my sister was still mad that I had been mean to Ali Shekari so we rode in silence.

Do you remember his pockmarks? The splatters of white that looked like they had eaten away the skin on his left side? Maybe you don't, I dunno. But that morning, I asked him. We were playing soccer in the courtyard while I waited for my mom and sister to come down. Everybody was already at the places they would be for the rest of the day. All of Hotel Barba was in a constant state of waiting for papers to come in. No one went out. No one lived any kind of life. They just waited and hoped some country would take them. There was nothing else to do.

As I waited, I saw Ali Shekari, who was trying to fix a bicycle he had found in the landfill behind Hotel Barba, under the mountains of trash.

"Ali Shekari, wanna play?"

I had a soccer ball I was going to take to meet the American family since they had a boy my age.

Ali Shekari jumped right up and played with me. He had his sleeves rolled up. The marks had eaten gashes out of his forearms.

As he kept the ball away and I chased it, a couple times he put his hand on my head as a joke. I hit it away. We were laughing, I promise. But once, I grabbed his side, cause he was shielding me from the ball—and he winced.

Ali Shekari was as tall as a man, so I stopped, because nothing that light should have hurt him. I wasn't as strong back then as I am now.

"It's okay," he said. "It's fine."

But he sat on a cinder block.

"Sorry," I said.

"It's okay. It's okay." He laughed.

Ali Shekari was Kurdish. He was a Kurd. Did I tell you that already? I think I did. Did I tell you about the Kurds? Am I falling apart?

The Kurds are nomads—like the Roma, who everybody calls gypsies. They, the Kurds, live in the hill country between Iran and Iraq. They go back and forth because they've been living there since way before those borders existed and they have no paperwork because they don't belong to anybody. They're like refugees for every generation all the time.

In the myths that Ali Shekari told me, they are the tragic result of a demon king who wanted to eat brains. It went like this:

I said, "What happened?" and pointed to his pocks. "Do they hurt?"

I could see him wondering if he could get away with waving it off. But finally he decided to admit it, "Yeah."

It was Saddam Hussein, the king of Iraq, who had done it. Do you remember the part where I said Iran and Iraq had been at war when I was a kid and when Saddam's planes bombed our city, I was just a baby? I think I did. It was the legend of Khosrou, the fat sleepy baby who once slept through the building next door getting bombed to pieces. I told you that, I'm sure. My mom ran into my room and I was still sound asleep. I could sleep through bombs and tornadoes and everything.

Anyway, that guy, Saddam, practiced his bombing skills on the Kurds. His war planes would swoop into the highlands and spot a tribe of Kurds with their sheep and they must have thought it was funny to drop bombs on them. Who protected the shepherds? Nobody.

They dropped the bombs just to see how far the Kurds would scatter. And you might think the Iraqi pilots were ashamed, but they weren't. By the time Ali Shekari was thirteen, the war planes were practicing dropping chemicals instead of regular bombs.

As we sat in the courtyard of Hotel Barba, Ali Shekari, who was twice a refugee, said, "Agent Orange," which I didn't know back then was a chemical bomb that drops on shepherds and eats their skin. But I nodded and didn't ask more.

"I'll be fine," he said. "Those bleep bleeps."

That was all the story I got from Ali Shekari. I know in the *1,001 Nights*, there are stories within stories, but this is real stuff. Anybody who has watched a ball fall from the sky and burst into a cloud of acid that washed over him and everyone he ever loved is not somebody who tells the story to entertain people. He nodded over at a lady from Moscow who had run away from her husband and who never came down to the courtyard, but watched from a window three stories up. He nodded at her and said, "She's a finigonzon," cause I'd told him about my language.

And when I turned to look at her, he snatched the soccer ball from my hands and started to play again. That was when it went wrong. I think he was trying to impress her.

But now you know why Ali Shekari was scarred on over half of his body. And if you want the story in the story, I'll tell you the one Ali Shekari told me about the origin of the Kurds later.

For now we can get back to the accident, which wasn't *such* a big thing, except that it was the last thing.

And whenever you look back and realize something was the last of something—like the last moment you ever saw your grandfather's house or the smell of the street you lived on or Orich bars or whatever—it can be an ordinary thing, but it also becomes the only thing you have, the clearest memory, and it gains all this extra meaning. To me, the accident was just that Ali Shekari was extra excited keeping the ball from me and kicked it just a little too hard. It flew into the spokes of his broken bike and burst. It wasn't a real soccer ball. It was one of those cheap plastic ones that can deflate like balloons. But it was the only ball I had.

There was the pause right after it happened. My mom and sister had come out, finally. The babushkas stopped talking. The finigonzon at the window, the old men playing backgammon, it seemed like they all watched me.

Ali Shekari said, "Akh. I'm sorry. I'll get you a new one."

Maybe it was because we were going to meet the American family and this was the toy I had to share or something. Maybe it was just the feeling that none of us could ever have any unbroken thing. All I remember is that I never felt so poor as I did then. And I cried. I shouldn't have. But that was the whole accident. A ball. It wasn't like he broke my thumb or anything. I didn't even know back then that men you looked up to could do so much more damage.

I made Ali Shekari feel like scum. He was so embarrassed he said, "I'm sorry," to my mom. He was probably even worried that he could be kicked out. I kept crying. And when he put his hand on my shoulder, I wrenched away, probably because I was embarrassed by that point too. But I should have forgiven him. I should never have treated him like he wasn't my friend.

My mom told him it was okay and took us to town, where we caught that bus. Everyone in that courtyard must have glared at Ali Shekari for hurting a little kid—but reader, please, he did nothing wrong. That was the last time I saw Ali Shekari. People came and went at the Hotel Barba without good-byes. The papers would come in and you'd run out. He probably got his papers to Australia. When we got back that day for dinner, the Zuppa Guy called me over and handed me a baseball cap. It was Ali Shekari's hat. He had left it for me. And my mom got me another ball eventually. I never got to say I'm sorry, Ali Shekari. I wish I was still your friend.

"**THE ORIGIN OF THE KURDS,**" said Ali Shekari one afternoon, to me, as we sat eating peaches the way friends do, beside a tree, with all of Italy blooming down the hill, "is this. This is how Ferdowsi tells it.

"First there was Zahhak, the villain king who brought an end to Jamshid's honorable reign, and who later chased Fereydun into the care of the rainbow cow. A rainbow cow, you must understand, is not a silly cow with big painted stripes. It is a splendid cow, like a peacock, with every hair a different shimmering color."

He had to tell me that, because I had interrupted him with giggling. He went on, "Zahhak was such a vile punk murderer that Eblis the devil took notice and came to his court disguised as a cook. He made Zahhak lamb stewed in wine, veal with saffron and garlic, and kebab—all of it was so delicious that Zahhak said, 'Tell me, strange cook, what gift I can give you and you will have it.' This is always a dangerous moment in a story, because the king is not a djinn, and a wish that is an insult can quickly become a curse. Another way to put it is—don't ask for anything that'll make the king mad.

"The cook was the devil, though. So he said, 'O King, all I want is to kiss your shoulders.'

"And the king said, 'Okay.'

"Don't think that just because this was hundreds of years ago that this was totally normal. It's still kind of weird to ask to kiss his shoulders when you could have asked for a mansion and a rainbow cow or something.

"When Eblis walked up and kissed the king on his shoulders, two things happened: The devil disappeared into a sudden burst of smoke, and the king grew two snakes from his shoulders.

"This is how Saddam became the serpent king. When he cut them off, they grew back. When he slept, they whispered wildness in his ears. And when they were hungry, the king would sacrifice two young servants so that the serpents could eat their brains."

He was neither a god who spoke nor a god who listened.

Like most kings, he was a god who only ever devoured.

"It went like this for some amount of time—enough for the weeping and mourning of the people to drown out the birdsongs and even the chorus of the east winds. Every day the king's serpents ate brains, until two heroes arrived, also disguised as cooks. They stood in the castle kitchen drawing up a plan. They couldn't just use sheep brains. The snakes knew the taste of human brain.

"Never believe that villains are hurting people by accident. They want to get better at their craft of breaking jaws just as you want to get better at art or music.

"So the cooks had to settle for something half-good.

"Every day, when two unlucky people were dragged from the nearby towns into the kitchens, the cooks thanked the soldiers and offered them tasty treats in the other room. Quickly, they would take one sheep and mix equal parts human and sheep brains into the two bowls for the snakes. Then they would help the other person escape through the cellars of the castle, with some hard bread, a wheel of dried fig, some dried beef. They would tell them to go, run off into the hill country and hide.

"Every day, they saved one.

"Every month, they saved thirty.

"When they had two hundred people hidden away in the hills, the cooks gave them some animals and showed them where they could live in the desert. And in Ferdowsi it says, 'The Kurds—who never settle in towns—are descended from these men.'"

I ate my peach.

"See," said Ali Shekari. "The Kurds are half a people."

He must have been trying to tell me something with that story. Maybe it was that somewhere, if you go back enough in history, everybody comes from ancestors who wandered around looking for refuge. Everybody was poor at some point.

I dunno.

Maybe it wasn't about me.

Maybe Ali Shekari looked at his own scars in the mirror and thought that he was half of a half. That a patchwork life was all he was ever going to get.

Maybe he was counting his own memories, holding on to them with trembling fingers. Or maybe he was thinking about the cooks, who were heroes, sure, but still had to kill and serve one person every day to the serpent king in order to save the other. Maybe half-good is as good as it gets in this life. And maybe that's why my mom was so interested in the next one.

I don't know.

Like I said, I never saw him again after we got back from the school.

MRS. MILLER SAYS I HAVE "lost the plot," and am now just making lists of things that happened to fill space. But I replied that she is beholden to a Western mode of storytelling that I do not accept and that the *1,001 Nights* are basically Scheherazade stalling for time, so I don't see the difference.

She laughed when I said this.

It was one of those genuine laughs you get and for a second you see the person they are when they're not a teacher. Like the same laugh she might have at a movie or something. She said, "That was a wonderful use of 'beholden.'"

And I said, "Thank you."

Have you noticed my English is super good now?

The point of the *Nights* is that if you spend time with each other—if we really listen in the parlors of our minds and look at each other as we were meant to be seen—then we would fall in love. We would marvel at how beautifully we were made. We would never think to be villain kings, and we would never kill each other. Just the opposite. The stories aren't the thing. The thing is the story *of* the story. The spending of the time. The falling in love.

All the good stuff is in between and around the things that happen. It's what you imagine I might be like when I'm not telling you a story, but we're sitting together in silence. Would my hands be fumbling with themselves in my lap? Would I be nervous? Would I love it if you asked about *Final Fantasy*? And would I say yes if you invited me to your house?

Look how much you know about me.

I bet if I told you that my dad came to Oklahoma with just one surprise for me, a friend from my past, back from the dead, you'd probably even know what it was even before I told you.

THE LEGEND OF MY MOTHER is that she does not stop. And if you don't stop, you're unstoppable.

I know I told you that already, but you didn't understand it the first time. I know you thought you did. But you didn't. Trust me, reader.

I love you with all my heart, but you just don't know.

For instance I bet if I asked you, "What is the toughest stuff on Earth?" you'd say, "Diamonds." But you'd be wrong. You should have said, "Your mom."

And if I said, "What is *toughness* anyway? Is it being an unbreakable rock?"

You'd say, "Yes," because you'd still be thinking of it wrong.

And I'd say, "But isn't it harder to break water?"

And you'd say, "Well, yes. You can't break water."

I would try not to smirk here, because Mrs. Miller says that's why I don't have many friends. And you'd say, "But at the molecular level, everything is eventually breakable—even an atom."

And you'd be right, because being breakable has nothing to do with toughness. Everything breaks. Everything is whirling around in a big bunch of motion and energy crashing into each other at the size of atoms and icebergs, and will crumble eventually.

But then you'd say, "So what makes you think your mom is so tough?"

And I would say this part slowly, cause I've said it before. I'd probably even whisper, "Cause she's unstoppable."

Every rock smashes into everything else and breaks. That doesn't matter. What matters is whether the rock keeps going the same direction it was going when it smashed. Do you see what I mean?

What keeps going?

What do you know that keeps going?

Never distracted? Never bored? Never deterred?

Beat up and threatened, sure.

Humiliated and ignored, often.

But never never stopped.

That's right. You get it now.

My mom.

HERE IS SOMETHING THAT only makes sense now that you know what you know.

In a refugee camp, it's the waiting that will kill you.

The whole point of a refugee camp is that there are *actual* people trying to kill you.

But really, it's the slow numbing death of hopelessness that does it. You have to imagine a room that's just a cement cube—nothing beautiful in it. If you're not careful, this is also what becomes of the parlor of your mind.

The room is your room in Hotel Barba. It has a bed. No lamp. One light in the ceiling. There is a bathroom with a shower, toilet, sink. Nothing else. No glass. No mirror. White walls. No art.

You leave the room and enter a hallway of doors that look just like yours. Nothing else. A fluorescent light above makes faces look green.

If a door opens while you're out in the hall, the face in the doorway is unsmiling. It won't speak what you speak. It's scared, like you. Down the cement stairs, there is nothing but an entryway. The staff are not your friends. They're good people, most of them. But other people before you were thieves maybe, or liars, so they've become hard. They police you. If they find out you put cinder blocks in your shower so you could sit down while you wash, they will shout at you and take them away. So you stay away from them.

You don't have any money. You're not allowed to get a job. Even if you're a kid who speaks Italian and looks like the other kids in town and could carry groceries or dig a trench or something, make mug rugs, I dunno—they won't let you. You can't travel. You have to wait.

There are a million papers shuffling across a million desks under a million upturned noses. Eventually, one of them will get stamped and you'll be told you can go be poor in Canada. But that's still weeks or months or years away. You have to wait.

There's nothing to do. No TV. The radio plays gibberish. No library in the words you read. Obviously no video games. No Game Boy. No comic books. You might have a ball, but if it pops you shouldn't cry. No art supplies. No yo-yos or whatever.

So what do you do, you wonder. You wait. You kill time remembering some other place in your life. You count those memories. Maybe you were happy then. You cling to them. If you can—like if your family isn't dead in Kurdistan—then you write letters. You tell them to write back. You beg for news. Any news. New anything.

You have to wait.

Until your mind starts to betray you a little. You count minutes until the Zuppa Guy yells, "Zuppa!" and you can file into the cafeteria for food. You count seconds.

This sentence took you three seconds to read. This took two. One. One. One.

Add them together.

What else are you going to do?

You have to wait.

Five.

Six.

Seven.

You go till the number is so big you can't say it in your head in the space of a second, and so you fall behind.

Two thousand seven hundred forty-seven.

Two thousand seven hundred forty-eight.

But that took you three seconds to say, so you're really on two thousand seven hundred forty-nine.

You're losing time.

You don't care.

Little by little, you stop caring about most things.

Who cares if they ever let you go anywhere. What sadness you've seen. Maybe it never goes away. Maybe it's the most true thing. Who cares anyway. Who cares if the people of the world don't want Daniel.

Daniel doesn't need the world.

And he doesn't need the people.

But you have to wait.

It's dark now and you've eaten the begrudged food and counted thousands of seconds and become so angry. Your fists go stiff and you stagger up the cement stairs to your door in the unmarked halls to your cement room and you lie down. And you admit you do need stuff. You whimper that you want love.

And you wait.

You wait all night.

You wait for the Committee to find you.

You wait for some stamp to give you permission to go somewhere and live.

And that's what it looks like. Unless you're my mom. She doesn't wait.

She bangs, she doesn't whimper. When we got to Hotel Barba and she saw the dead eyes of the people—not even begging to stay alive—she told us, "No. No we won't do that."

Back then I didn't know what I know now. The people just looked sad to me. So I said, "Do what?"

"Wait," she said. "Waste time."

She said the Hotel Barba turned sadness into opium. It tricked you into thinking you were waiting to go live somewhere, when you were already living somewhere.

So that's how she found that family I mentioned, and saved her money for bus fare, and the rest of her money for two pencils and six erasers.

We took the bus to Rome where we thought the family attended school. But when we got there, we realized the giant building was their house.

We rang the bell.

A woman who could have been an Oklahoma mom opened the door, joyful and alive like she'd just walked out of the ball pit at McDonald's. "Ciao tutti!" she said. "Or should I say, hello friends!"

Her name was Karen and Karen was kind in the way that people can be, when kindness doesn't cost them anything. "Come in! Come in! You must be thirsty. Where did you come from again? It must have taken ages. Can she get you anything?"

"No, thank you so much," said my mom.

Karen waved to her housekeeper that she didn't need anything and the housekeeper ran away.

Back then we didn't know that if you wanted water in American homes, you had to ask for it.

Have I described Karen? Do you know what Barbie looks like? Can you imagine her twenty years later? She had an accent that I thought was Australian, but I know now was Texan. She said, "Well, I'm just delighted that they found y'all."

Let me cut to the chase. Because otherwise, this will take a while. It was a charity group that answered my mom's letters and found Karen's family—who had the kids our age, who were being home-schooled.

The program had six subjects and eleven workbooks in each subject. I was in first grade and could tell you that that was sixty-six books to complete over the year. Every book had about two hundred pages. So that's 13,200 pages. And there were two of us, so that's 26,400 pages. This becomes important later.

The house had marble floors so we didn't take off our shoes. As we entered, a giant man with shaved blond hair, a business suit, and a holster with a gun in it walked in. He looked like the security guards at the UN offices. He was getting his coat from a closet by the door, but when he saw us, he stopped. He didn't speak.

We didn't speak, because we were guests.

Karen laughed uncomfortably and said, "This is my husband, John."

John glared at Karen.

"Hello," said my mom.

John turned around and left without his coat. Karen laughed again, then swallowed it. "He's just very busy is all."

In the back of the house was a sunroom where we met Janet and JR. If this was a book in Mrs. Miller's class, she would point out that they were both named after John, which says something. And she'd point out that Janet being a finigonzon version of her mom, and JR being an angry kid who threw tantrums by tossing his super expensive glasses into bushes and making his mom look for them—that was all meaningful. But this isn't one of those books.

I sat next to JR. He had a buzzcut like his dad, and was using a paper clip to scratch into his desk.

"My dad is a spy," he said.

"My dad is a sayyed," I said.

"That's not a thing," he said.

"Then neither's a spy," I said.

"He can't talk to you."

"But I'm fun to talk to."

"They give him a lie detector test every day. He can't be around you."

This part was true. For the rest of the time we knew them, we came in through the back door, and if I needed to go pee or something, I'd check to see if anybody was in the hall first. I imagined the secret police of America would strap him to a lie detector and say, "Have you now, or ever before, played tag, freeze tag, blob tag, or oonch neech with Iranians?"

And he'd say, "Never."

"Have you even smiled at one?"

"Never."

"Even the little ones?"

"Never."

And they'd breathe a sigh of relief and let him into work for the day.

Other than that, it was normal.

Remember the 26,400 pages?

Karen was kind enough to sit us next to Janet and JR—and later, after JR complained—kind enough to let us sit in a back room.

Looking back, I didn't even need that soccer ball that Ali Shekari popped, because JR wouldn't have played with me anyway.

We would sit in a row in the back room—my mom, my sister, and me. My mom would take a workbook that Janet or JR had filled out already and go page-by-page, erasing every mark. Janet's were hard because sometimes she had essay questions, but JR's were harder because he liked to press his pencil into the paper so hard that it made mountains and rivers on the pages. She would erase as fast as she could and pass the book down. Then we would try to fill them out again.

I didn't have the heart to tell her that I could still kinda tell where JR had marked his answers. I told my sister and she said, "So? He probably got them wrong."

We only had two months before the school year was over and Karen's family would want to go skiing, so we had to finish the sixty-six books in sixty days. But really forty days, because those were the school days and we had to travel to Karen's house to use the books. I'm not going to try to make you cry by describing how it felt, or how they looked at us, or what they said in between all their kindness. Sometimes when you're a refugee, you have to give up the dignity you'd have if you said, "You know what, thank you, but no thank you. Your son treats my son like a dog, and your daughter says, 'Ew,' if we get near her, and we appreciate how smiley you are, but we'll figure out some other way to attend school."

But there isn't another way. This isn't America. You don't have options. So you have to bring cold hot dogs you stole from the Zuppa Guy and spend all your money on erasers and sit on a bus for two hours and sneak into some people's house who don't like you and beg for their trash, which they only let you borrow, and you sit a safe distance from their kids and you erase. You tell your kids to hurry, no time for breaks. If you do it as hard as you can for forty days, if you don't stop, then you complete the whole year in two months. But you have to erase 660 pages every day, and get a callus on your finger that won't go away for the rest of your life.

You can't stop for rest.

You can't waste time with dignity.

You have to scoop up every workbook as soon as it hits the ground like you're starving.

But also, unless you want to become an ungrateful person, you have to understand that Karen was probably doing her best. Nobody has to give anybody anything.

For forty days, my mom sat in the chair for eight hours each day and never stopped erasing. If you look at her hands, you can still see the bumps where it bled so much.

I'm telling you.

Unstoppable.

MY MOM IS THE UNSTOPPABLE FORCE. The power beam you get when you hit level-99 in *Final Fantasy* and learn the Ultima spell that goes through the crust of the planet like it's the crust of a pie.

My dad is the immovable object.

In Oklahoma they put two-ton winches on the fronts of their trucks to rip out tree stumps and even then, some of them won't move.

But my dad watched his wife and kids leave on a plane, and didn't budge.

At this point in the story, my mom, the unstoppable force, had run face first into the fist of Ray, and my dad, the immovable object, had flown to see us for the first and only time.

They were neither of them, themselves.

And my sister and I were lost.

Mrs. Miller, if you get this, you can't tell anyone what happened.

THE DAY MY DAD ARRIVED, I stood at Will Rogers Airport, wondering what he would look like. It was six years since I'd seen him. He probably wouldn't even recognize me. I was a crybaby when he last saw me, who couldn't even dive into a pool. But now I could do a 360 back kick, and had eaten tornadoes, and dug trenches and, little by little, like Mithridates—I had become unhurtable.

I made sure not to stand too close to Ray, so no one would think I had chosen him to be my new dad.

My mom was at home, making a giant lunch.

My sister had gotten into a fight with Ray in the car over the radio, so she was standing much farther off.

As people walked out of the tunnel, I imagined he was somewhere in the back of the plane, telling the flight attendants stories, making everyone laugh, and us wait.

In times like this, Ray didn't say much. He just stood there. If you said anything to him like, "It's taking forever," he'd just say, "Gotta learn to wait."

And if you said, "He'll probably have lots of bags," Ray would say, "Oh yeah?" like, You think so? And suddenly you wouldn't think so.

Finally, my real dad walked out of the tunnel from Iran into the middle of Oklahoma.

"KHOSROU! BEYA BEYA," HE SAID.

Gigantic smile. Big bushy mustache. Shorter and fatter than I remembered. His red hair had gone beige and white. He laughed and said, "You dog children, come here," which is hard to explain, but is a nice teasing thing to say.

"Baba, don't be so loud," my sister said.

He had already scooped us up into a hug. My sister and I never touched each other, so we pulled away.

Whenever I imagined this moment, Ray wasn't there, so I never thought of what they would say to each other. Maybe when Ray looked at my dad—who looked so much more like a dad than Ray did—he thought of his own. I don't know. They shook hands and said hello. We walked past a Cinnabon and my dad said, "Akh oonah khooban?"

Are those good?

"Yeah," I said.

He said, "Dar New York, messlesh dashtan."

Which meant he had eaten some in the New York airport.

"Baba!" said my sister, "Speak English!"

My dad made a funny embarrassed face like, "Excuse me, princess," and I laughed. In Farsi, he said, "Forgive me, Madame, but your father prefers the language of Ferdowsi."

"Then don't be so loud," she said.

My dad nudged me, like, You've been dealing with this?

It was so quick, becoming a family again. We hadn't even reached the baggage claim and he had his arm around me, needling my sister with his embarrassing behavior. It was so quick that he became human to me again, in the real world of Oklahoma, where you could buy cinnamon rolls at a stand in the airport.

Before that, he was a voice from the other side of the world.

And before that a memory of a face, and a smell.

And before that a myth, a poem of what his father had been, what fathers could be, what place we took in the story of our people. He was all of Ardestan—all the saffron fields, all the walnut trees, the platter of pomegranates and wedges of cheese. He was the lonely mountain and the snake, the pheasant in the mulberry tree. He was the bull and the boulevard of jasmine. And tea. He was the house with the birds in the wall and the Ferris wheel in the desert. He was the fountains of Isfahan, the steps in the stone, cut by the hand of Farhad. He was the city of kings, and the voice of Scheherazade, the whirling dervishes that leap, the fire worshippers, the nomad Kurds, and the eighteen sheep. He was the sizzling kebab, from the land that once belonged to Cyrus, the late great shah-in-shah. He was the rug and the flaw.

And now he was so small.

I HAD TO ADMIT THAT Ray could beat him up if they got into a fight, and I had to make sure they didn't. As we waited for his bags, I watched him as closely as I could without him noticing, and I wondered how come he had gotten like this—his nose swollen, his legs waddly. He wore khaki pants with too much stuff in each pocket. He made jokes to

Ray about the trip, the way you might talk about the weather before you've decided if you're friends with somebody or not.

When the carousel started and the bags from New York started to flow past, like a river of barrels, everyone had those new black suitcases with handles that come up so you can roll them behind you.

If I was Scheherazade, I wouldn't stop here, because it isn't much of a cliffhanger to tell you, his came out and it wasn't.

It didn't even have wheels.

It was the size of a van door, maroon, and leather. Maybe it was German, I don't know. It lumbered out of the entry and seemed to slow down the river just by sitting on it. I could practically hear my sister's low frequency scream of humiliation as she tensed every muscle. My dad must have felt it too. That every person in the airport was watching the ogreish bag and wondering what third-world goons could possibly own it.

When it reached us, Ray jumped ahead to be the host and get the bag. Also to show how strong he was, to lift a suitcase that probably weighed more than he did. As he put it down, he said, "Nice."

And honestly, I couldn't tell you if it was a "nice" like you do if you're admiring how nice the bag is, or a sarcastic "nice" like somebody just wet themselves. I have no idea. I looked at both their faces and couldn't tell.

I leaned over to my sister and said, "Is that a nice bag?"

And she said, "Let's just get out of here," which she would have said either way.

In the car, my dad told stories of his travels, but not of Iran. It cost so much money to come to America, especially to pay everyone for the proper papers. Maybe he didn't want to mention his new wife, who had answered the phone of our house when I had called for American Father's Day and she whispered, "Don't call here again, you dog children." It's hard to explain, but when *she* said it, it was an ugly thing to say. Then she hung up. When my dad called a few weeks later, upset that I hadn't called on a holiday they don't even celebrate, I told him and I think she got into trouble. She never spoke to me again. Her name is Mahsa or Morteza, and I guess she's my stepmom.

Anyway, he spoke in Farsi, "They have these cakes here—incredible—I bought fifteen in New York."

"Chocolate cakes?" I said. We were driving down the highway, past the brown grass part of Oklahoma that squats next to the airport. There wasn't much to look at.

"No," he said, "Yellow cake, with cream inside."

"Cream puffs?"

"Yeah. Twinkles?"

"Oh. It's Twinkies."

"Twonkles?"

"No, I'm sure it's Twinkies."

"They're incredible."

I looked out the window.

Behind the overpass rose a tangle of neon blue tubes—three giant water slides behind a billboard: White Water

Rapids. The park extended into flume rides, wave pools, and a lazy river. From the highway, you could only see people far away like ants and hear the tinny music playing on the loudspeaker.

"That looks interesting," said my dad.

"You should take the kids," said Ray.

My dad nodded. "They have something like that in Paris," he said.

Turns out he'd gone to Paris with Morteza the previous summer.

THE TIME IT TOOK to get my dad out of the car and into our house almost killed my sister. All through the ride over, she'd said, "Speak English," and he'd said, "Basheh meekonam," which is "Okay, I will," but not in English.

When he entered the house, he looked around at the blank-faced walls, the two prickly bushes outside the window—the tan shag carpeting, the lack of books, the tiny stove. On his face it said, "How did my kids end up here?"

When he spoke, he said, "You don't have a TV?"

Ray said, "We keep the living room for family conversations," which is true, I guess, since we never had any family conversations.

"It's in my room," I said.

My mom had been stalling by putting something in the oven, but she finally walked over. The last time they had been together, in Dubai, they were married to each other. Now they were married to Ray and Morticia.

She walked over, but stopped short. They bowed to each other, like a gesture of affection, but no touching.

I said, "What did you bring?"

Everyone was more than happy to jump right into the suitcase.

Happy reader, honorable friend, I can tell you, he brought back my heart.

MY HEART HAD BEEN broken beyond the repair of King Khosrou's greatest weaver, and carried in it a hole so big it could be said to be made up entirely of one big flaw.

I STOOD IN OUR LIVING ROOM—while my mother looked through the papers she had asked for, and Ray opened the tray of baklava from the Tehran airport, and my sister inspected her inlay jewelry box—holding Mr. Sheep Sheep.

His face was just as I remembered. Big round eyes, smiling as if he was happy to see me. He'd forgiven me, even though I had betrayed him. And he was happy to see me. He wasn't white anymore. A hard life had turned his wool gray. His arms still stretched out wide for a hug, but his left one drooped a little. But that wasn't the news. The news was that his throat had been slit, all the way around his head. It would have fallen off if not for the jagged black-thread stitching. It was sloppy, like a dentist who didn't know how to sew had done it on a plane, after some agent in the airport had ripped the sheep open to see if he'd been stuffed with drugs.

As Mr. Sheep Sheep looked up at the lights of the plane cabin, lying on a cold tray table, it must have felt like an emergency clinic in Dubai.

I stared into Mr. Sheep Sheep's eyes and wondered if he was still alive in there, or if the journey—all the ugliness he'd seen—had killed the light in him. I looked at my dad, who seemed like a nice man, and who wanted me to be happy. I don't know why I did it—maybe I realized everyone in my memories was already gone—but I ran to my room and sobbed into Mr. Sheep Sheep until he was soaked.

OH, AND HE BROUGHT Orich bars.

They taste pretty much like Mounds bars.

I WOKE UP THE NEXT morning with Mr. Sheep Sheep's head dangling off his body like a pinky finger caught in a door. The stitching had come loose overnight.

I got into the car, because I had missed the bus.

My mom—who had cut her hair short for the convenience—was still messing with it in the rearview mirror, and still frustrated.

Then we drove to the Economy Lodge Motel to pick up my dad, because it would have been inappropriate for him to stay at our house. Also, there was no room.

At one point she said, "I can fix Mr. Sheep Sheep if you want."

I shrugged, "Whatever."

They had sheep in Oklahoma and sheep farmers.

But what did I know about it, without a Baba Haji to explain? Besides, I was too old for stuffed animals.

"Do you want me to cancel with Mrs. Miller?"

She meant the visit from my dad to Mrs. Miller's class.

I said, "No."

Like the demons who believe in God, I had accepted my fate. To be outside the place where He speaks or listens. To know and remember and to never be believed.

To be punchable by Jareds and untouchable by Jennifers.

Maybe the truth of it is that Persians are sinners, and lying is just another one.

Are you even still there, reader?

No?

Maybe you've gone and the only eyes are the ones who flipped to this page accidentally. Or you've skipped ahead from someplace in the beginning and missed all the parts that explain me to you—from there to here.

Maybe I'm the patchwork text.

Maybe I deserve to be hit all the time.

Maybe I'm a liar.

Maybe I don't deserve a welcome.

And maybe I never had anything good.

Maybe even this.

I'm sorry I wasted your time.

ANYWAY, WE PULLED UP to the motel where we would stay the night, sometimes, when Ray was mad and they were getting a divorce.

My dad shuffled out of his room holding a bag that looked vaguely foreign. Like it wasn't Nike or Adidas. It was morning, but he was already sweating through his short-sleeve button-down shirt. Keys jangled in his pockets.

"Good morning, weepy boy!" he said as he collapsed into the front seat.

I didn't say anything. "This place is great," he said. "I already made friends with the 7-Eleven guy. He's open all night. I wanted a Twinkie cake, but all I had was a hundred dollar bill, and he didn't have that much change."

"You could have bought comic books," I said.

"I went outside to see if anybody had change, but nobody walks around here, so all I met were police who wanted to know why I was walking around with all this money."

"You got stopped by cops?"

"Yeah, no problem, Khosrou. Don't worry. I asked them if they had change for a hundred, and they laughed."

My mom couldn't help but laugh too.

He told the story as if he was an adventurer on the Silk Road. "I returned to 7-Eleven and bought one hundred dollars' worth of Twinkies," he said. "I gave some to the police. I'm friends with them now."

He pulled out a Twinkie and tossed it to me. My mom sucked her teeth. In the entire time we had been in Oklahoma, she had not bought a box of Twinkies. Too expensive.

"Save it for lunch," she said.

"Oh eat it now," he said. "Who cares. The whole world will die someday and who cares if you had a bad breakfast?"

"How many have you had?" I asked.

"Seven," he said.

I decided to save mine for lunch.

We—me, my dad, and his weird bag—walked into the school toward Mrs. Miller's class. I wished for genies to be true, and for me to find one someday, and for it to come back in time and make all the Kellys and Jennifers stay home sick today.

My dad walked through the halls like he had been there a thousand times, and every time someone had told him he looked handsome.

His back was straight, belly out. He nodded hello to the custodian, the vice principal, and the office ladies. He didn't ask anybody permission for anything.

The classroom was a cement cube. But it had streamers and wavy cardboard on the walls, and posters about kindness that really mean calmness.

Everybody was in there. Mrs. Miller was at her desk finishing her notes. Jared S. sat in the front, because otherwise he'd flick the ears of the person he sat behind. Kelly J., the girl who had made my heart, little by little, immune to poison, sat in the back with Jennifer L. and Jennifer S. Daniel W., who was born a Daniel, sat beside them and helped make fun of

Michael M., who had been home-schooled until this year and didn't know any of the chill expressions people use. He didn't keep notebooks.

"Introduce me to your friends," said my dad in Farsi.

"Kyle's in a different class," I said.

He said, "What're you, a squirrel, hoarding friendship?"

Or something like that. It was a phrase I didn't know, so I made up that meaning based on how it sounded.

Mrs. Miller looked up and saw us. "Hello," she said, and walked over to give my father a handshake. She got the kiss-kiss on the cheek from my dad, which isn't a real kiss, but they don't do it in Oklahoma, so she said, "Oh!" and laughed like she was nervous.

"Everyone," she said, "This is Daniel N.'s dad . . ."

She paused, so he'd say his name.

He didn't say anything.

My dad just smiled.

It was at this moment—standing in front of the whole class for a presentation on Iran—that I knew for certain, he didn't speak English.

"**HIS NAME IS MASOUD,"** I said.

"Muh-zood?" she said.

"Mah-sood," he said, cause he recognized his name. But he said it too loud. When you're speaking a language you don't know, you forget how loud to make the words.

In the *1,001 Nights*, you have to imagine at least once or twice that Scheherazade loses her place or realizes she's already used the genie-turns-into-a-mouse trick, and she goes blank. Her eyes—black, begging—stare at the king. He doesn't know what has happened. The river has run dry.

There is a pause that lasts almost an entire night, that for Scheherazade feels like the rest of her lifetime.

Good reader. Wait. No one is good but God alone. Decent reader. Reader who is kind to sheep and wears tasteful hats. Wise reader.

This was like that.

We stood before the class as if they were agents behind glass.

Finally, Jared S. said, "So he's a dentist?"

"Yes," I said.

"Does he have a magic carpet?"

"No."

"I do have a carpet," said my dad in Farsi.

"A magic one," I said to him in Farsi.

"Well I could tell them about one," he said.

"Why are you answering for him?" said Kelly.

"He doesn't speak English," I said.

"Of course I speak English," said my dad in Farsi. "Why did you say that?"

"You don't," I said.

He turned to the class, "I—espeek—Engleesh."

"Baba," I said.

"Are you famous there?" said Jared.

"I never said he was famous," I said. Jared was trying to make me seem dumb.

"Of course," said my dad, speaking through his barrel chest and mustache. "Very famous. Are you famous?"

"No," said Jared.

My dad turned to Kelly and said, "Excuse me, miss, do you know this boy?"

She laughed at his playful seriousness.

"Yes."

"Do you know he is a little . . ." He rolled his eyes and wiggled his eyebrows. It could have meant anything, like he's silly or kinda dumb.

Kelly burst out laughing. "Yes!" she said.

My dad turned to Jared S. "See? You are famous."

Jared had to smile when my dad made a show of shaking his hand as if he was a movie star and saying, "Thank you, famous man. Thank you."

The whole class was laughing by then.

He answered more questions in his broken English, sometimes turning to me for translations.

Was it true we had a house with birds in the walls?

"Of course. Their great-uncle had five pools with swans. And falcons in the roof."

Did his great-great-grandpa really get his weight in gold?

"Yes. He was no—Khosrou, what is the word for 'giant man'?"

"Hulk."

"He was no hulk like me, so not too much gold."

"What about saffron fields?" said Jennifer.

"What about saffron fields?" said my dad.

"Do they exist?"

"Yes."

"Did you own them?"

"Khosrou's mother's mother's mother, yes, but no more."

My dad turned to me and said in Farsi, "Khosrou, tell them this. They don't understand what stories are for."

"What are they for?" I said.

"For remembering," he said, "Tell them this. Rostam, do they know Rostam?"

"I don't know." Then I said in English, "Do y'all know Rostam?"

"Persian Hercules," said Daniel W.

I turned back to my dad, "Yeah."

He said, "When the poet Ferdowsi finished his great book, he said, '*Keh Rostam yalee bood dar Sistan, manesh kardam Rostameh dastan.*' Tell them that."

"Uh."

"You didn't understand."

"Just the poem part."

"Do you know Sistan?"

"No."

"It's a small town."

I turned to the class. "Okay, everybody. Sistan is a small town in Iran."

Jared said, "So?"

"Stay with me," I said. I smiled at Mrs. Miller, who stood beside us at the front of the room the whole time smiling—not to herself like she had some joke about us in her head, but at us, like she was beaming her happiness right into us.

"Okay," said my dad in Farsi, "He says, 'Rostam was just a local hero of Sistan when I met him.' Ferdowsi means when he began his poem, Rostam was a real person, famous in a small town. But do you know '*dastan*'?"

I shook my head, even though I knew it. I wanted to hear him say it, in person and not on the phone.

He said, "Story. Dastan is the land of stories. The world that we speak."

I turned to the class. "Okay, so Sistan is a small town, and dastan is a storyland. When the poet ended his book, he said, 'When I met him, Rostam was just a local hero of Sistan. I'm the one who turned him into the Rostam of dastan.'"

"Yes," said my dad in English, and dropped a meaty paw on my shoulder. He said to the class, "Stories are stories. Life is life. They kiss and they marry, but they die alone."

Then he thought about it some more and added, "And death is not the end. They kiss more in paradise."

I waited for questions.

"That took forever to explain," said Jared S.

"Yeah, it does," I said.

"Your dad's awesome," said Daniel W.

Then my dad put his European bag on Jared's desk and pulled out a tray of baklava—which, if you don't know by now, is layered pastry soaked in rosewater syrup and stuffed with cardamom and walnuts. He had bought an extra tray at the Tehran airport for my class. He was thinking about it way back then.

The whole class stood up and rushed to the front.

"Hold on, everyone," said Mrs. Miller.

I handed out napkins and my dad served pieces of gooey, crispy baklava.

Kelly J. looked at hers and said, "What is it?"

Jennifer S. said, "Just eat it. It's so good." She had already swallowed hers. My dad gave her another.

He winked at me as the whole class turned into a party, and whispered, "Sugar."

Which was his way of saying a good storyteller gives the people what they want. And it's kinda funny, cause he's a dentist, so a good storyteller also makes sure to keep them coming back.

Kelly brought it up to her lips. I watched and waited for her judgment. Even though I do not love Kelly J., I wanted her approval. She nibbled the pastry as tentatively as a deer. "It's amazing," she said. She put the rest in her mouth and smiled.

I would have jumped like a fool at the chance to offer her another piece. But my dad put his hand on my shoulder. He said to Kelly, "He can make."

"Wow, really?" said Kelly. "You can make this?" Reader, she looked at me as if I was Abbas the Baker himself.

I can't really make baklava so I shrugged. In Farsi I said, "I can't make baklava."

"Your mother can teach you," said my dad. "That's practically the same. It's more of a promise. You could make it if she asked."

It's not like she became my girlfriend.

But I did learn to make baklava later, just in case it comes up again.

As everybody ate and laughed at my dad's jokes, I took the biggest and best piece of baklava from the middle of the tray, walked to Mrs. Miller, and gave it to her.

I thought about the long year and everything she'd done for me. How she had always known which to be—a teacher who speaks or a teacher who listens—and I said, "Thank you, Mrs. Miller."

She was the best teacher I ever had, and she was crying a little, so I walked off before she could hug me or anything.

A **FEW MONTHS AFTER WE** finished the workbooks in Italy, the President of the United States said we could have asylum—but only if an American family vouched for us and promised we wouldn't become the kind of people who live on welfare and steal from Americans.

It took another few months, but an old couple in Oklahoma said they would. They were retired already—Jim was a NASA engineer and Jean was a school teacher, and if you want to know the details, it's because their church had a program with Ellie's church (remember Ellie is Sima's mom exiled in London), and the word got to them that Sima and her kids weren't thieves and would be good people. So they signed up. Can you believe that? Totally blind, they did that. They'd never even met us. And if we turned out to be villains, they'd have to pay for it. That's almost as brave and kind and reckless as I can think of anybody being.

Reader, if you think anything of Oklahomans, I hope you'll remember Jim and Jean Dawson, who were so Christian that they let a family of refugees come live with them until they could find a home, and who made them sandwiches with Pringles chips, which is the best chip any place has to offer, and means you're welcome, and who let them play with their grandson's Nintendo.

WHEN WE GOT OFF the plane, it was nighttime, so I had been asleep, and when we left and got into Jean's car after we met her and everything, I realized my hat—the one Ali Shekari left me before he disappeared, to say sorry for bursting my soccer ball—was left on the plane.

There was nothing left of Ali Shekari but my spotted memory.

In the back of Jean's car, driving from the airport for the first time toward Edmond, I cried. In my pocket I had three peach pits from the orchards of Mentana, and four Micro Machine cars to jump over them as if they were boulders. I had abandoned Mr. Sheep Sheep in a field, lost my kite in Dubai, and forgotten Ali Shekari's hat in an Italian plane.

"You don't need any of that," said my sister. She meant the peach pits and the cars. "Look what they have here."

I looked out the window, where she was pointing, at the giant water slides of White Water Rapids. It looked like the kind of place that, if you were from Oklahoma, you'd remember as a mythical paradise. For that car ride back to Jean's house, before we met Ray and had to leave them, I thought that was exactly where we had landed.

"Just don't go diving in the shallow end," she said.

I NEVER WENT TO WHITE WATER Rapids until my dad took us. After the last day of school, Kyle went to California again for the summer, before I could prove to my dad that I had a friend, or to my friend that I had a dad.

That's okay.

In the *1,001 Nights*, sometimes characters wander in and out of the story as if a sleep-deprived Scheherazade had forgotten to give them a purpose.

It was the first Monday of summer, after the Sunday when my dad visited church. This is important because the fight that would come later, the one that finally separated us from my dad, began there.

Pastor Hamond, you may not remember, is the one in the Dallas-made suits. He shook my dad's hand. My dad smiled and nodded, then he leaned over to me and said, "All his teeth are fake. Every single one."

I laughed. Jonboy, the youth pastor, avoided us, probably because he thought I'd told my dad about him pulling out my thumb. I hadn't, but it was nice to be protected.

So even though my dad could have just said he was feeling sick from eating five dozen Twinkies, he still attended the special evening service, where Pastor Hamond stood in front of the tiny congregation and preached his sermon directly to my dad.

I don't mean that he looked at him every once in a while. I don't mean that he made references to "other" people from other backgrounds in his examples. I mean he got on the pulpit and said, "Brothers and sisters, we are lucky enough to welcome Muzoo Niari tonight, all the way from Iran. And Muzoo, if you'll permit me, I'd like to speak just to you tonight. Because if a shepherd has a hundred sheep, but even one is lost, he doesn't abandon it, but goes looking for it, to save the one."

There is nothing more true-blue than a pastor of a small town making a sincere speech directly at you in a room full of forty people as if they aren't there, and expecting an uncomplicated handshake deal to come of it. And there is nothing more exactly Iranian than to sit there nodding agreeably. That's that tarof I told you about—the polite self-annihilation. The way of saying, "In your glory I turn to elemental dust, and hope only that it does not make you sneeze."

Or my dad was just super weirded-out, cause it was super awkward.

Pastor Hamond didn't look at anybody else, not even me, sitting right next to my dad. But you could tell he was aware of the audience. He was performing it all for them.

"Muzoo, I ask you, have you felt the freedom of the Lord? Have you felt it? He's nodding, folks. Is that a yes, Muzoo?"

"Yes," said my dad from the front pew.

I whispered in Farsi, "Do you know what he's saying?"

"Doesn't matter," he said. "Look at him. Let him enjoy himself."

I looked over my shoulder. Everybody was looking at us. To my left, Ray was stiff. I don't think he was listening, just festering.

Pastor Hamond went on. My mom had her Bible in her lap, underlining passages that the pastor hadn't even mentioned. She was smiling to herself, mouthing a prayer to God.

Reading is the act of listening and speaking at the same time, with someone you've never met, but love. Even if you hate them, it's a loving thing to do.

You speak someone else's words to yourself, and hear them for the first time.

What you're doing now is listening to me, in the parlor of your mind, but also speaking to yourself, thinking about the parts of me you like or the parts that aren't funny enough. You evaluate, like Mrs. Miller says. You think and wrestle with every word.

It's like when you're hearing a great story from Scheherazade and you're seeing past the thing to the main thing—past the adventures of the orphans to Scheherazade herself, begging to stay alive another day. The same way, in a small-town church in Oklahoma with a kinda dopey pastor, my mom could look past the thing he was saying, to the source of it.

She was replenished by the same thing that amused my dad. And that infuriated Ray.

By the end of the sermon, the pastor had convinced himself that he'd converted my dad, because my dad kept nodding and saying yes to everything.

"Have you had your heart softened, Muzoo?"

"Yes."

"And would you like to change your life before you leave here?"

"Yes."

"And would you like to take the real plunge?"

"Yes."

"Uh, Dad," I said.

"Would you like to be baptized?"

"Yes."

Uh-oh, I thought.

"Did you hear that, folks? That's the rejoicing of angels."

Everyone but Ray clapped.

Pastor Hamond smiled like he'd sold the car in the far back corner of the lot.

"Alright then, let's get a towel for Muzoo."

Everybody stood.

We watched as my dad followed one of the deacons into a room that led around the stage, up to an elevated pool that looked out over the crowd. If you're from Oklahoma, you know what I'm talking about. If you're from Iran, imagine a big bathtub on a balcony, center stage, behind a pulpit, under a giant cross, and three grown men in white hospital gowns getting in. One of them is hairier than the others. That one's my dad.

The other two were the pastor and the deacon. They were both necessary, cause the next step was for my dad to renounce Satan, and then they'd dip him backward (like action movie heroes do to ladies when they tango with them), and it would take both men to lift my dad back up out of the water.

Just like that, like Mr. Sheep Sheep, he was born again. When he came out of the water, the congregation cheered. "Muzoo," said Pastor Hamond, "You've been washed in the blood."

My dad, soaking wet, said, "Yes. Good. Yes."

I think I never wanted something to be true more than my Baba believing, and being saved, and moving to America, and being in heaven together after that.

I know it wasn't going to happen. It's just how I felt.

So I was happy, is what I'm saying. And I even hugged him when he came out, even though I don't hug people. Even the pastor. I hugged him. That was the only time I ever touched that guy.

In the fellowship hall, everybody had cookies and coffee. I walked up to my sister's table, where she was selling mug rugs.

"What do you want?" she said.

"Nothing."

"Wanna walk around and ask if they want to buy mug rugs?"

I shrugged and picked up a couple.

"Do you think he'll move here?" I asked.

"Baba?"

"Yeah."

"No. Of course not."

"He can't go back if he's Christian," I said.

She rolled her eyes. "He did that for you, idiot."

I put her mug rugs down and walked to the bathroom with my eyes pointed directly up at the ceiling.

"Be careful," she said. "Ray's mad."

THE NEXT MORNING, WE PICKED up my dad, who had bought another hundred dollars' worth of Twinkies. It was just my mom, my sister, him, and me.

I don't remember much of the car ride except my mom was quiet. I said to my dad, "Are you really a Christian now?"

And he said, "Yes!" and laughed. "I'm your father. I am humanity. I'm everything to everybody."

I didn't say anything after that.

I guess that was my dad's favorite myth, that he was everything to everybody.

WHITE WATER RAPIDS IS EXACTLY as tubular as the commercials tell you. Extremely.

It smells like chlorine, and the water is extra blue so it looks cleaner than it is. The walls of the park are giant logs tied with white rope, like you're inside a ship. The snack shops can turn an ice cream cone completely upside down to dip it in chocolate without anything falling out.

You're supposed to wear flip flops if you're walking from the tide pool to the lazy river, the flume ride, the group inner-tube ride, or the slides. But the paths are made of a smooth surface with little holes in it, like lava rock, so it's no big deal if you're barefoot the entire time.

The first thing you do when you get there is say good-bye to your mom.

Then you pay $28 per person, which only our dad would do in our family. On the other side of the turnstiles, there are giant floaty tubes for rent. The blue circle ones are the smallest, and you might want the green long ones for two people, but that would be a huge mistake, because they go much slower.

Then you walk to one of the lounge "beaches," which have no sand, but green turf, and a ton of lay-down chairs, and lockers for your clothes and shoes.

My mom would never come here, because she would never be seen in a swimsuit. I don't even think she has one, and she'd want to save money on the lockers. So she would say, "Go. I'll stay with the clothes." (And the sandwiches she would have packed to save on buying corn dogs.)

My dad stuffed our stuff into a locker, plopped onto a lounge chair, and said, "Go. Have fun."

"Are you coming?" I said.

"I don't want to wash off my baptism. Go. Do you need money?"

I nodded. White Water Rapids also has an arcade with *Street Fighter II*, which is the greatest arcade game of all time. He took out a tube of bills. "Do they take a hundred?"

"No."

He unrolled it, and leafed through, looking for some other bill.

"Do they sell Twinkies here?" he asked.

"No."

"Baba," said my sister, "Stop showing everyone."

"Akh!" he said in Farsi. "Is my money too foreign now? It's dollars."

She stopped scolding him just so he'd stop speaking Farsi. He found a five and gave it to me.

"If he gets five, I want five," said my sister.

He found another and gave it to her.

"Go," he said. "If you see a waiter, send him to me."

There are no waiters at White Water.

My sister and I looked at each other for two seconds, then turned and walked in opposite directions. I went straight to the arcade. Later, I would make it my mission to show my dad I wasn't avoiding the rides or scared of pools now or anything like that.

Street Fighter takes two quarters, because it's a super premium game. Five dollars gets you twenty quarters, which is a ton to put into swimsuit trunk pockets.

There were a bunch of big kids at the machine. But they didn't know I had spent three years in Oklahoma already and only got two quarters from my mom to spend on a whole day, so I knew all the tricks to make a game last. And with twenty quarters, I could probably play *Street Fighter* for twenty hours.

I was using Blanka, who is a monster with a hairy chest. I'm best with him. Ryu is great too, and can do kicks that Ray can do. I used to call him Rayu.

Anyway, Mrs. Miller says I can't write about *Street Fighter* because good writing cares about keeping the audience interested, so I'll skip all my sweet moves.

I would beat a kid, and turn to him to say, "We can still remain friends," which you do by nodding up at them, like you're pointing at them with your chin, and you say, "Good game, bro." Or if you'd like to show extra respect, "Good game, big dog."

I was the ultimate champion for a while, until a high school guy showed up and knew how to counter my electricity move with Chun-Li's heel stomp. When he beat me on my last quarter, he said, "Nice game," with the nod I told you about, and that felt good, cause he was almost in college even. Then I felt a punch, right in the middle of my back, between the shoulder blades where it stings the most.

I turned around and saw Brandon Goff from bus 209, and I didn't even have shoes on.

OVER THE NEXT THREE SECONDS of life, I wished to all the djinns in the White Water area that I would become Jean Claude van Damme, and these would be my options:

1. Blood fist to Brandon Goff's chest, which he would just take. Then he'd pound my face until I died.
2. A 360 back kick into his guts. That would drop him for sure. But then he'd catch me as I ran out, cause he was between me and the door, or the friend standing

next to him would, and they would pound me and break my feet.

3. Scream, but I told you I had just made a new bud. He was still playing, but he'd think I was a wuss. And then Brandon, plus his goon, would pound me.
4. Beg my new pal to save me.
5. Shriek like a howler monkey, and start slapping myself like I'd gone wild and maybe see if I could scare them away.

The options were getting worse and worse until Brandon said, "You look like you're about to whiz yourself."

I was. That was the next option.

Brandon laughed at the look on my face.

"Relax, dude. We're cool."

"We are?" I said. One stomp would have broken all the little bones in my bare feet, so I wasn't very chill.

"Yeah man. How's the summer going?"

He had his head shaved, and that made him scarier.

"Good!" I said. This was loony town stuff. This was the guy who pantsed the vice principal on the same day he stabbed Tanner in the hand with the round metal brace that holds the eraser on the back of a pencil. He was just standing around, shooting the breeze with me, like, Isn't it cool to bump into old friends over the summer?

So I forgot the polite response for a second, but then said, "Uh. Good. How's *your* summer going?"

"Great, man," he said. "Oh. Listen, your dad told me to give you this. He thought you'd be out by now." And he handed me five bucks.

Brandon Goff handed me five dollars.

If I took it, I thought then maybe he'd jump me, smash my nose, and tell everyone I stole it.

"Go ahead, take it."

"Why wouldn't you just keep it?" I said.

"There's twenty bucks waiting for me if I don't."

"Ah," I said.

He handed me the five bucks.

"Your dad's kind of a boss," he said.

I got back to the lounge area around the same time as my sister—I guess she got a delivery too. He was lounging back with his silk shirt open and sunglasses on. A can of Coke rested on his hairy belly.

"Baba, what are you doing?" said my sister.

"Nothing," said my dad. "Do you want fries?"

"No. Why are you talking to people?"

"I like people."

A kid ran over with a plate of fries from the concession stand. My dad slipped him a twenty. He ran off.

"Well stop it. It's embarrassing."

"It's embarrassing to give people money?"

"Yes!"

"Well too bad. I like French fries. Have you ever considered that you're embarrassed of yourself?"

My sister looked around and saw everybody casting glances at my dad, lying on his throne. Kids were milling around, waiting for him to want something. I knew what she was thinking. Even when he was being a boss, he was doing it in a way no one else did around here. Back then, all she wanted was to be "normal," to speak English perfectly and go to business school, and never seem strange to anybody.

But that was the moment I realized that myths are just legends that everybody agrees on, and legends are just stories that got bigger over time. The story of my dad—who for one day became the king of White Water Rapids—was just another myth in the making. The way everyday concerns didn't bother him, the rules he followed that weren't the normal rules for heroes, all of that—made him interesting. He was the god who spoke and spoke and spoke, and you never got tired of it.

But unfortunately for my sister, he was not a god who listened.

THAT IS MY LAST MEMORY of my dad.

The same day, we took him back to the airport.

It was obvious he wasn't welcome to come again because of Ray. He had his other life. And laws started to keep Iranians out of America—even just to visit.

He went back to being a voice from the other side of the world who called me Khosrou.

I wonder sometimes what his story will be.

Why he let us go.

Why we weren't interesting enough or fun enough to hold close. I'm not a baby anymore. I know a stuffed sheep is just a toy. But I loved that thing so much I would have done anything to be with Mr. Sheep Sheep again.

I'm not sure why I'm so much less valuable to him.

Maybe you're reading this and you know.

Maybe you see the reason I don't. Like maybe I'm a bad person, and I don't realize it, and I don't deserve a dad.

I don't know.

If you do, and you see me someday, I hope you'll tell me.

But I'll tell you one thing now. If I ever have a kid, I wouldn't let them go, ever. Even if they had to leave Earth, and I had to follow them into airless space, I'd hold on to them and suffocate, but at least I'd have held them close. And I wouldn't hit my wife either, not for any reason, not even if she hit me.

SO WE COME TO the hitting.

THE MEMORIES ARE ALMOST all done now.

THAT DAY, AFTER WE TOOK my dad to the airport, we got home to find Ray was in his bad mood. What happened was the last best memory I have of my sister. She's still around. She's not dead or anything. I just mean it's the memory I'll keep, instead of all the other ones.

He was furious.

We knew that because he was working on his car, throwing tools around the garage, and he didn't say anything as we walked into the house, even after my mom said, "Salaam," three times.

"Go ahead," she said to us. But we knew there would be less fighting if we stayed.

"No," said my sister.

"It's fine," she said.

"No. You come in," I said.

My mom is the hero of this whole story, in case you were wondering. She always did what heroes do. The law that applied to her was the law of sacrificial love. The legend was unstoppable belief. The myth was the strongest person you have ever known. Not Hercules. Not Rostam. Not Jean Claude van Damme could protect and love as Sima, my mom, who was our champion, and who—like Jesus—took all the damage so we wouldn't have to.

She walked into the house with us.

In moments like these, when you know something is about to happen, everyone finds some reason to stand around and wait for it.

Ray stalked into the house.

They fought.

I will spare you the details.

Fighting is never poetry.

It is always bad storytelling.

The characters say something and mean something else, but the connection is so obvious it embarrasses the reader.

It might be, "We still don't have soy sauce. You didn't have time to get soy sauce?"

And that means, "You've spent too much time attending to a guest I don't like."

But it escalates.

They shout. He approaches her so he can look down and she has to look up.

He looms over her.

His hands are at his hips, but cocked and loaded.

She doesn't back down, and can't back away—her back is to the kitchen counter.

She says, "Go to your room," to us, but we don't.

He turns and says, "Go."

But my sister says, "No."

Her arms are crossed.

He says, "What'd you say to me?"

My mom explodes to get his attention. She slaps his back and shouts, "Don't you talk to her!"

He grabs her by the shoulders, lifts her, and pounds her into the side wall of the kitchen. The whole kitchen rattles with her bones. The dishes in the cupboard.

He does it again so hard her head slams into the wall and her knees buckle.

My sister screams, "Stop! What're you doing, you animal."

Ray must be in a movie in his own mind at this point.

He turns toward us.

I look at him and try with whatever look I have to tell him that someday I will know all the moves, and will be strong enough to break all his bones, and that future me will remember this. But he looks past me and storms at my sister. She doesn't move.

He juts his jaw down at her and says, "Say it to me again."

And she juts hers up at him, eyes directly pointed into his, and says, "If you touch me, I will call the police and they will put you in a cage."

He looks like a panther staring down at a parrot. He looks like he wants to kill her. And Dina, that's my sister's name, stares back unafraid, and dares him to do it.

ANYWAY.

I DON'T KNOW HOW MY MOM was so unstoppable despite all that stuff happening. I dunno. Maybe it's anticipation.

Hope.

The anticipation that the God who listens in love will one day speak justice.

The hope that some final fantasy will come to pass that will make everything sad untrue.

Unpainful.

That across rivers of sewage and blood will be a field of yellow flowers blooming. You can get lost there and still be unafraid. No one will chase you off of it. It's yours. A father who loves you planted it for you. A mother who loves you watered it. And maybe there are other people there, but they are all kind. Or better than that, they are right with each other. They treat each other right.

If you have that, maybe you keep moving forward.

IMAGINE YOU'RE IN A refugee camp and you know it'll be a year or more before anything happens. It's going to be a tough year. But for the person who thinks, "At the end of this year, I'm going somewhere to be free, a place without secret police, free to believe whatever I want and teach my children." And you believe it'll be hard, but eventually, you'll build a whole new life—that's like winning the lottery. It's like saying you'll get one hundred million dollars at the end of the year.

But if you're thinking every place is the same, and there will always be people who abuse you, and about how poor you'll be at first. The sadness overtakes you; it's like saying you'll get a soup and a sandwich at the end of the year, and that's it.

Here's the thing, you'll both have the same year at Hotel Barba. But one of you will be looking around with joy and anticipation, wondering what you can do to prepare your kids for the new world. And the other will be slumped in the courtyard, surrendered to the idea that it's all one long river of blood. I don't know which belief is true—nobody does. But what you believe about the future will change how you live in the present.

That's how she did it.

MY MOM DIDN'T WANT to go to the hospital because she had already gone twice that year, and we couldn't stay in the house, so we went back to the Economy Lodge Motel next to the 7-Eleven in the part of town where neighbors don't really talk to each other.

Ray had stormed out and slammed the door.

But we knew we had to escape again.

My sister didn't talk about it. We just got our things. I grabbed my school backpack, dumped out the books, and put in some clothes and Mr. Sheep Sheep, and my Micro Machines, and the peach pits. This time, I had my own suitcase.

We got in the car and drove around until nobody was crying and our eyes weren't so red. Then we went to the motel so my mom could lie down, cause I think she was still dizzy.

The room was just another cement cube. One brown bed, one bathroom, one window with brown curtains. But it also had a TV with channels we'd never seen before. Dina said, "Let's get candy and watch stuff."

We bought Twinkies, and Pringles, and Mounds bars at the 7-Eleven with money our dad left us. I bought a comic book of Wolverine, the second greatest hero of all time. We watched TV late into the night, until my mom woke up. My sister was asleep. I was watching an action movie by myself.

She said, "Are you okay?"

I said, "Yeah."

I had been thinking about the *1,001 Nights* and wondering what would happen if Scheherazade was sick or dizzy one night and fell asleep right in front of the villain king. Or what would happen if she ran out of stories, her mind went blank, and she knew if she didn't keep talking, he would kill her. Would she start recounting her memories?

Right from the beginning, would she start with her grandpa and grandma and tell all the family stories? Would she run up, eventually, to her own life? To the fruit trees when she was a kid, the rivers and rooftops and mirrors and cats until she was telling him about himself, about the moment she met him, about the telling of that first story, and what she was thinking as she was telling it, and the way he was reacting? Would the memories curve into themselves into a perfect round river? A red river? A heart pumping blood in and out in perfect circulation? What if it goes on forever, the telling and retelling? When did all these words begin? Are they all just distant memories we are passing to each other?

And what if, like a rug, they are flawed? Memories are just stories we tell ourselves, after all. What if we are telling ourselves lies?

I don't know.

Maybe I was just scared that I would never be strong enough to protect the people I loved. I was crying in her arms while I was thinking all this. She said, "It's okay."

There was a long time of silence.

Eventually, I said, "Do you remember Baba Haji?"

And she said, "Of course."

"No," I said. "Do you remember the time I was a kid. I walked around into his courtyard, and there was a bull they wanted to kill for a feast for me. All the men were struggling with it. Is that real? Did that happen?"

I was terrified of what she'd say, because all this time, I had held on to that one memory like a peach pit in my pocket. It was mine, and it was the only one I had of my Baba Haji. If it was untrue, I don't think I could take it.

"No," she said. "It wasn't like that."

I closed my eyes, because I had lost my Baba Haji.

"That wasn't for a feast for you. The bull had gone mad," she said. "It was going to kick someone or kill one of the farmers. So they went to your Baba Haji. He was so strong, they all went to him for this kind of thing. He took care of everyone who worked for him. And it was a mercy to kill the bull, because it would thrash and break its own neck if they didn't."

"Really?" I said. "And did he come out and hold my face?"

"I suppose so."

"And were his hands red with blood?"

"Oh no. He would never have done that. You must have imagined that."

"But he smiled at me."

"Of course. You were his. He would have also made a feast," she added. "But it would have been a sheep. He would have spilled the blood. You have to understand that means a blessing. It's ancient. To step over the river of blood, to accept the sacrifice and be thankful. Then we could eat, only after we understand the cost of joy. And he would have washed his hands."

We sat in the dark motel room with the light of the TV flickering. I knew we would be whole one day.

Maybe it would take a thousand years.

But we'd get there, little by little.

author's note

Hello, Reader. It's Khosrou again, but this time I am thirty-six years old, with a beard, and a job where everyone calls me Daniel.

Around thirteen years ago, I was living in New York City, when my dad called with the news that my Baba Haji had died. I knew right then I would never have another memory of my grandfather, other than the three I recounted in this book. All I ever wanted up till then was to return to Baba Haji's house in Ardestan, to learn how to be a man, to farm, and to reclaim the eighteen sheep he had given me on my fifth birthday.

That was the moment I began to write this story.

I figure you want to know which parts are true. The short answer is all of it is true. I have changed the names of some people simply to avoid calling them out, combined others into a chorus of Jareds and Jennifers, and played a tiny bit with the timeline. But the elements are all—to my recollection—true. Ah, but remember, a patchwork text is the shame of a refugee. I am afraid I did not have access to family records, historical documents, or even most of my family members. I relied on interviews I made of my parents. And, of course,

I spoke only, ever, from and about my memories. Even the stories of the generations before were from the memory I had of hearing them. My mother would like me to tell you that her father was not nearly as bad as I remember him. Perhaps I misunderstood a great deal, in the way that a child misunderstands, but those are the myths I believed at the time.

This was my life, as I experienced it, and it is both fiction and nonfiction at the same time. Your memories are too, if you'll admit it. But you're not a liar. You're just Persian in your own way, with a flaw.

I have a son now. He is the exact age I was when I freed Mr. Sheep Sheep, and I can't imagine ever losing him. I pray that he will be rich in memories of me holding him. He is named after my Baba Haji.

acknowledgments

IT HAS TAKEN much of my adult life to write this book. In that time, a great many people showed me undue kindness, and deserve my love and gratitude. My mother, first and foremost, is truly the hero of this story. Without her unstoppable bravery I'd be unrecognizable to myself. My wife, Alexandra, and son, Gideon, have given me the love that kept me intact while revisiting all these moments of shatter. Carey Wallace is the reader whose opinion I have relied upon at every step.

Stacey Barney was the friend and advisor who told me to write this from the perspective of my younger self, and opened the floodgates as result. It was Namrata Tripathi who advised me, and invited me to her company dinner even though I was just a stray at a book conference.

As most people do, I made a fool of myself the first time I met Arthur Levine. His mythology is well-known, and I wanted so badly to win his esteem. He was gracious and encouraging—exactly as you'd wish heroes to be. He was the first and only editor to see the book and his guiding hand made it far better than I could have on my own. Thank you, Arthur. I imagine Khosrou and Arturo would have been friends, and I hope this book makes you proud.

Thank you to the entire team at Levine Querido: Meghan Maria McCullough, Antonio Cerna, Nick Thomas, Semadar Megged, and Alex Hernandez. I'm so proud to be a part of your adventure. To have been the first book of Levine Querido feels like I have been given a part of history.

Thank you to Elizabeth Parisi for art direction and infinite patience. Thank you, David Curtis for art unmatched. Thank you, Anamika Bhatnagar for the most thorough and encouraging copyedit I've ever had. Thanks also to Allison Elsby, Shona Burns, and everyone else at Chronicle Books.

And now we come to Joanna Volpe. Reader, I wish you knew what I know. I wish you understood what I mean when I say Joanna Volpe is, hands-down, the best agent in the industry. Jo is a visionary who speaks, and one who listens. She's a kind friend and I'm honored she'd choose to work with me. My greatest gratitude to her, and to Pouya Shahbazian—a Persian brother in arms. Thank you, Meredith Barnes, who is so talented I have dreamed of working with her for ages, and who showed up for this project like some sort of genius ex machina. Thank you to the entire New Leaf family: Suzie Townsend, Hilary Pecheone, Joe Volpe, Abbie Donoghue, Veronica Grijalva, Mia Roman, Kathleen Ortiz, JL Stermer, Janet Reid, Jordan Hill, Cassandra Baim, Mariah Chappell, Madhuri Venkata, Kate Sullivan, Dani Segelbaum, Devin Ross, Jordan Hamessley.

And thank you, reader. Time is an unrenewable resource and you have given some to me. If ever you see me, consider this your invitation to say hello. You deserve my thanks in person.

That's enough from me.

Thanks, everybody.